IN THE ABSENCE
OF LIGHT

JILLIAN CAREY

Dedicated to Caroline, who is the reason I fell in love with writing

CHAPTER 1

THEO

My life hasn't exactly been all sunshine and kittens, and I'm not just saying that for sympathy points. It's been a snowball of crazy horribleness, actually. Especially for these last few years. But right now, standing at the edge of the forest with an Avis in front of me — I kind of feel like the luckiest guy in the world.

I know this is insane. On several fronts. For one thing, the luckiest guy in the world probably lives somewhere in Udula, sitting at the top of one of those sky-scratcher-things and drowning in money, not struggling to make ends meet in a cramped little house occupied by only three people. But it's also insane because logically, an Avis shouldn't *be* here. And I know

I'm not as smart as Ren, not as well-read (or… I guess *learned*, would be a better word here), but I'm not an idiot either. I know Avi are native to Volant, bred to be giant, bird-like war-machines, but that doesn't change the fact that one of them is right here in front of me, somehow sitting on a branch that it looks too heavy to actually be sitting on.

This can't really be happening, right? Avi don't just show up in Silva. They don't come wandering into the depths of the forest, don't escape from Volant for a bit of fun. I should try to figure out if I'm hallucinating, should climb back down a bit because who knows? Maybe the air really is thinner up here, like Ren always says, but instead I call out, "Hey birdy!" driven by some kind of stupid impulse of mine.

The Avis cocks its head. I think it's a girl, because the guy ones are supposed to be colorful, and this one's feathers are a mixture of dark grays and blacks, the only hint of color the glowing white designs of her beak. I smile at her as if a giant bird is actually going to be able to understand human mannerisms. But she's not doing anything to me, and she hasn't tried to kill me, and I really want to get closer to her. You see, I've always been adventurous. Maybe a little too adventurous for my own good, I don't know. But ever since my parents passed away, there's so much work to do, so many loose ends that are constantly unravelling further, and any chance I can get to have a little fun is something I usually grab and hold on to.

And riding one of the famous Avi sounds pretty damn fun.

"Here, birdy, birdy," I say, scooting closer to the Avis. Up here, the branches get really thin and bendy, and it feels like I could fall at any moment, though I never do. I guess that's a Silvan trait, but it just seems funny to me that not everyone can walk and jump and run around in trees like we do. I've never even been on the real ground before. No one's seen the bottom of the Silvan forest — it's said to be as dark and mysterious as the ocean, and I believe it. We all live right around the middle of the trees, where the branches are thick and sprawling and we can build houses in and around the trunks.

The Avis blinks at me. It's a little unsettling, because she's got these beady eyes and her beak's all long and pointy, looking like it could take my eyes out with a good peck. Avi are meant to look intimidating though, considering they're bred for war. This one flaps her wings a couple times, keeping balance on the branch she's on, and I startle, pausing where I stand. Her wings are *huge*, each one a good few human-lengths long. I wonder how she even got in here, past all the branches.

"Do you need help?" I ask her now. I don't actually expect her to respond, because I know animals don't go around talking to people, but I feel like I have to say something as I creep closer to her. All of the sudden, she gets this fierce look in her eyes and flaps her wings again; it scares me so bad that I stumble back a step.

That's my mistake.

I'm usually really good at maneuvering around here, but then again, I'm usually not standing opposite an Avis. My foot slips off the branch and I windmill wildly, flailing desperately for balance before I finally tilt a little too far and tumble.

It's terrifying. I've never fallen before. Didn't even think I could. Branches and leaves whip past me, scraping my arms and face, and I wonder when I'll hit a branch, and then I wonder if I *won't*, if I'll just fall all the way to the forest floor.

I'm probably going to die. Maybe it's fitting, dying just like my parents did.

Mind you, this all flits through my head in about half a second, and I'm screaming as it does, twisting and tumbling through the air with my heart in my throat and tears in my eyes. And suddenly, there's something warm and firm under me. It doesn't feel like a branch, or like I've died and am being carried by an angel, so I grab on for dear life — and then it takes me upward. I'm pretty sure I'm not getting yanked up into heaven, but if I am, I might just let go again.

Then I realize I'm not getting taken to heaven. And it's really not an angel under me. It's the Avis.

I have no clue how she's moving through the trees like this, flying and hopping and twisting all throughout the branches until suddenly we're higher than I've ever been before, breaking through the canopy of leaves and into the sky. I can see the entire forest, stretching out for miles and miles, and now I really can't breathe, because it's *amazing*. I can hardly believe what I'm seeing, and I know no one else is ever going to believe me either. Crap.

That's also when I remember I have things to do tonight. Like, I promised my little brother I was going to actually make dinner instead of picking something up on my way home again. And Ren had made this disbelieving noise when I said it, so now I want to do it twice as much. Except I'm flying in the air on the back of a giant war-bird and I don't really know if I'm going to make it home for dinner. Man, Ren's gonna be pissed.

By the time I get home I'm sweaty and dizzy and high on adrenaline. I know no one's going to believe me if I just outright say that I was flying around on a giant bird, so I'm going to have to use drastic measures.

The door slams behind me, and I'm already calling for Ren before I can even get my shoes off. "Ren!" I shout. "You have to come see this!"

"I'm fairly certain he won't see whatever it is," Hector says pompously, wandering out of his room. He looks freshly awoken from a nap. He's going through this phase right now where he likes to sound more important than he really is, but I'm letting him get away with it. I'm trying to let him be a kid for as long as I can, and it's actually a lot harder than you would think.

"Ha-ha, very funny, Hec," I say blandly, and Hector gets this little smile on his face, because even though I say it sarcastically, we both know I really am amused. "Seriously, where's Ren?"

"He went to pick up dinner since you forgot," Hector says. It's not malicious or biting — just eleven-year-old honesty, plain and true — but it jabs through me all the same.

"Oh, shit," I say, and then immediately correct myself. "I mean, shoot. I'm so sorry, I meant to get home earlier—"

"It's okay," Hector says, already walking toward the kitchen. The table's been set, and I don't know if Ren did it before he left to make some sort of point to me or if he just asked Hector to get it done it before he got back. There are only three places, which makes sense since there's only three of us, but it still looks wrong to me. "I kind of wanted Arlo's anyway."

Hector's at that age where he can eat anything at anytime without it affecting him whatsoever, but I really don't want him eating fast food and takeout every night. Of course, since that's the case, I should probably stop feeding it to him all the time. It's just hard, leaving enough time at the end of the day to make a proper dinner for all of us. I work all day busting my ass and getting paid less than I should. Everyone takes advantage of the fact that they can pay people less if they don't have a high school diploma. I've been working since I was fifteen — ever since my parents died — and I really think it's about time I got a raise.

The door opens and Ren steps in, looking pissed. I mean, he looks pretty neutral, like he always does, but I can still tell that he's pissed. I've gotten good at reading him, especially since he rarely makes any facial expressions. I don't know if it's something he trained himself to do or just something that's native to his people, since none of them can see anyone's facial expressions anyway, but at first, it'd really freaked me out. Now, it's just Ren. He always says that if he can't gain insight by seeing people's facial expressions, why should other people be able to do so from his? So I guess it makes sense.

Anyway, I don't need Ren to glare at me to know he's mad. It's the way his shoulders look stiffer than usual, the way the door slams behind him when he never slams the door, the way his shoes stomp against the floor as he comes toward the kitchen.

"Hey, Ren," I say meekly, because I've always hated getting on Ren's bad side.

"Hey," he says shortly, and then we all sit down for the most uncomfortable dinner ever. I don't think Hector really notices the tension — he goes on about some project he's been working on in school, and I get this bubble of pride in my chest because he's so smart and I love him with all my guts — and by the time we're done eating I tell him he can go to his room and that I'll do the dishes tonight. It's always been a chore for Hector, but I'm hoping to get Ren to stay behind so I can talk to him. I need to apologize about dinner, and I still kind of want to tell him about the Avis.

Thankfully, Ren knows I want to talk to him. Or maybe he wants to talk to me. If that's the case, he doesn't exactly make it easy, harshly washing the dishes and sharply placing them back in their cupboards, glasses clinking and clanking off each other. He stumbles on the leg of a chair on his way back to the sink, his expression hardening even more, and that's how I know he's definitely mad.

Ren doesn't stumble. I mean, not usually. He may be blind — all Covans are — but that doesn't really put him at a disadvantage. His hearing is like a bajillion times better than anyone else's, and I think he "sees" similar to a bat or a whale or something. I don't know if it's because of the sound of his footsteps or what, but Ren's always been perfectly fine at navigating.

I can still remember when I first met him.

I was ten at the time, and it'd started out as just another day in Silva. Everyone's pretty lax around here — it's the kind of place where you can walk down the street and recognize everybody you see. That's why it's never been strange for kids to go out and play on their own; everyone knows there's someone around looking out for them.

What *had* been strange was seeing somebody unfamiliar. Even back then, I'd been obsessed with pushing the boundaries, trying to climb higher and farther from home than I had the last time, and the time before that. I'd always had this notion that I was the only one who really did that, that no one else could claim they'd ventured as far as I had. That's why it was so surprising when I came across this little shelter out in the middle of nowhere.

It was teeny tiny, for one thing, barely big enough to stand and move around in. Plus, the roof had been all shoddy and full of holes — totally impractical for when it rains, which is pretty often here in Silva.

At first, I'd thought it was some kind of fort another kid like me had built, and I'd been ready to investigate to make sure, but then someone had said, "Go away." Before I saw him, I'd thought Ren was older than me. He'd sounded all gruff and scary when he'd said that, but maybe it's my fault for never having been cautious enough for my own good, because instead of heeding the advice of the person who obviously didn't want to be bothered, I'd investigated further.

Ren had been sitting inside his little makeshift home, his back against the tree behind him and his chin resting on his knees. He'd been looking blankly in my direction, body tense, though I hadn't realized at the time that he couldn't see. Ren used to say that that was because I'm unobservant, but I think he underestimates how good he is at pretending he *can* see.

Sometimes, even now, I swear we're making eye contact when I know we're not.

"What are you doing here?" I'd asked him, squatting in front of his fort. It may have taken me a while to realize he was blind, but it took me even longer to realize he was homeless, living all on his own. Maybe Ren was right about me being oblivious.

"Minding my own business," he'd snapped at me. "Why don't you try it sometime?"

Back then, Ren had been super defensive. I hadn't understood it, but I hadn't really understood a lot of things. Despite being a year younger than me, Ren had known a whole lot more than I had about the real world, although I guess that tends to happen when you're abandoned as a nine-year-old. I'm still not entirely sure about his situation with his parents because he'd always been really private about that, closing up whenever I tried to pry, but I'm like ninety-nine percent sure that his parents were horrible people who kicked a little kid out of their home. It's no wonder he wandered so far away.

Still, I think part of why he never told me was because he didn't want me to realize he was Covan. I know it's horrible, but no one really likes people from Cova. A long time ago, there was this huge war. Cova lost, and all the other nations decided to punish them. Since then, Covans have been living underground, and hundreds of years have passed. That's why they're all blind, you know. Instead of creating lights, they just let all their other senses grow sharper.

It's all pretty crap if you ask me. Covans aren't any different than everybody else, and anyone who's met Ren can attest to that. He was just another kid like the rest of us, after all. Except for the fact that he was homeless and had snuck into Silva to escape the harsh, abandoned plains of the land above Cova.

Unable to take the hint, I hadn't left Ren alone. I'd just frowned, and never one to waste the chance of making a friend, I'd said, "I'm Theo, what's your name?"

To this day, I don't think Ren had actually wanted to be left alone. I don't think anyone does. That's why instead of ignoring me or telling me to go away again, he'd said, "Veloren."

I'd scoffed. "That's too long," I'd informed him.

"What?! *Yours* is too *short*," Ren had immediately countered, before hesitating and then adding, "*Theodore*."

Offended, I'd spluttered, "I'm gonna call you Ren!" Unsurprisingly, it'd stuck. My whole family had started calling him that. You know, after I'd started bringing him around. We'd never outright mentioned that Ren was Covan (or homeless) to my parents, but I think they knew. And they totally didn't care. They were always encouraging me to invite him over for dinner and sleepovers, telling him over and over that what was ours was his.

Now, with them having been dead for three years, what's ours really *is* his. He'd moved in the second I'd asked him, crying after failing yet another test and burning Hector's dinner for the third night in a row. The two of us had ended up getting jobs, which meant I stopped going to school and teaching what I'd learnt Ren in the afternoons, but it also meant that we could pay the bills, and that Hector could keep living a normal life. You know, as normal as it can be when you're being raised by your older brother and his best friend.

It's all still worth it to me. I think I'd do anything when it comes to Hector. He's the only family I have left.

"Ren," I say now, placing a hand on his arm. Instead of stiffening, Ren relaxes. He always does. I think it's because he's blind. Like when I'm touching him, at least he knows I'm really paying attention, you know? Maybe it grounds him. "I'm sorry I forgot about dinner. I can make it up to you."

Ren doesn't turn to look at me, because he doesn't need to, but I know he's listening. "How?" he says finally.

"What if I show you why I forgot?"

Ren sighs. It's because of this sigh that I know he's going to go with me. See, Ren can preach about duty and responsibility as much as he wants, but he really can't resist doing the fun things I manage to find. I think he loves a good adventure as much as I do.

"Fine," he agrees, and I can't hold back my whoop of excitement. I practically drag him through the house while he grumbles at me, because he hates being dragged around. I call out a goodbye to Hector while I'm at it, scarcely waiting for his reply. Moments later we're out the door and traversing the trees, climbing away from the busy village center, higher and farther.

"Where are we going, Theodore?" Ren sighs, climbing with ease. You'd think a blind guy would have a hard time navigating the trees, but he doesn't. He's lived here almost as long as he lived in Cova, now, but even in the beginning he'd gotten around fine. Still, I keep an eye on him, not wanting him to trip and fall up here on the bendy branches.

"You'll see," I promise him. "She's around here somewhere."

Ren stops in his tracks behind me. "*She?*" he says incredulously. "Theodore, who did you leave up here?" He's the only one who calls me that. Theodore. If anyone else did it, it'd totally gross me out, but it's fine with Ren. I'm used to it.

"Not who. *What*," I correct him, looking around me. I definitely left the Avis here somewhere. I told her to stay and it seemed like she was going to, so I hope she didn't up and run on me. I really want to ride her again.

"Theodore," Ren says sternly, and I can hear a bit of panic in his voice. At first, I think he's panicking because I'm being crazy again, but then I realize he can hear something I can't. I turn around to look at him, searching for the Avis even harder.

And then I see her.

She's below us, but she's steadily making her way up, jumping from branch to branch and looking for all the world like she belongs in the forest, despite likely having lived her entire life in the sky and on the desert plateaus in Volant.

The Avis hops onto a branch opposite me and Ren, balancing there delicately and watching the two of us with a cocked head. Ren looks shocked — his eyes are wide, as if that might help him see the creature before him, and his lips are parted. I love seeing his emotions expressed like this, considering how I'm so used to staring at his blank face. Even when he's insanely happy, he usually only shows it with the barest of smiles.

And then the Avis opens and closes her beak a few times, making this loud, rapid clicking sound, and Ren looks *terrified*. He stumbles a few feet backward along the branch, toward me, his hand extended. "*What is that?*" he hisses.

"It's an Avis," I say proudly, and the Avis is looking at me kind of like I'm looking at her. I think we're equally as excited to see each other, to be honest. I bet she came from the actual Volant military, which is no doubt incredibly boring for awesome creatures like her. She probably felt just as locked up and trapped there as I do here sometimes, and I don't blame her for wanting to go on an adventure.

"No, it's not," Ren says sharply, because he obviously doesn't want to believe it's true. He still looks scared, which makes sense. He's always been a lot more cautious than me.

"It is," I say convincingly. "She was just out here in the forest. She let me ride her."

"Tell me you're lying," Ren says.

"I'm not lying. She's friendly, I promise."

"That thing could hurt us," Ren says, and the Avis makes an angry sound. I don't think she likes being called a 'thing'.

"Icarus wouldn't hurt a fly!" I declare, and I swear Ren's eye twitches.

"Icarus…? You *named* it?"

"I named *her*," I correct. And I only just named her, really. It was a heat of the moment kind of thing, but it felt like something I had to do.

"That's a boy name," Ren points out.

"It's a girl name," I argue immediately. I can be annoying like that. Arguing with Ren has always been fun for me. I like pushing his buttons, riling him up. It's my only way to act like a kid anymore, seeing as I've been forced to grow up without my parents around. "Because Icarus is a girl, and that's what I named her."

Ren presses his palms against his temples, rubbing harshly. He's stressed out, and I don't want him to be. I want him to forgive me for not making dinner tonight, and then I want him to fly around on Icarus with me.

"You're crazy," Ren finally says. "I just — there are so many reasons why this is insane. She's either a wild animal and dangerous, or a trained animal and *twice* as dangerous. If you get caught with her you'll get in trouble, probably by two governments this time, and—"

"*And* she's awesome," I interrupt. I'm not in the mood to hear about all the kinds of trouble I could get in. I feel a little invincible right now. Icarus chose *me*. She showed up in the forest for me; took me on a ride in the sky. I feel like it's important. "Plus, she's not dangerous. Me and her totally get each other."

18

Ren takes a deep breath, sounding like he's gearing up for a speech, so I keep talking before he can really get going.

"Here, I'll show you," I say. "Just watch."

"I can't," Ren says, deadpan, and I roll my eyes despite the fact Ren can't see it.

"Here goes nothing," I mutter to myself, quiet enough that there's a chance Ren didn't catch it, and then I jump straight up into the air and off the branch, tumbling through the trees for the second time today.

No sane Silvan would ever jump out of the trees. I can hear Ren screaming my name from somewhere far above me — I've already fallen a lot, in just a second or two — but I don't call back, mostly because I couldn't hope to speak past all the air whipping into my mouth even if I wanted to.

Luckily, I know I'm not gonna die. I can see Icarus already zooming toward me, expertly avoiding the branches once more, and it's kind of a terrifying sight, seeing a full-grown bird of war diving toward you. Instead of skewering me with her beak or swallowing me whole, however, she swoops under me and I land on her back, clutching her feathers as her giant wings beat once, twice, and then she's hopping and flying back up through the trees again, toward Ren.

I feel horrible the second I see him. His face is streaked with tears, his eyes red as he gasps for breath, and I wonder if maybe there was a better way to show him that Icarus was a nice bird, but it's too late now.

"See?" I call desperately, and I know Ren can hear Icarus, can probably feel the wind generated by her wings.

"No!" he yells, but only because he's stubborn and angry and maybe a little distraught.

He needs to believe me, though. I'm suddenly sure of it, and desperate because of how sure I am, I say to Icarus, "Get him."

Ren hears me, because every strand of his DNA was basically *designed* to be able to hear me, and he shakes his head, hard. "No," he says, but that doesn't stop Icarus from zooming through the air, from shoving her beak between his legs and flicking her head back, sending Ren flying over her body. I reach up and snatch his hand out of the air, pulling him down firmly onto Icarus's back as she starts to move again, and Ren clings to me desperately, breathing heavily into my shoulder.

"Put me down!" he demands.

"Just wait," I say.

"I hate this," Ren growls, still clutching me tightly. And I think I get what he means. I bet I'd be scared too, if I were blind and suddenly completely lost my sense or orientation. I bet the loud sound of Icarus' wings beating isn't too helpful either. But I don't want him to be scared of this.

"It's okay," I assure him. "We're above the trees now, but just a little. I could probably jump off from here. I can see all of Silva."

Ren relaxes a bit, some of the tension easing out of him. Okay, so he definitely likes knowing where he is. But his expression is still pinched, and that kind of makes me happy. He shows emotions a bit easier when he's just with me, I think.

"We're going to have to do something about this," Ren says, his voice serious. Now he has just one hand clutching my shirt and the other resting against Icarus. She's soaring above Silva, and she seems delighted to be able to fly like this. I wonder how often the Avi in the Volant military get to fly for fun.

"What do you mean?" I ask, and I'm not playing dumb. That's the thing about me and Ren, though. He's always thinking three steps ahead of me.

"We can't keep an Avis," Ren says. "We'll get in trouble."

"No one has to know," I plead, my voice already taking on a desperate tone.

Ren opens his mouth to answer, but before he can there's a loud sound from down below, immediately followed by a broadcasted voice. "Avis riders, we respectfully request that you land now. Otherwise we'll be forced to consider this a Volation attack and will respond with our full military might."

CHAPTER 2

THEO

The head of the council isn't happy to see me. He looks really angry, in fact. He's this guy named Nicholas Barfung, and he hates me with a passion.

It isn't all that rare for him to show up at my front door, usually with some kind of warrant in hand. I tend to get in trouble a little too easily, which is maybe why I underestimated the severity of everything I've done today. I mean, I've never gotten in *real* trouble before.

But now, Barfung is glaring at me like I've gone and killed his cat or something, and a whole crowd of people have formed where we landed. They're all balancing on the branches above and below us, but it's the council that's truly surrounding us, each of them looking as stern and angry as Barfung.

"This is the last straw, Laurent," Barfung hisses. He likes to do that — throw my last name out there as if to show that I've really done it this time. He's not just glaring at me, though, he's glaring at Ren, too, which is ridiculous. Everyone knows Ren's never done anything wrong.

"Sir," I begin, straightening my back and gearing up to explain this whole thing away, but Barfung is already shaking his head, and then he's talking again before I can get the chance.

"There won't be any 'ands' or 'buts' this time," he says seriously, jabbing a finger at me. "This is a real criminal offense, going and stealing an Avis from the Volations."

Indignation bubbles up in me, wild and quick. "I didn't steal her!" I protest. "I found her in the forest!"

A whole chorus of scoffs seem to surround me, and I know not a single person here believes a word out of my mouth. "I'm serious!" I say, desperate.

"Save your lies for the judge," Barfung orders, and something cold slithers down my spine. The judge? Like, in a *court?*

The next thing I know, council members are ushering forward with ropes in hand. Panic grips my lungs and I back a little toward Icarus, her startled squawk indicating that she knows what's going on just as much as I do.

"No, stop!" I beg, but they throw the ropes over her anyway, and then they're twisting and pulling and she's crying out in pain and no one's doing anything about it. It's like they don't even see her as a living, breathing creature — just some kind of war machine.

"You're hurting her!" I scream, but someone else is holding me back, and I realize it's Ren.

"There's nothing we can do," he says quietly, his hands firm on my arms, and the fight drains out of me. I feel like my entire body is filled with metal, every part of me heavy and slow, which is almost unbelievable, considering how weightless I felt just minutes ago.

"We'll be by to collect you in the morning," Barfung informs me nastily. "Then your fate will be in the court's hands."

I resist sticking my tongue out until he turns his back, but once he does, it's tongue-out city — glaring and wiggling and everything. I hate him with my entire being.

"Come on," Ren says, and it sounds quiet and dejected. He should sound mad, should be yelling at me for being stupid and reckless again, but he just sounds tired. This isn't fair to him, I realize. I have to stop dragging him along and getting him in trouble with me. Hell, *I* need to stop getting myself in trouble, especially if I want to get any better paying jobs.

The walk home is slow and quiet, and in the silence I can hear Icarus crying out in distress. I wonder if I'm imagining it or if Ren can hear it happening for real. I consider asking him, but I know he'll lie to me if it's the truth.

On our street, almost everyone's curtains are drawn. I see a few pairs of eyes peeking out at us and I glare back at them, straightening my shoulders.

We used to be on good terms with our neighbors. Back when my parents were alive, anyway. They would say hello whenever they saw us, had traded leftovers sometimes for dinner. Now, they barely even look at us.

I know what people say about me. That I'm a delinquent. That I'm reckless and dumb and a danger to our community.

They're wrong. I might be a little too adventurous for my own good, but I never put anyone else's safety in jeopardy. And I'm a hard worker. I work harder than any of my neighbors, and it's all for Hector. I just want him to live a normal life, to go to school and have a lot of friends and do what he was meant to do with his life.

The front door closes quietly behind us, the both of us kicking off our shoes in the entrance. I line mine up against the wall automatically, not wanting Ren to trip over them later, and then we make our way to our rooms. Ren bids me goodnight and slips into his own, and I open Hector's door, poking my head inside. He's still awake.

"Hey Hector Shmector," I say, leaning against the door jamb. Hector's room used to be *our* room, but now it's all his. It looks pretty much the same as it used to. All the lights are on, despite the fact that I've been telling Hector we need to save on the electricity bill, and he's lying on his stomach with a book propped open in front of him.

"Hey Theo," Hector says, sitting up after he sees me. "I thought you'd be Ren."

"Ren comes in here?" I say, amused.

"Yeah, sometimes," Hector says. "Usually to say goodnight, but sometimes to tell me to turn off the lights. He says he can *hear* them."

I smile. I know Ren has crazy wicked hearing, but even now I'm not totally sure when he's pulling my leg. I'm pretty sure he can't actually hear the lights, though.

Finally, I step into the room, closing the door behind me. "I got in trouble today," I tell him.

Hector's expression drops, and my heart drops with it. I hate disappointing him. "Again?" he says, almost disbelievingly.

"Yeah," I say. "I'm going to court early tomorrow, so I might not see you in the morning."

Hector purses his lips. It takes more strength than it should not to reach over and pinch them together. Annoying Hec is kind of my job as the big brother, although I feel like a lot of my big brother jobs have disappeared in the face of my parental guardian jobs.

"It was worth it, though," I add suddenly, grinning. "I flew on an *Avis*."

Hector scoffs. "No way!" he says, but he's grinning, and his eyes are alight with excitement. I know he wants to believe me.

"Yes way," I promise him. "Night Hec. I'll bring something good home for lunch, okay?"

"Okay," Hector says happily enough, obviously satisfied with the promise of food. "Just don't be in too much trouble," he instructs.

"I won't be," I tell him, and I hope to the Stars I'm not lying.

I wake up to pounding on my door. For a second, I think it's the council and I bolt upright in a panic. But then I realize the knocking is just on my bedroom door — my parent's old door — and I say, "Come in."

The door opens, and it's Ren standing there. He already looks dressed and ready, totally composed.

"You should start getting ready," he tells me. "We'll want to look nice for the trial."

He's right, of course, so I get up and get dressed for the day. It's a good thing he woke me up when he did, because before long the council really is knocking at the door. I peek into Hector's room but he's still sleeping, so I decide not to bother him, vowing to bring him home something really good for lunch today. I'm gonna get him cookies, too.

Opening the door reveals Barfung and I'm frowning before he can even say a word. Ren is better behaved out of the two of us and he greets Barfung cordially, despite the lackluster response Barfung gives him.

"Let's go," Barfung says shortly, turning and starting toward the town square without bothering to make sure we're actually following him. "The hearing will begin the moment you two arrive, so we'll need to walk quickly."

I think Barfung's trying to make us look all sweaty and disheveled by the time we get there, but Ren and I have been running errands and doing laborious work for years now. It's gonna take a bit more than a brisk walk to get us winded.

When we arrive, my legs turn into jelly. We're having a public hearing apparently, and it seems like the entire town is here. People are sitting and standing in a ring all the way around the town square, except for where the judge is sitting. There are two vacant chairs in the very middle.

Barfung doesn't even say goodbye to us, nor does he have the courtesy to tell us that those chairs are, in fact, for us, so Ren and I just make our way over to them anyway. I feel puny, sitting here in front of everyone like this. I'm shaking all over, although I try my best to sit still and look calm. Ren does it easily. I almost believe he's not freaking out as much as I am, but he is. Even though his face and posture seem totally neutral, I can see the way he's rubbing his thumb and forefinger together. He's anxious.

"Ladies and gentlemen," the judge suddenly calls, and what little conversation was happening in the crowd ceases. "We gather today to examine the crimes committed by the accused, Theodore Laurent and Veloren Selcouth. The crime is as stands: undocumented travel from the lands of Silva and to the lands of

Volant, theft of a Volation war creature, and crimes of terror against the Silvan people."

My mouth is hanging open. Like, eyes wide, jaw dropped, the whole thing.

"How do you plead?" the judge says.

"Not guilty!" I answer immediately. "I didn't do any of that!" I can tell no one believes me, and it just makes me angry when in reality I should probably feel terrified. "I never left Silva — I found the Avis on the outskirts of our forest. And Ren wasn't even there, he had nothing to do with this!"

"Shut up," Ren mutters to me. He still looks entirely unaffected by everything.

"If I may speak, your honor?" a council member says, having already gotten to their feet. The judge waves them on. "The boy lies," the council member says, waving a hand flippantly at me. "Avi are highly trained militaristic creatures — one wouldn't wander into Silvan territory unprompted. Besides, Laurent has been in trouble countless times now. It's clear our previous punishments aren't teaching him any lessons."

My mouth's gone dry. I need to defend myself, need to try to explain everything that's happened, but no one wants to hear me out. The judge is nodding, looking pretty convinced himself, and I have no idea what to do.

"My decision is made," the judge announces, and all my protests die in my throat. *This is totally unfair.* "Veloren Selcouth," he continues, and what little murmuring had arisen in the court silences. "Innocent. He remains on good standing with the court, this being his first offense." Despite how anxious I am about my own sentencing, a little sigh of relief escapes me. At least Ren is innocent.

But Stars, what are they going to do to me? Put me in jail? I can't provide for Hector in there!

"Theodore Laurent," the judge's voice rings out, and I sit up a little bit straighter, hoping and praying with all my might for everything to just go my way for once. The silence and the tension builds; I can hear the creaking of chairs as people shift in their seats, the breathless anticipation as we all wait in unison for the judge to make his decision. "Guilty."

Panic rushes through me at full force. I'm trying to decide what I'm going to do, if I'm going to be able to earn wages in prison and send them back to Hector, how he's going to react when he hears his big brother is behind bars—

"And exiled to Restore the Light," the judge adds.

Silence falls like a blanket over the court, except for a single gasp. At first, I think it was me, but then I realize the sound came from Ren, and that his hands are clenching the sides of his chair as he leans forward in his shock, as if he somehow heard the judge wrong.

"You— you can't…" he says, except it's horribly quiet, and I'm sure I'm the only one who's heard it. Guards are already heading toward me, and I can see handcuffs in their hands. What, it's happening *now*? I don't even get to stop to get my stuff? Don't get to say goodbye to Hector?

My throat tightens and my eyes feel hot, but I push it all down and turn to Ren, desperate. "Take care of Hector," I beg, and Ren's face turns toward me, his blank expression gone in favor of shock and fear. Someone pulls me to my feet and I feel something cold click around my wrists. "Ask Mr. Johnston for my paper route. Hector can help you fill out the bills. Make sure he turns off the lights. Take care of him!" I say that last part over my shoulder, because my hands are cuffed behind my back and I'm already halfway across the square. Ren looks horribly small, sitting there alone in the middle of the town square. Hector's almost as tall as him nowadays and a bizarre thought flits through my head — *who's going to do the measuring wall now?*

"Let's go," grunts one of the guards, and I stumble over my feet as we move away from the town center. Here, all the branches grow so thick and wide it's almost like walking around indoors on the floors we built ourselves.

The guards walk briskly, going fast enough that I find myself tripping a couple of times, unable to get my balance with my hands tied behind my back like this. I don't know what I'm going to do. We're getting closer and closer to the edge of the forest and I should probably be devising some sort of plan but all that's going through my head is the judge's words ringing out over and over again. *Exiled to Restore the Light.*

They don't expect me to return.

The don't expect anybody to, once they're sent off to Restore the Light. It's all some big joke, some impossible task no one's actually capable of. A way to tell me to fuck off without sounding quite so callous.

You see, Darkness has been encroaching on our lands. No one knows where it's coming from, but there are places all over where the sun doesn't shine, a cloud of dark that light can't penetrate. They're supposed to look perfectly normal at night, mind you, but once the sun comes up... Darkness.

And no one knows how to fix it. The people that go in don't come back out, and I'm probably only being sent to Restore the Light because everyone's growing desperate at this point. A dark spot has been encroaching on Silva these past few years, after all, and a section of our forest has died, unable to receive sunlight anymore.

"Uncuff him," one of the guards says behind me, and there's a click followed by the sudden release of pressure. I find myself rubbing my wrists, not even having realized they were sore.

"We'll watch you leave Silva from here," the other guard says. I can see the edge of the forest from where we are. Looking down, I think I can see some dirt, some of the actual forest floor. There's a prod at my back and I stumble forward a step, the branch below me bending warningly. I've never been this far from home, I realize. That's when it all finally hits me.

"What am I supposed to do?" I demand, turning to look at the guards behind me. "Where am I supposed to *go*? Stars, where do I even start?"

The expression on one of the guard's twinges just a bit, and he looks sympathetic. Pitying. But I don't need pity, I need *guidance*.

"Sorry, kid," he says. I think he might really mean it, but that still doesn't help me.

They're just watching me, and it's not like I can keep standing here all day, so I start walking. I feel like I'm walking the plank, straight to my death, and I'm really freaked out. Still, I try not to look too pathetic, because I don't want word getting back to Hector and Ren that I was a wimp about this. I want them to think of me as being strong, I want them to believe I'll come back.

I want to believe I'll come back.

So I square my shoulders and run the rest of the way. It's scary jumping from branch to branch when they're this thin, when I can actually see the ground below me, but I do it anyway. And when the next branches are too far for me to reach, I jump anyway, and I keep running after my feet hit the ground despite how jarring it is. It feels so *different*, hard and firm, and I can run on it even faster than I can run in the trees, not having to worry about where I can safely put my feet.

Another moment later and I'm out — the forest of my home is behind me and before me is a vast expanse of open fields. I've only ever seen anything like this in textbooks before, but I keep going anyway, trying to be unphased. So what if I don't have any supplies or money or means of travel? So what if I have absolutely no idea where to start in order to Restore the

Light? I'll do it anyway. I've got myself, got my brains. I may not be as smart as Ren, but... I can still do it. *Don't be afraid,* I tell myself.

I walk for a while.

I have absolutely no idea where I'm going, obviously, so I just head straight, hoping I'll figure something out along the way. My stomach's already growling, and I wish I'd had the foresight to think I might be skipping more meals than just breakfast today. And poor Hector... soon he's going to realize that he's missing a lot more than just a nice lunch.

It takes me by surprise, when it happens. I think I've been walking for a couple hours — at least, the trees seem pretty distant behind me. I'd been idly wondering if I was going to end up dying of lack of water before I'd even had a chance to Restore the Light when a screech splits the air and has me looking up.

A shadow covers me as Icarus flies overhead, blocking the sun. I can't help the smile that takes over my face — I'm not alone!

"Icarus!" I yell out, grinning up at the sky like a lunatic. "What are you doing here, girl? How'd you escape?"

She doesn't answer me, obviously, but she starts to descend, flying in circles as she drops lower and lower through the sky. It's not until she's beating her wings heavily in order to slow down that I realize she's not riderless. Her legs hit the ground and dust kicks up from her still beating wings and I just stand there gaping at Ren, who's clinging to her back in terror, eyes clenched shut as if that's going to help him not see any more than usual.

"*Ren?*" I finally manage to get his name out of my mouth, and his face turns toward mine.

"Hi Theodore," he says breathlessly. Gears are turning in my head, attempting and failing to put together what the hell is happening right now. Finally, I decide to just come out and say it.

"What are you doing here?"

"I couldn't let you go alone," Ren says, his voice hardening with surety.

And I'm touched — really, I am — but, "What about Hector?!"

Ren's expression closes off. I hate it when this happens. Hate that he hides even from me.

"He'll be fine," Ren says, but I'm shaking, because now I'm not just scared for me, I'm scared for all of us. Ren, who's now definitely exiled with me, seeing as he *actually* stole an Avis, and Hector, because he shouldn't have to do this! He shouldn't have to be alone, shouldn't have to worry about taking care of himself... "He'll be fine," Ren repeats, stern. "You know he's a smart kid."

"He shouldn't have to be alone," I protest. I can't breathe. It feels like my ribs are pressing in on my lungs. How is Hector supposed to survive all on his own?

"Hey," Ren says, and I don't know how he can tell my face is crumpling, tears coalescing in my eyes when he can't even see me, but he does. "He's going to be all right, okay? I went home before I stole Icarus. I told him what's happening. He's going to stay in school and use our savings — we can't use them while we're exiled, anyway — and he's going to be *fine*. We'll be back before he can even make a dent in them. Okay?"

I sniff. It's not okay, not really, but there's no way we can change any of it now. "Okay," I agree weakly, and I think I get it. If it'd been Ren who was exiled… I couldn't have left him to do this on his own. Then again, I couldn't have left Hector behind in Silva either. At the very least, I'm thankful Silva won't provide any dangers for him. He's going to be safe in there, even if me and Ren are risking everything in an attempt to Restore the Light out here.

"Get on," Ren says, his voice softer now, and he scoots over on Icarus' back. I think about how terrified he was to ride her, how scared he clearly still is, and I'm touched. He did this for me.

Icarus kneels and I scramble up her back, shoulder bumping against Ren's. He has a bag on his back — thank the Stars he stopped for supplies.

I clear my throat a couple of times, getting comfortable on Icarus for what'll likely be a long ride ahead of us. "What do we do now?" I say quietly, turning to look at Ren.

Ren's fingers tighten in Icarus' feathers. "We Restore the Light," he says, and Icarus shoots into the sky.

CHAPTER 3

VELOREN

I hope Theodore doesn't ask why I followed him. I'm bad at lying, you see. The thing is, I figured after abandoning our home and stealing an Avis to travel with him, he'd just draw his own conclusions, which I'm pretty sure he has.

I can think of all sorts of lies for why I might've followed him, too. Like maybe I don't think he can actually manage to do this on his own. Or maybe I finally started craving adventure like he always has. But no matter how many excuses I think of, I know they'll fall flat. So if he asks me, I mean *really* presses me for an answer, it would have to come down to one of the two truths I have, and I don't want to tell him either of them.

The first is that I'm in love with him. It's something that I try not to think about, but I feel like I've known it for as long as I've known him. That probably sounds crazy, but there's just something about Theodore. I don't know how everyone he comes across doesn't feel the exact same as me. Anyway, I couldn't have let him do this all by himself — not when I know it's so dangerous.

And even though I never want to tell him any of that — I can't even begin to imagine how he'd react — I know I'd spill it all to him before ever telling him my other reason.

I don't want him to Restore the Light.

I know I haven't lived with my people for years, but I still feel loyal to them. I'm still *one* of them. When I hear people talking badly about Covans, I bristle. When I hear talk about Restoring the Light, knowing what I know, I hope to the Stars that no one figures out how to do it.

I don't know what I'm going to do. I need to get Theodore and myself unexiled without Restoring the Light. I have no idea how I'm supposed to accomplish this, but I know I'm definitely not going to be able to figure anything out from up here.

I'm trying not to show it, but the Avis terrifies me. I have no idea where I am. It's so loud up here that I feel disoriented, lost. And it's like a constant earthquake, this giant bird moving relentlessly with each beat of its wings. I'm holding onto its feathers for dear life, honestly, but it's not entirely out of fear that I say, "I think we should find a town to land in soon."

"What? Why?" Theodore says, already sounding defensive. He enjoys flying too damn much for a Silvan.

"We have no idea where we're going, or even where to start," I reason. "We need to talk to people and gather information. Can you see any towns nearby?"

I know where we are in theory. The lands in between the four nations used to belong to the Covans, before we were forced underground. In the centuries since then, it's become a land of nobodies. Askund, we call it. Here live the people who don't belong to any nation, along with those that have been exiled from them. If I can't figure out an alternative way to end our exile, this is where we'll end up.

"I think there's some sort of town in the distance," Theodore says, though he sounds unsure.

"If it is one, we should land before we get too close," I say. "We won't want to announce our presence with a Volation war-bird."

Icarus squawks, her body moving with the sound, and I cling to her all the harder.

"Don't listen to him," Theodore says in that infuriating baby-talk voice he insists on using with the bird. "You're so much more than that, aren't you? *Aren't you!?*"

The Avis squawks again and I groan at the sickening lurch of her body. Maybe I'm scared of heights. Sure, I have no idea how high up we are, but I don't have a hard time imagining slipping off Icarus' back, nor the feeling of my body plummeting through open air…

"Hey!" Theodore says suddenly, and he slaps me on the shoulder to get my attention, as if I'm not constantly listening. "It *is* a town!"

"Thank the Stars," I mutter, but Theodore doesn't hear me. He's too busy talking to the bird, encouraging her to land so we can walk to the village.

Thankfully, Icarus really has taken some weird liking to Theodore, so she brings us to the ground. The second her feet make contact I feel relief flood through me. Theodore grabs my hand without me even having to ask and he tugs me after him as he scoots toward the edge of Icarus' back. We slide off her, my stomach momentarily catching in my throat as we fall, but then our feet hit the ground with a jarring impact and I stumble forward a few steps, releasing Theodore's hand as I do.

For a second, I just stand there, amazed. It's been a long time since I could stand without feeling the ground moving minutely beneath me. Creaking and swaying and shifting and settling. Here it's just firm, hard ground, like that from which I came.

"You all right?" Theodore says, his voice somewhere off to my left. Icarus is making that creepy clicking sound, presumably with her beak, so I think Theodore's doing something with her. Maybe he's leading her into hiding.

"Yeah," I say, turning to follow him. I stop when my foot lands in grass, taking a step back so I can stand on the hard ground of the path again.

"It's weird, right? The ground," Theodore says, coming back to me now. "*Stay*, Icarus," he adds.

"Not really," I say, mind drifting back to foggy memories of my days in Cova. I think Theodore's forgetting that I came from ground like this. It's not the same, though. Underground, it was always cool and damp, and eyesight was a thing that came up very rarely. I didn't even have a real concept of it before I met Theodore.

He hums in acknowledgement before nudging my elbow with his own. "I think we're about a mile away," he says, and he starts walking. I fall into step beside him. "I hope you're right about all this."

"I am," I assure him. "What better way to get information than by talking to people?"

And this is true, genuinely, but it's also a means for me to stall. If someone down there actually has a good idea about how to Restore the Light, I'll have to try to lead Theodore away from their suggestions.

I feel horrible about all this, but what can I do? If I let Theodore Restore the Light, my people will suffer. And if I don't, *Theodore* will suffer. It's like a lose-lose situation, the only solution being circumventing the problem entirely. I just have to figure out how to do that.

"What if we need some sort of verification of travel?" Theodore frets, drawing me out of my thoughts. It's probably a good thing. They just seem to be going in circles.

"Theodore, we're in *Askund*," I say. "This entire place thrives on crime. You really think someone's going to try to stop us at the gates?"

"You're right," he breathes. "I need to calm down." And despite that declaration, he finds several other things to panic about on the duration of the walk. I'm almost relieved by the time we make it to the little town, despite disliking not knowing exactly where I am.

The town is loud, and therefore disorienting. It takes a lot more concentration for me to navigate normally here, and I think even then I must be failing somehow, because Theodore keeps grabbing my arm. I know he doesn't want anyone to realize I'm blind, because that'll just cause us trouble, so I try to keep my head up, despite the fact that it's a bit easier to concentrate on the influx of sounds when I don't have to worry about what I look like, too.

"This place is weird," Theodore murmurs to me. I can only imagine what it must look like, probably bustling with people of all kinds. I imagine the buildings are all in the process of falling apart with homeless people lining the streets. From the snatches of conversation I've picked up, I think the both of us underestimated just how crime-ridden this place is. People everywhere are talking about odd jobs and deals, and someone passing by us mentions a 'target'. I can only hope they're talking about some sort of shooting practice and not a person.

"How are we supposed to figure anything out in here?" Theodore says lowly. He grabs my arm suddenly, yanking me away from some unknown tripping hazard, and then he keeps his hand there. I have to replay his question in my head.

"We have to find the right crowd," I say.

"I think this is *all one crowd*," Theodore hisses, and I don't doubt him. I don't think we were really prepared for what Askund entails. I'm just about to suggest that we leave — maybe take some time to regroup and figure out a plan — when Theodore says, "*Woah.*"

I hear it a second after he sees it. There's a massive crowd somewhere in front of us, tons of voices meshing together in what could be either anger or excitement, considering how loud it is. The idea of walking into a crowd isn't an ideal one to me, but Theodore's already dragging me forward and into some building — probably a bar — before I can get the chance to object. His hand slides from my elbow to my wrist to my hand, his fingers slotting carelessly with mine, and I feel any urge I had to protest dissipate. So what if we're pushing further and further into a crowd? Feeling completely disoriented isn't *that* bad.

In moments, I can feel people pressing in on all sides, and a few of them grumble and say stuff like, "Watch it!" but Theodore doesn't pay them any mind, so neither do I. I still have no idea what we're heading toward, but that's not an entirely unexpected feeling when Theodore's the person you spend all your time with. I've learned to be patient, so I simply let myself be strong-armed through the crowd until Theodore suddenly comes to a stop. "Woah," he says again.

He's managed to get us to the front. Everything sounds a lot clearer up here.

"You're cheating," a man growls, his voice deep and angry. A girl lets out a pretty, tinkling laugh, and I realize it's her he's talking to.

"You're just a sore loser," she says lightly, sounding almost flirty in her response. "Do you want to play again?"

"What's going on?" I ask Theodore. I know there must be some kind of bet or game happening, but I can't figure out any more than that on my own.

"This girl has, like, a pile of money," Theodore tells me. And then, sounding reverent and almost breathless, "She doesn't look like she's from around here."

I don't glower — I rarely make any facial expressions, if I can help it — but if there were a cloud floating above me reflective of my mood, it'd be storming right now.

"But what are they doing?" I demand.

"Some sort of bet, I think," Theodore says, and then the noise of the crowd around us builds again. Whatever the two of them are doing, it's happening now.

"How about we make things more interesting?" the girl says, her voice easily picked out of the cheering crowd now that I know what I'm listening for.

"How?" says the man, sounding impatient.

"You correctly guess which hand the coin is in, and I'll give you back all your money."

"And if I guess wrong?"

Without a moment's hesitation: "You double it."

Stupid. If the guy's already lost this many times, there's no way he'd—

"Deal."

Idiot.

At least now it's clear what kind of game is going on here. The crowd is still loud as the girl presumably starts her trick, although Theodore falls silent beside me, likely watching with rapt attention. I step closer, curious, and listen intently. If she's like anyone else in this line of business, she's cheating somehow. She seems so confident that she'll win, so she has to be.

And then—

Clink.

It's small, and barely noticeable, but it's there. The sound of two small, metal objects hitting each other. You'd have to really be listening for it to hear it, especially over the sound of the crowd, but I doubt anyone's trying to listen anyway. They're all just using their eyes, attempting to follow the coin and decide which hand it ends up in.

"Theodore," I say quietly, just as another *clink* sounds from her direction. "Is she wearing any jewelry? Bracelets?"

"What? No," Theodore says, distracted. I'm sure of it, now. This girl has two coins, not one.

She slaps her hands on the table, the sound of her palms almost loud enough to obscure the sound of a coin smacking the table under her hand, but not quite. It's on the right side — her left — although I'm sure no one else thinks so. She probably did some fancy sleight of hand, something distracting and showy that everybody fell for.

"Which hand?" she asks.

"*This one*," the man says, sounding confident.

I can only imagine the look of triumph on the girl's face as she delicately responds, "Sorry," probably opening up her other hand for all to see. The man roars in anger and the crowd grows louder again too, amazed or bewildered or furious themselves.

"Anyone else want to try?" the girl calls loudly, confident.

I don't know what I'm doing, but I've stepped forward before I've even had a chance to think it through.

"I'll play," I say, and I hear Theodore say, "*Ren*," from behind me, sounding alarmed, but I ignore him.

"Yeah?" the girl says. "What'll you bet?"

"I win, you give me all your earnings," I say, and a hush falls over the crowd. I still can't quite figure out why I'm doing this. Maybe I'm trying to prove something — this girl's really gotten on my nerves, and I want to impress Theodore more than she had. Plus, the money wouldn't be so bad. We can always go somewhere else to try to gather information on the Darkness, but we won't make it very long if we have to steal every time we want to eat.

"And what do I win?" the girl says, sounding incredulous now. She doesn't think I have anything to offer her, and I don't, really, but…

"An Avis," I say.

"We are *not* giving up Icarus," Theodore says hotly, still somewhere behind me.

"Deal," the girl says after a moment's pause, and I can't place the tone of her voice. "Ready?" she says.

I nod, aware that she's watching me, and then she begins. The clinking of her coins is still there, faint but present, and I hope to the casual observer it looks like I'm watching with all my concentration. Really, I'm just listening as hard as I can, ignoring the murmuring of the crowd around me.

She slams her hands on the table. It's under her left hand again.

"Her right," Theodore whispers. He's not too close to me, but I could pick out his voice anywhere.

"Your left," I say. The girl pauses.

"You sure?" she sings confidently, and I know she's bluffing.

"Her *right*," Theodore whispers again, a little louder this time.

"I'm sure," I say, and the pause drags on even longer this time. She's thinking, I'm sure of it. Trying to figure out a way to show me her hand without showing the coin in it. "Show me your hand," I demand, tired of waiting. Finally, she does so, and I know because of the gasp that ripples through the crowd.

"I thought it was in the other one," someone says.

"I've never seen her lose," says another.

"Theodore, help me with our winnings?" I say, turning to face him, and I feel him rush by me. He chuckles nervously as he collects our money, apologizing awkwardly to the girl, and then he's by my side again.

"Let's go," he says, and I don't hesitate to follow him, the two of us weaving through the crowd together as quickly as we can. The second we're outside the bar, walking along hard dirt again instead of creaking floorboards, Theodore huffs out a breath, and I drop my hand from where I'd been holding onto his jacket.

"That was insane," he says. "What were you thinking?!"

"I was thinking that I could win," I say gruffly. And I did, didn't I?

"But offering up Icarus like that?" Theodore demands.

"I wouldn't have given her up," I promise him. Theodore doesn't seem placated, and he mumbles grumpily under his breath as we make our way back through the town. I'm not too worried about it. I figure he'll forgive me by the time we're back with Icarus.

That's one of the things I love about him. Theodore feels everything so *fiercely*. It's like all his emotions are constantly fighting to be the most present inside him. When his parents died, he was so sad, longed for them so horribly, that I was sure

48

he'd be bedridden and depressed for months. But he loved Hector too much for that, so he pushed back on every ounce of sadness with three ounces determination, and he picked himself right back up and stayed strong for his little brother.

He's just like that, constantly thinking about other people before himself. He always knows what to say to make me laugh, even when I'm in a bad mood. Hell, the fact that he can *tell* when I'm in a bad mood is pretty astounding in itself. I feel like I never even act any different than usual.

It's just… everything about him. How strong he is. The way you can hear his smile in his voice. How he'll start to laugh at something he's saying and not be able to get through it, even though no one else knows what he's laughing at yet. The way he *always* manages to burn whatever he's cooking, and the way he claims he's not scared of anything even though he's clearly terrified of thunderstorms. He always gets really quiet during them.

Stars, I can't think of a single thing I don't love about Theodore. I think when I first realized that was when I realized I loved *him*. I hadn't known what to do with that information. Still don't, really.

I shake my head, realizing I need to stop getting lost in my thoughts. I can still hear the sound of Theodore walking a step ahead of me, but that's when I realize that's not all I can hear.

I listen to people walking every day. The sound of their shoes on the ground (or trees, usually) and their clothes brushing against their bodies. I can hear people walking faster and people walking slower, can tell what direction they're going in and who's walking together, based on the cadence of their footsteps. And right now, I hear three people walking together. Me and Theodore and...

Who's walking with us?

I open my mouth to tell Theodore, and I'm in the process of speeding up to get next to him, but it's just then that someone grabs my arm. There's a hand over my mouth by the time I'm yanked backwards and I can't get any words out, can't call out to Theodore. I struggle against the captor, trying to escape their hold on my face, my wrists, but it's no use. No one on the street calls out or says anything, so this kind of thing must not be out of the ordinary for Askund.

Before I know it, I've been dragged away, and my captor shoves me harshly against a wall. The air feels different here — colder, breezier — so I assume we're in an alley.

"Who are you? What do you want?" I gasp the second their hand leaves my mouth. They still have a hold on my wrists, managing to pin them against the wall above my head.

"Forget about me that easily? Come on, what do you *think* I want?" comes the answering scoff, and recognition floods through me. It's the girl from before. The con artist.

"I won that money fair and square," I bite out, glaring at her.

"Don't be an idiot," she hisses. "I don't care about the money. I want the Avis."

"Yeah, you still didn't win," I say. "Why the hell would I give you the Avis?"

"How about because if you don't, I'll use *this*—" she's holding something up, I'd bet money on it "—on your pretty little eyes."

No one's ever called my eyes pretty before. I actually blink in surprise, and then I wish Theodore were here so I could ask him if that's actually true. And then I wonder why I even care.

"Look," I say, hoping I seem confident and not just totally oblivious to the fact that she's probably holding some sort of knife in front of my face. I hope she doesn't use it, because even though I don't use my eyes, I still appreciate having them. "The Avis is our only mode of transportation, so you're out of luck. Plus, it's not even my Avis to give."

"Well it wasn't yours to take, either," the girl scoffs. I'm not about to get into it with her, not about to explain the whole wild Avis on the loose schtick, so I just shrug my shoulders.

"I'll give you your money back, but I won't give you the Avis," I say, trying to placate her.

This crazy girl actually *growls*, and finally she says, "How about you just let me hitch a ride back to Volant with you?"

And it takes a second for everything in my brain to click, but finally it does. "You think we're Volation?" I blurt out.

"Um. You're not?"

"No?" I say. "We're Silvan." The lie rolls of my tongue easily. Sometimes I almost think I *am* Silvan, considering how long I've lived there.

The girl huffs, then, and I can hear the dejection and disappointment in that breath. She really wants to get back to Volant, for some reason. Not that they'll let her in, if she's been exiled like us.

And suddenly, I can hear Theodore — thank the Stars. He's calling my name, sounding like he's getting closer and closer to the alley. I wonder if the girl is still holding a weapon to my face or if she put it down sometime between the origin of the threat and now.

"*Theodore!*" I call when I think he's close enough to hear me, and the girl gasps quietly. Theodore stops calling my name, and I'd bet it's because he's running.

"Damn you," the girl mutters to me, seconds before Theodore bursts into the alleyway with a shout of, "Ren!" And then, "Oh — it's you. Um. We can't give you your money back. We... spent it all, already," he lies terribly.

"I don't want the money," the girl says. "I want you to take me to Volant on your Avis."

"Uhh," says Theodore.

"I'll pay you," the girl says. "Or I'll — I'll help you. Whatever you need. Just take me to Volant."

"Well, we weren't really *planning* to go to Volant..." Theodore says uneasily.

"Please," the girl says desperately, and I'm shaking my head, because we don't need an extra problem in our lives right now, and surely Theodore will listen to me, even with that overly large heart of his—

"Sure," Theodore says, making me groan.

I *hate* this girl.

"Oh, thank you so much!" she says, her demeanor changing completely. She lets go of my wrists and I hear her walk away from me, and Theodore laughs suddenly, and I just *know* they're hugging. Theodore and I never hug. Why don't we hug? "I'll be a good traveling companion, I swear! You totally won't regret this. Oh, and I'm Eleanor, by the way."

"Like the Lost Princess," Theodore comments. He's always been good at that. Joking with people he hardly knows and carrying on conversations without any of those awkward silences that seem to follow me around. I don't know how he does it.

"Exactly," Eleanor says. "Eleanor became the most popular baby name in Volant, so you can find about a hundred of us anywhere you go."

"Then we'll be sure not to add anymore Eleanors to our group. You can be our only one, I promise."

Eleanor laughs, and Theodore laughs too. I think I might be trying to eviscerate Eleanor with my mind. I'm standing well off to the side, my arms crossed over my chest.

"What was I thinking?" Theodore says, a moment later. "I forgot to introduce us! I'm Theo, and this is my best friend, Ren."

"It's nice to meet you both," Eleanor says pleasantly, as if she weren't threatening to gouge my eyes out mere moments before.

"Yes, very nice," I say blandly. "Are we sure the Avis can even carry all of us?"

"Oh, a full-grown Avis could carry four, maybe five people for an extended period of time," Eleanor says immediately, sounding like she's rattling something off from a textbook. "Even a young one could carry the three of us. How old is it?"

"I'm not sure," Theodore says. "But she's got those military markings on her beak, so she's old enough to have gone through training, I guess."

"Crude, isn't it?" Eleanor says. "I wish they'd find some other way to mark them."

Theodore agrees enthusiastically, and my huff of annoyance goes unheard. I didn't even know Icarus *had* weird beak markings.

The two of them start walking without any prior warning so I fall in step behind them, blood boiling. Theodore's telling Eleanor all about how he found Icarus and how he was exiled to Restore the Light because of it.

"That's horrible," Eleanor says. "And they just sent you off? Without your brother?"

"*Yes*," Theodore says emphatically, his anger apparent in that one word alone. "So I *have* to succeed. I have to get back to him."

"Maybe you should stop in Udula," Eleanor suggests. "They probably have hundreds of books on the Darkness."

"You're right!" Theodore gasps, sounding excited, and I feel something inside me deflate just a little bit more. I still don't know what I'm going to do. I *can't* let him Restore the Light, but how else can I get Theodore un-exiled? It all feels so hopeless.

CHAPTER 4

ELEANOR

"Oh, she's beautiful!" I say once we've finally crested the ever-sloping hill. The Avis stands up, rising from where she'd been hidden in the tall grasses, the second we reach her.

"I know, right?" Theo says breathlessly, and I don't think it's because of the hill. He's looking at the Avis with such admiration in his eyes, so I look back at her too.

She seems perfectly healthy. No injuries or indications of abuse; no reason for her to have abandoned her post. From the markings on her beak, I can tell she's from the defense quadrant. Nothing adds up.

It doesn't seem like she recognizes me, but I guess it's pretty presumptuous to assume that she would have. It's not like I can tell her apart from the hundreds of other Avi back in Volant, either.

I realize then that Theo's still talking to me, rambling on about the Avis, who he keeps calling 'Icarus'. He's clearly fond of her, and I've always heard that how a person treats animals is indicative of their character, so I relax slightly in his presence.

But only slightly. Because even with all these good signs, I feel like I can't trust these guys. I just can't buy that an Avis would leave Volant for absolutely no reason. That makes me think that Theo somehow stole her, but I can't see how anyone could've actually managed that.

And then there's that Ren character. His whole demeanor puts me off. Every time I look at him, he looks so expressionless. And I feel like he's never looking me directly in the eyes. Plus, I'm still kind of mad at him for scamming me out of my hard-scammed money. I have no idea how he didn't fall for it — two coins, lots of flashy movements, and a quick switcheroo at the last moment. It works every time! After I put the coin in my final hand, I drop it into my sleeve and flick the second coin, hidden in my other sleeve, into my palm. Maybe it was just luck, but somehow Ren won when everybody else normally loses.

Still, whether or not I trust these guys doesn't matter. They're my only hope of getting back to Volant, which I've been away from for far too long now — not that it was my choice.

Although I guess that's all in the past. After all, there's nothing I can do to go back and change the fact that my fiancé tried to kill me in order to steal the throne.

Yes, it's surprising, I know. I'm not just *one* of the Eleanors in Volant — I'm *the* Eleanor. Eleanor Breindal, daughter of King Robert Breindal III, very exciting. It's been so long since anyone has connected my name with the name of the Lost Princess, though, and had I known Theo and Ren weren't native to Askund, I would've given them a fake name.

Out here in Askund, not many people know much about what's going on inside the nations, meaning it doesn't matter if I use my real name or not. Nobody knows who I am, although that's definitely a good thing, if you ask me. Askund is probably the most dangerous place for anyone to know my identity. This place is full of savages, and I don't doubt the lengths they'd go to to use me as some kind of bargaining chip.

Then again, maybe my own kingdom is full of savages too. I'd never really *loved* Warren, but I'd respected him, and I'd respected the fact that it was tradition to marry some man you didn't know all that well in order to do good for the kingdom. Surprise, surprise, it turned out not to be so great of an idea to marry your one and only daughter off to someone who was practically a stranger. He got rid of me at the first chance he got — hit me over the head and shoved me in a boat to drift aimlessly away from my kingdom, though I suspect he meant to kill me. It's been nearly a year since then, a time filled with me trying my hardest to find some sort of way back, so there's no way I'm going to squander my chance now.

"Can you say hi, Icarus?" Theo says, his voice in a higher pitch than usual. The Avis squawks at me, which I take as a hi, so I pat her on the beak. Appeased with this course of action, Icarus lowers herself to the ground for better access.

"Ladies first," Theo says, and he offers me a hand. I take it, despite the fact that I've mounted Avi countless times in my life, and settle on her left side. Theo climbs up after me, and then he reaches out a hand for Ren. "You next, dude," he says. Ren raises his arm in the air, looking kind of imperious if you ask me, and Theo leans forward and grabs his hand before pulling him up.

Ren bumps into Theo as he's climbing onto the Avis, and Theo directs him backwards. "You're behind me now," he informs him. Some emotion flashes across Ren's face, too quickly for me to catch, and then we're all settled.

"Ready?" Theo says, sounding excited. I don't exactly blame him — most people outside Volant never get to grace the skies.

"No," Ren mutters, moments before Theo urges Icarus into the air. Ren's eyes are clenched shut, one hand balancing on the Avis and the other fisted in the back of his friend's jacket. He must be scared of heights.

It quickly becomes apparent that Theo and Icarus have a bond very much unlike the ones that form in the military between commander and Avis. There, everything is strictly professional between both parties. Affection isn't really allowed, because attachment would mean depression if anything were to happen to the other in battle.

So seeing this is totally different to anything I've ever seen before. There's no barking commands, no orders for what Icarus should do. Theo doesn't even seem entirely sure of how to control her, he just kind of talks to her like she's a person, hoping she'll do what he wants. He's lucky Avi are so smart.

"I was thinking we could stop at Udula first," Theo says, looking up at me. "And then we could take you to Volant after." It makes sense, considering how close we are to Udula and how far we are from Volant, so I agree, because there really isn't any room for me to argue, despite how much I want to get home.

With that, Icarus flies with more purpose, moving through the air like she's really meant to. We're only an hour's flight out from Udula, so it won't be long until we get there. That'll give us a good few hours in the libraries before they close for the night, at which point we'll have to figure out what we're doing about our sleeping arrangements. Not to mention, we'll need to find somewhere to hide the Avis.

"So," Theo says conversationally, after about a minute of silence. Or rather, the absence of conversation. It's kind of hard for silence to occur when wind is rushing past your entire body. "Volant, huh? What's that like?"

I frown. It's not that I'm not used to idle chit chat — I am, having experienced thousands of pointless conversations with various stuck up royals in our ballroom — but it's been so long since I've had to participate in it. In Askund, everything is different. Nobody talks to you without a purpose, and you can never let your guard down. Maybe that's why mine's still up, even though Theo, for some reason, sounds genuinely curious.

Maybe he's trying to figure out my kingdom's secrets. He has one of our Avi, after all. But then, he must think I'm just some sort of random citizen, so there's really no reason that I'd have any good intel for him. Which means he really *is* just curious.

I've never known anyone like this. Anyone that's wanted to talk to me without some ulterior motive. Without the idea of getting on my father's good side or leeching information from me or trying to make themselves feel important.

Is this what people are like in the real world? Not like what I've come to expect is Askund, where you have to steal and cheat if you want to stay alive, but everywhere else. Are people just… genuine?

"It's nice," I find myself saying, a smile sneaking across my face. It's been a while since I really let myself think about home. A part of me always feared I'd never make it back there. After all, what chance did a princess stand when thrown into the tumultuous culture of Askund?

I miss all of it. My home, with its countless hallways and secret passages, with the gardens that I'd always get lost in in the evenings, a book in hand. My home, with the bustling servants who smiled and waved to me every time they happened to walk past and the soldiers who almost constantly followed me from a distance, probably assuming they were much sneakier than they actually were. My home, with the sprawling streets of the city, always loud and crowded with my people busy going about their days. I can hardly count the amount of times I'd snuck out of the castle to mingle among them, a hood pulled far over my face and the guards at the castle probably sounding the alarm at my sudden disappearance.

I wonder if that's what they think happened to me. That I snuck out of the castle one too many times. That some evil peasant finally got the chance to kill me. Warren probably told everybody some kind of version of that story.

"There's always people out in the streets, even at night," I finally continue. "And it's so hot during the day, up on those plateaus, but once the sun goes down it gets so cold that we need heavy coats."

"Volant sounds cool," Theo says, and when I look at him, he's grinning. I grin back.

"It is," I inform him. "What about Silva? Do you like it there?"

The smile slips off Theo's face. "I miss it already," he says quietly. "I miss the way the branches bounce under my feet. I miss all the colors — leaves and moss and bark and flowers. And the *smell*." Theo sighs sadly, head tilted up at the sky.

"And the sound," Ren pipes up. I turn back to look at him, but Theo just throws himself backward, head landing in Ren's lap as he looks up at him, the happiest expression painted across his face.

"Yeah?" he says, excited.

Ren clears his throat. "Yeah," he says. "You know, the sound of the wind in the leaves. And branches creaking. And insects…"

"*Stars*, I miss it," Theo huffs, still staring up at Ren.

"Me too," Ren says quietly. "Plus, the trees blocked out the sun. It's so hot out here; I feel like I'm getting a sunburn."

"You *do* look a little red," Theo says with a frown, and he raises a hand, pressing the backs of his fingers to Ren's cheek. "Does that hurt?"

"Nope! I think I'm good!" Ren says quickly, and he grabs Theo's hand and pulls it away from his face. I can see it now — he *does* look red. We should probably try to find some sunscreen for him in Udula. Not that I actually care about his well being, or anything. These people are still strangers, I'm not going to trust them just because they seem as homesick as I feel. Plus, Ren *still* won't meet my eyes. He hardly even looks in my direction, and it's starting to piss me off.

I don't want the conversation to die, though, now that it's started. It's… nice.

"So how long have you guys been in Askund?" I ask. Theo's sitting up again now, and Ren's no longer holding onto his shirt, instead having both of his hands splayed over Icarus' mixture of feathers and fur.

"Well let's see," Theo says, and he holds up his hands, folding fingers down as he counts, mumbling to himself. "I'd say, about… seven hours? Well probably less for Ren — he didn't have to walk on his own for a while."

For a second, my entire mind silences. And then, "*What?*" I exclaim.

"What?" says Theo.

"You've only been out here for a few *hours?*"

"Well, yeah," Theo says. "I found Icarus yesterday, and this morning I was exiled. And then I walked for*ever*, and Ren stole Icarus, and then we flew to that town where we found you. Yeah, seven hours sounds about right."

I feel dizzy. I'm in the company of *amateurs*. They have no idea what life's like out here in Askund! They've never slept without a proper shelter over their heads, never had to make it on their own. I feel like some sort of babysitter now.

"Do you guys have *any plan at all?*" I demand.

"*Yes*, we have a plan," Ren bites out. "We know where we're going, we got some money—"

"My money," I mutter snidely, still pretty hung up on that.

Ren hears me, though, and he scoffs. "That *I* won."

"Yeah, how the hell did you do that, by the way?" I finally ask him, twisting in my seat to look at him just in time to see his jaw snap shut. That 'sunburn' of his is coming back and I want to roll my eyes. He may be good at keeping his expressions locked away behind some sort of indifferent mask, but even he can't control the color of his face.

"I'm not telling you," Ren says.

"We're traveling together now," I reason. "If we're going to scam people, I need to know how you saw through it."

Ren snorts. For the life of me, I can't figure out what's so amusing. "They won't see through it," he promises.

"*You* did."

He just shrugs. "They won't. Although you should let people win every once in a while. You know, make it seem a little more authentic."

I don't answer, but that's because he's right. That's probably how he won, after all. Noticed some kind of pattern happening. Whatever.

"Hopefully we won't have to scam anyone else for money," Theo says placatingly. I'm not surprised — he doesn't really seem the sort to cheat people out of their money. Then again, I never expected that of myself either.

"Hopefully we'll get to Udula soon," Ren mutters darkly, mimicking him. Despite how long we've been flying, he looks no more comfortable with being up in the air than he had earlier. Luckily, we aren't too far. Icarus is making good time, and I think I can see the very tops of Udula's famous skyscrapers rising in the distance.

With a sigh, I lean back on my hands and settle in for the remainder of the flight. With any luck, I can help them find some information to help with their journey and then we'll be on our way.

CHAPTER 5

THEO

As the unofficial leader of the group, I declare that it's time for a dinner break the second we step into the city. Some of us have been traveling all day after all, and maybe eating together will get rid of that *tension* between Eleanor and Ren. I don't know exactly why, but I get the feeling they don't like each other.

I can't deal with the two of them not getting along for the rest of our time together, especially right now. I'm already uneasy enough in the city, and not just because we had to leave Icarus behind a second time and sneak past Udulan guards since none of us have any traveling documents. It's just that this place is *weird*.

It's absolutely nothing like Silva. I didn't actually expect it to be, seeing as these people don't live in trees or anything, but there are no similarities *at all*. Everything here seems cold and pristine — the people included. The buildings are gigantic, making me dizzy whenever I try to look to the tops of them, and hardly anyone seems to talk to one another, yet it's somehow still so *loud*. Everyone's walking like they have somewhere to be, and I'm doing everything in my control to make sure none of them bump into Ren.

I bet he hates it here. The noisiness of Askund is nothing compared to this place, and Ren is suffering because of it. His head keeps whipping around, like he's trying to hear something, and more than once he's reached for me instead of it being the other way around. I'm hoping whatever place we find for dinner is quieter than the streets of Udula.

"How about this place?" Eleanor suggests, stopping right in the middle of the sidewalk and pointing to it. At least three different Udulans snap at her as they navigate around the sudden roadblock, but Eleanor doesn't pay them any attention. I look inside the building.

Everyone in there seems to be eating their meals with utensils — things like soups and salads and pasta. Those foods are harder for Ren to eat, so I'm hoping for the kind of place that serves finger foods. Something that he can eat with his hands.

"I'm in the mood for a sandwich," I inform Eleanor, and she just shrugs, so we start walking again. Again, Eleanor is the first person to spot a place to eat, but this time it's a deli, so I agree. The three of us squeeze into a tiny booth, me and Ren on one side and Eleanor on the other.

It's so much quieter in here than outside that Ren's relief is noticeable — to me, at least. The tension has melted out of his shoulders and his face no longer has that sort of pinched look it was sporting before.

"What can I get you three?" an older, kind-looking server asks us. It looks like he's the only one in here, so maybe he's the owner as well.

"Steak and cheese, please," Eleanor says.

"Ham and turkey," I say.

"Same as him." Ren nods at me.

"Two ham and turkeys and a steak and cheese, comin' up!" the man says cheerfully, and he shoots a wink at us, making me grin. I look back to the table as he crosses the room, finding Eleanor squinting suspiciously at Ren. He's looking right back at her, or at least, it seems that way, and I clear my throat loudly, drawing their attention.

"So," I say. "What's our plan?"

"Eat and then find the nearest library," Eleanor says immediately. "We'll gather as much information as we can and be on our way. I doubt we'll be able to afford any hotels in this place, so our best bet would be to camp out in Askund for the night." I have to admit, it's pretty nice having someone so experienced with us. Even though what I'm meant to do is still daunting, the task seeming to loom endlessly over me, I feel like

I've finally got my footing. It's only a matter of time, now, until I Restore the Light.

"Sounds good to me," Ren agrees, no doubt eager to be out of the city already.

The food comes quickly, which I'm thankful for, considering I haven't eaten all day. The three of us devour our sandwiches in no time — they're toasted perfectly so that the bread still has a good crunch, and it's so delicious that I momentarily pause, my heart clenching, when I remember my promise to bring a good lunch home for Hector today. No matter, I try to tell myself. I'll just get him something when I really do come home.

We end up leaving a generous tip with our twice scammed money and head on our way. It takes four separate tries to find someone patient enough to actually give us directions to a library, and at that point Eleanor's fuming about how rude everyone in Udula is and Ren's equally as angry, having tripped over at least three different uneven sidewalks. I'm surprised they still aren't getting along.

Luckily, the library's as quiet as a library is supposed to be, and I can't help looking all around the place. The ceilings are high, and the shelves go almost all the way up. Eleanor looks as surprised as I feel, and even Ren seems impressed. He can probably tell how huge this place is through sound alone.

"Where do we even start?" I say, and even though my question is a whisper it echoes unnervingly around the cavernous room.

"Can I help you?" another voice calls out almost immediately, and we all jump. "Make your way to my voice."

Except it's not that simple, because the woman's voice echoes around thrice as much as mine had, and we end up wandering around quite a bit before we finally find her. She's sitting behind a desk, reading glasses perched on the end of her nose with chains dangling from the sides of them, looping behind her ears. Her hands are folded on the surface before her, fingernails long and painted purple, lips pulled up in a smile so polite it's almost unnerving.

"Um, hi," I say. "We're looking for books on the Darkness."

Eleanor, looking pained, adds, "We're doing a research project on it."

"Well, I can certainly help you there!" the librarian says enthusiastically. She gets to her feet, the chains on her glasses swinging rapidly as she hobbles away from us. Without any other instruction, we fall into step behind her.

"These books used to be really popular, when the Darkness was still relatively young," she informs us, in that way old people always seem to want to share the knowledge they have. "They don't see much use these days, though. Seems as though people have just given up."

I try not to let her words affect me, but I can feel something in the pit of my stomach *sink*, hearing that. Even people in Udula — supposedly the smartest people around — gave up. What chance do I stand, then? How can I honestly

70

expect to Restore the Light and return to Silva when hardly anyone thinks it's possible?

I don't know how he does it, but Ren can tell I'm upset. I know this because he bumps into me as we walk, and it's too quiet in here for that to have been an accident — he can hear exactly where he's going. I appreciate it, though. I appreciate having him here with me, knowing that I'm not alone in all this, not alone in trying to Restore the Light. I think as long as I have Ren with me, I'll be able to accomplish anything.

The librarian's still talking — I accidentally tuned her out — but I start listening again just in time to hear her say to Eleanor, "You know, you look kind of familiar…"

Eleanor laughs, but it sounds nervous. "Really?" she says. "I guess I just have one of those faces."

The librarian hums. "Say, what did you tell me your name was?"

"Aliyah," Eleanor says immediately. I frown. Eleanor turns to me and shrugs exaggeratedly. And then, whispering so that the librarian can't hear her, "I'm thinking we should use aliases."

"How come?" I ask.

"Just in case we don't want anyone to know we were here."

I nod, because I guess that makes sense. You never know when you should've hidden your identity until after you didn't hide it. So, "I'm… Exaltor," I add importantly, when the librarian looks at me expectantly. "And this is…" I look at Ren. I panic. "Red."

Ren can't even see me, but if looks could kill…

"Yes," Ren says dully. "It's also my favorite color."

"How... unusual," the librarian comments, and Eleanor snorts. I glare at her. *It could be a name!*

She's not paying attention to me though, and I suspect it's because she's trying to remember where we're going. The library is like a maze. We're led down several aisles, each identical looking, before we finally stop at a section of tables paired off together, enclosed in yet more shelves. No one else is in this seating area, plus I haven't seen a single other soul in the building, which leads me to wonder if anyone besides us and the librarian are even in here. For a type of people who are supposedly the smartest, Udulans sure don't spend a lot of time reading up.

"This shelf should have a lot of information on the Darkness," the librarian continues, pointing. "And this one over here has a section about Restoring the Light. If you hit electricity, you've gone too far."

She disappears into the stacks after we thank her. Immediately, the three of us plop our supplies on the nearest table.

"Let's divide and conquer," Eleanor instructs. "Theo, help me with the Darkness section. Ren, you could get some books on the Light."

"Um," I say loudly, because obviously that's not going to work, although Eleanor doesn't know that, and we don't *want* her to know that…

"Come on," she says, and she starts dragging me toward our shelf. I snatch Ren's hand and pull him after us, and as we pass the shelves for the Light, I shove him into it. I don't know what else to do, but hopefully he grabs some of the right books. I hope to the Stars he doesn't come back with ones about electricity.

I'm so distracted thinking about Ren that I have a hard time browsing through my own shelf. I just grab the first few I see, and when Eleanor starts heading back to the table, I turn and follow. Ren hears us and joins us, holding an armful of books and looking uncomfortable.

"Okay, let's see what we've got," Eleanor says, setting hers out on the table. They all look important, having titles like *Darkness and its Attributes* and *The Leading Theories on the Darkness*. None of mine look as useful, and when Eleanor questions me on *Darkness: A Government Hoax?* I insist that it could be important.

Ren, on the other hand…

"How the hell are books on *lightning* supposed to help us?" Eleanor demands. Ren flushes. He crosses his arms and stands there defensively, though he doesn't actually say anything to defend himself.

"Actually," I say quickly, feeling like I have to remedy the situation somehow. "Ren's illiterate." Ren's mouth tightens ever so slightly.

"What?" Eleanor says.

"Yep!" I say, sticking to my lie. Or — I guess it isn't really one. It just isn't the truth, either. "Can't read a thing, this guy!" I laugh, throwing an arm around Ren's shoulders. He shoves me off.

Eleanor looks vaguely uncomfortable. "I could teach you sometime, if you want," she offers hesitantly, which surprises me. Offering to teach someone to read doesn't seem like the kind of thing you do when you don't like someone. Maybe I've been reading her wrong.

But, "I have no interest in learning," Ren lies. I can tell he's angry with me, but I didn't know what else to do. It was the best thing I could come up with, even though it probably makes Ren feel stupid. I don't want to make him to feel that way — he's one of the smartest people I know. Plus, I just hate making him feel bad in general.

With that, he marches over to the table and takes a seat, and I sit down beside him. Eleanor returns to the stacks to get more of the books we actually need, and I pull one of the books on the Darkness over to myself, flipping it open.

"She hates me," Ren mutters quietly, slumping in his chair.

"You hate her back," I counter, and Ren sits right back up.

"What reason do I have to not like her?" he says.

"I don't know," I say. "Maybe you're jealous."

At that, Ren splutters. And then he clears his throat. "Jealous? W-why would I be jealous?"

I scoff. "As if it's not obvious," I say. Ren looks like he's shrinking in on himself beside me, so I decide to have mercy. "Look, I promise you can sit up front on Icarus next time, okay? I was just trying to be polite."

"Sit up front…" Ren mutters. "I mean, yeah," he says. "Okay. Good."

"See? There's no need to dislike each other. We should all just get along."

"Right," Ren says, and then Eleanor's back, crowding the table with even more books. She pulls a couple toward herself, and I decide to finally start reading the one in front of me. I pull it closer and read it out loud so Ren can know about it too. He's better at remembering this stuff than I am anyway.

There's just one problem. We're moving through lots of books, picking and choosing the sections to read that seem relevant to us, but I'm starting to notice a pattern. None of the authors even begin to suggest a solution for the Darkness, for one thing, but hardly any of them offer any examples as to how it started, either.

"Eleanor," I say. "Have you found anything about the origin of the Darkness?"

Eleanor frowns. I don't know if she was thinking about it before, but she definitely is now, and she starts skimming through the books with purpose. I stop looking for anything else, too, just flipping through pages in a desperate attempt to find some mention of its origin. I don't know why, but I suddenly feel like this is something we have to know. How can we figure out how to end something without knowing how it began?

"This doesn't make sense," Eleanor says. "You'd think there'd be something about the Darkness' origin in here. I mean, it hasn't been around *forever*. Is it some kind of secret?"

Ren scoffs. "If it is, we'll have to go to Ilma," he jokes.

"That's a good idea," I point out. Ilmans are known for their secrets, along with their healing prowess. Many people don't trust them because of this, constantly feeling like something's being kept from them.

"No, it's not," Ren protests immediately.

"It is," Eleanor agrees with me. "Plus, they're Volant's neighbor. You could stop there on your way to dropping me off."

"It's settled!" I say, excited, and I gratefully shut the book in front of me. I hadn't been able to concentrate on it, anyway.

I can't sleep.

I've never slept away from home before. Normally when this happens, when I can't get my mind to quiet down, I'll sneak out of the house and climb up high in the trees. There, I'll make myself comfortable on a branch and look up at the Stars, just waiting to get tired enough so that I can go back home and crash in my own bed. More often than not, I wouldn't make it back, falling asleep right there where I laid before I even registered getting tired.

After my parents died, I didn't leave at night anymore. Hector has nightmares a lot, now, so I like to be around so that he can crawl into my bed with me when he's afraid. He always pretends that he's not scared, that he's just coming to keep me company since he's awake anyway, and I never call him out on it. Thinking about it now, I feel sick to my stomach. What if he has a nightmare tonight when I'm not there to comfort him? He'll just have to sit there all alone in our house, the wood creaking, the branches scratching against the windows. I can't stop thinking about how scared he must be, left all alone at eleven years old. Stars, I'm the worst big brother in the world.

"Can't sleep?" Ren whispers, his voice breaking through the silence surrounding us. It's no use lying to him — my breathing or heartbeat or something is probably giving me away.

"No," I admit, and I turn in my sleeping bag to face him. Eleanor's on my other side and Icarus lays curved around us, her body forming a crescent above our heads. We only landed here a little while ago, having flown for a few hours after the sun set, wanting to get a head start on tomorrow's journey to Ilma.

"Me neither," Ren says, and he turns to face me too. His eyelids flutter open, revealing his pale blue eyes. They're almost startling to look at, how noticeable they are even in the dark of the night, and I get the urge to reach forward and brush his hair in front of them, like it usually is. They're too entrancing otherwise, much too beautiful for a person who doesn't even use them.

"It's weird out here," I say, because that's part of it, at least, and Ren doesn't need to sit through my fretting about Hector any more. I can't quite place my finger on it, but something's off. Maybe it's just the new atmosphere, the absence of everything that's familiar about Silva, but my body feels too keyed up to sleep.

"It is," Ren agrees softly. "Too quiet."

I grin, because that must be it, and I'm glad Ren's feeling it too. There's a moment's silence, and then—

"Really? Because it seems pretty loud with you two talking."

I shut up after that, and I see a flicker of annoyance flash across Ren's face before he turns over in his sleeping bag with a huff. "Goodnight Theodore," he says pointedly.

"Night Ren," I answer.

A pause.

"Goodnight Eleanor," Eleanor adds, and I laugh, repeating the sentiment before I force myself to sleep, feeling a little bit better than before.

I wake to a scream. I sit up, heart already pounding wildly in my chest, and look around desperately.

It doesn't work.

"What's wrong?" Ren demands, sitting up somewhere to my right. I can't see him. I can't see anything, it's so dark.

"What's *wrong*? It's fucking dark, is what's wrong!" Eleanor yells.

"Big whoop," Ren scoffs. I hear him lay back down. "I hear that's called 'night'."

"Don't be a smartass," Eleanor bites at him. "I can't even see the moon anymore — I can't see anything. What's going on?"

Something anxious bubbles in the pit of my stomach, an idea, a realization, and then—

"Eleanor," Ren says carefully, a tinge of alarm hiding in his tone. "Who's sitting beside you?"

"What? No one," she says.

"No," says Ren, firm. "Theodore's next to me, and you're next to him — who's *next to you*?"

"*No one*," Eleanor repeats herself, and a moment of silence passes, a second where everything stills, and then Eleanor shrieks. I feel her fling herself over me, Ren's groan announcing that she's landed on him as well, and I can feel my breathing coming quicker.

"Guys," I say quickly. "I think we're in a dark patch."

"How is that possible?" Eleanor demands. "We could see just fine last night!"

"Moonlight can penetrate," I explain hurriedly. "Just not sunlight. We have to get out of here!"

After that, it's a mad scramble to get to our bags and feet. I shove things into a bag I'm not sure is mine and stumble in Ren's direction. I collide with him and gasp out an apology as his hands come up to my shoulders to steady me. Ren makes a clicking sound in response.

"What?" I say, confused, and Ren repeats himself, a grating repetition of clicks sounding off right next to my ear, almost similar to the clicking Icarus makes with her beak but chillingly *not*. I shake my head. "Ren, I have no idea what you're saying."

"I'm not saying anything," says Ren from somewhere behind me. I yell, shaking off the *thing* and stumbling backwards, in the direction of the real Ren. Something grabs my wrist and I yank, *hard*, but Ren goes, "Theodore! It's me!" so I stop struggling and clutch him back.

"What are these things?!" Eleanor demands, and she's nearby so I reach out and grab her too, pulling her toward Ren and me.

"I have no clue," I say. "I didn't even know things lived in here! I guess that's why they say when people go in, they never come back out…"

"Don't say that," Ren hisses, and he starts marching the three of us off in a random direction. I guess it's not random to him, though, because unlike Eleanor and me, he can navigate perfectly fine right now. He keeps yanking us from side to side, no doubt avoiding figures he knows are there, and Eleanor and I are clutching onto him and each other so hard we're bound to leave bruises.

"There's so many of them," Ren whispers, and I can hear the underlying horror in his voice. "It's like they're multiplying — I can't even tell where they're coming from."

"How the hell can you see right now?" Eleanor demands, sounding confused and scared and angry. Ren and I ignore her as we continue to march on, but then Ren starts speeding up, and suddenly we're jogging, then running. I have no idea what's chasing us, or how close they are, or how many of them are after us. I don't know what's worse — being completely in the dark like me, or being horrifyingly aware of what's out there like Ren.

The terrain isn't making it any easier to get away. The grass is long and unkept, tall enough to touch our hands as we run. I keep tripping over dips and knots in the rolling ground, and at one point Eleanor falls to her knees, but Ren and I yank her back up before she can truly hit the ground.

"Crap," Ren hisses out. "Run faster!"

We break apart a little, no longer holding on to each other except for our hands, swinging wildly between us as we run for our lives.

Suddenly, something catches onto the back of my shirt and *yanks*. I go stumbling backwards, hands slipping away from my friends, and collide into something hard. I struggle as foreign arms lock around me.

"Theodore!" Ren cries out, but the last syllable is cut off as something presumably grabs him, too, and then Eleanor screams.

"Where's Icarus?!" I gasp out, because maybe she can get us out of this. I elbow whatever's holding me in the gut and it chitters angrily, its grip momentarily loosening. For a second, I'm free, my body lurching forward in a desperate attempt to escape, but then its hand clasps around my thigh. Its fingers must be abnormally long, and I can feel its sharp nails — claws? — pressing into the front of my thigh.

Panicking, I wrench my bag off my back and whirl it through the air behind me. It collides with the creature, hopefully smacking it right in the face, and it clicks furiously right before its claws dig into my leg, twisting and *slicing*. I scream, the sound mixed up with a gasp as the pain truly hits me, and then I swing my bag into it a second time, harder, and it finally lets go.

I stumble away from it, ignoring the throbbing in my leg with every step, and call out Ren's name. "Over here!" he says. Eleanor's made it to his side again, too, and I crash into them gratefully, holding back the sob that tries to climb out of my throat as I bear my weight against them. Absently, I press my hand against my injury, thinking I should probably put some pressure on it, but I have to swallow down bile at how wet it feels. I can feel my blood oozing past my fingers, thick and hot.

"Icarus!" I yell, shoving the distraction of my pain away and concentrating on her with all my might. I pray to the Stars that she hears me, and I sob in relief when she calls back from somewhere up above us. I wonder if she woke up in the Darkness too. She must've gotten scared and flown out of it, not that I blame her. I almost feel bad asking her to come back in, but I don't think we can make it out of here on our own. "Icarus!" I call again, and Ren and Eleanor join in.

Ren's still pulling us through the Darkness, jerking us from side to side to avoid the creatures. Occasionally, I feel them snatch at my bag or clothes, but I just press closer to Ren, and he urges us forward a little faster.

"How are you doing this?" Eleanor gasps out again, impatient. I'm thinking we might've gotten out of the thick of it, because Ren doesn't seem to be pulling us as desperately anymore. Maybe the creatures come in waves.

Still, neither one of us answer her, and I can feel her becoming more and more agitated. "Seriously, Ren!" she says. "Can you see right now? What's going on?!"

I hear Ren's annoyed breath, and I can't think of a single excuse for the life of me, so I know it's coming. "I'm Covan, all right?" he snaps. "I'm blind. I don't need my eyes to get around."

Eleanor falls silent. She says nothing, and I feel Ren's hand tighten around mine. I don't know what he's thinking.

I open my mouth to say something, to try to dispel the tension somehow, but then a huge, taloned foot wraps around me. It's Icarus, thank the Stars, but as the giant beat of her wings thrusts us into the air I feel a painful throbbing in my head. My thigh hurts less now, but I can't tell if that's because I'm losing less blood or because the adrenaline of everything is obscuring the pain.

We're flying higher and higher, Icarus' body perpendicular to the ground, by the feel of it. I'm gripped tight in her claw, and the air is rushing around me, and I think we're higher than we've ever been before.

And then, suddenly, we're out of the Darkness, just like that. The light is blinding, making my eyes water as I clench them shut, but I wrench them back open again as I register that Ren's hanging from Icarus' beak by the back of his shirt. Now that I can see him, I register that he's speaking. He's curled into himself with his hands pressed over his ears, muttering, "Put me down, put me down, put me down," over and over again.

Eleanor is in Icarus' other claw, and she looks even more dazed than I feel. She glances over at me, then, and I'm about to offer some kind of greeting when she gasps.

"Theo!" she shouts. "Your leg!"

Oh, yeah. Forgot about that.

I look down. My hand is still pressed against my thigh. It's red all over, and there's blood on my pants, seeping steadily down my leg.

"Oh Stars," I say, suddenly dizzy.

"What's wrong?" Ren demands, overcoming his fear of dangling from an Avis' beak in order to speak. He's removed his hands from his ears.

"He's bleeding!" Eleanor cries.

"Yeah," I agree helpfully. My tongue feels thick in my mouth. Heavy.

"Wha— how? When did — how much blood have you lost? Can you do your seven times table?" Ren rambles, the panic evident in his voice. I look over at him, and he almost looks angry. Almost.

I shake my head, because the thought of thinking hard enough to do *math* right now is definitely not a fun one. But then I realize Ren has no idea that I'm shaking my head, yet I still don't say anything. My entire body feels too heavy, too impossible to move. I just want to sleep.

"We have to land," Eleanor says. "He needs bandages. Maybe a doctor…"

I tune her out. Just listening to them is tiring, so I let my eyes slip shut, my head coming forward to rest against Icarus' talon. I just need a nap, is all.

CHAPTER 6

VELOREN

I'm soaking wet. The bird pushed me into the lake, and I can't tell whether she was trying to play or whether she's mad at me for letting Theodore get hurt. *I'm* mad at me for letting him get hurt.

I tried so hard to keep everyone safe, but it was impossible. Everything happened so fast, and the number of creatures just kept increasing. They were everywhere, surrounding us, and both Theodore and Eleanor had been depending on me.

Finding out that Theodore was injured was scarier than all of that combined, though. It'd felt like my heart had crawled up into my throat, my ears stuffed and sounds muffled as I'd panicked, wondering what was happening to him, what was *wrong* with him.

Thankfully, Icarus had listened to me when I'd told her to land, even though she usually only listens to Theodore. I'd stayed with him as Eleanor had run into the town we'd landed by, getting all sorts of bandages for him. And when she had returned, she'd said, "I'm gonna stitch him up."

"*What?* Do you even know how to do that?!" I'd demanded, panicked, and rightfully so, because she'd said *no*.

Unfortunately, she was also right. He was bleeding a lot, and bandages didn't seem like they'd be enough to patch him up, so Eleanor had been forced to become an impromptu doctor. I'd hovered anxiously around the two of them the entire time, suddenly grateful for my inability to see. I was similarly grateful when Theodore managed to remain unconscious throughout the entire thing.

After Eleanor bandaged him, we'd loaded him back onto Icarus and taken off again. *Wherever the nearest water is*, I'd told her, and thankfully, she'd complied. Now Eleanor's at the top of the hill with Theodore, checking his injury again while I collect water. At least it isn't too hard to do from inside the lake.

The second all of our canteens are full, heavy and no longer noisily gulping in water, I straighten up and screw their caps back on, anxious to get back to Theodore. I speed up about halfway up the hill, suddenly convinced I can hear two voices.

"What's wrong?" Theodore says, his voice persistent enough that it means this isn't his first time asking the question. I recognize it because I routinely fall prey to the same needling whine. It's hard for Theodore to not get what he wants when he sets his mind to something.

I hear Eleanor sigh. "Just — he's Covan?" she says, sounding incredulous. "I mean, you hang out with a *Covan*."

It takes me a second to realize that I'm not walking anymore, just standing completely still a little more than halfway up the hill. My body feels a thousand tons heavier.

I don't know why I thought this wouldn't happen. That Eleanor might not be like everybody else, for some reason. That she wouldn't mind, because it's only thanks to me that we even got out of the Darkness in the first place.

But who was I kidding? I'm Covan, and this is just how it is. How it'll always be.

Theodore sounds angry when he speaks. "Yeah," he says harshly. "And he saved your *life*. Keep talking like that and he'll be the only person I hang out with."

And somehow, just like that, everything's fine again. Who cares what other people think about me, about Covans? Who cares about other people *at all* when I have Theodore? Theodore, who's always on my side, always looking out for me.

Yet I feel happier still when Eleanor responds, sounding properly cowed. "You're right," she says quietly. "I guess I was just… surprised."

I finally crest the hill, and I can't tell if my face is as impassive as it usually is. I think I might be smiling. "I got the water," I announce.

"Thank the Stars," Theodore croaks, and I'm suddenly glad I filled all three of these things. I rush to his side immediately, and I can't help the way I reach out for him, am always reaching out for him. My hands flutter over his body anxiously, touching his shoulder, his chest, just barely cupping his cheek. My heart's pounding with relief, my whole body flooded with the knowledge that he's okay, that he's safe.

"Here," I say, pressing a flask into his hands, and I help him sit up, a hand firm on his back. I want to scoot behind him, want to wrap my arms around him and let him lean back into me — his back to my chest, his head on my shoulder — but I don't. Because we don't do that. We aren't like that.

"I'm thinking we should stay here for a while," Eleanor announces. "I don't really think Theo's fit to travel right now, plus the easy access to water is nice."

"Can't argue with that," I say, and Theodore gasps as he finishes chugging a flask of water. I hand him the next one.

"You know, lake water isn't so bad," Theodore says, actually taking the time to breathe between sips now, but I can't for the life of me concentrate on what he's saying. Now that I know he's okay, the blinding panic from before has dissipated, leaving entirely too much room for other thoughts to creep in.

This is all my fault.

I should've known we were in an area of Darkness. All the signs were there — the feeling of unease, my inability to sleep, the fact that we'd traveled to the damn place at night. It's been so long since I've experienced it, though, and I honestly thought I never would again. I certainly hadn't *wanted* to.

There's more to being Covan than most people know. Yes, we're all genetically blind, but it's not because being underground for so long without light blinded us, as everyone else seems to think. It doesn't really work that way. The truth is that when the first Covans were forced underground, they were confronted with the fact that they weren't alone.

No one had believed them, of course. They'd just been defeated in war and the other nations were angry, unforgiving. *The Covans'll do anything to try to escape their punishment*, they'd said. And so no one had batted an eye when the Covans had claimed to be in danger, saying that they were getting picked off and killed by creatures they couldn't see.

And they really couldn't see them, no matter what they did. Light didn't work down there. No match or flame could fight the oppressive darkness that surrounded my people. And angered that the Covans had even tried to be rid of the Darkness in the first place, it'd punished them; it took away their eyesight, and that of those who shared their blood.

We learned to live with it. The Darkness, that is. If we cooperated, we were fine. We ignored the creatures who clicked and creaked, whose nails stung sharp in your skin if you angered them. We accepted our fate and dealt with it accordingly.

It wasn't until the Darkness started encroaching on the abovelands that anyone bothered to care about it, and even then, only because it affected them. None of them know about how the Darkness residing underground, I'm sure. After all, they didn't believe my people all those centuries ago, and I'm certain word of our plight was never relayed through the generations.

I never realized how out of the ordinary living with the Darkness was until I wasn't living with it anymore. My mom had been mortally injured by one of the creatures — not because she angered it, but because sometimes the creatures were restless, and she just happened to be in the way — and Dad had sworn up and down that he was going to kill it. Kill them all, he'd said.

Mom, still clinging to life even as it'd escaped her, spilling out onto the floor and soaking into the knees of my pants, had cupped my face with her hands — similarly wet with blood, I hadn't realized until much later — while Dad had marched around our little home, slamming weapons and supplies into a bag as he'd cried, not quietly enough for the two of us to miss.

"My Veloren," she'd told me, a smile in her voice. I could hear the pain she was in, the strain of her words. "You must leave this place. It's not safe for us. It never was."

"M-mom," I'd said, my heart pounding in my chest, my breath loud in my ears. "I *can't*."

91

"You must," she'd insisted. "You leave and don't ever come back. Hear me? Escape this Darkness, Veloren. There's no destroying it."

"*Mom*," I'd sobbed.

"I'm serious, baby," she'd said. "Your father's angry, but even he knows he can't win. Not without dooming the rest of our people. So go. I'll never forgive myself if you die here, too."

Crying, I'd kissed her on the cheek, my tears falling onto her face, before getting shakily to my feet. There was no time to say bye to Dad; Mom and I both knew he would've tried to stop me. He didn't realize he was walking into a death trap. Or maybe he did and didn't care. All I know is I heard my mom stop breathing only a few short steps from our home, and though I wasn't there to witness my dad's death, I know he's gone too.

I'd escaped from one of Cova's many exits. They're all over the place, and our people have used them for centuries to get around from kingdom to kingdom much faster than everyone else, not that it does us any good. We're still hated everywhere we go, after all.

It's because of these exits that the Darkness is showing up in the abovelands.

But luckily, I'd chosen one near Silva. I hadn't been actively thinking about it, just trying to get to the nearest one I knew, and it was like my legs were carrying me with a mind of their own. I'd had this notion in my head that once Dad started fighting the creatures, they'd come after me too, which only made me move faster.

I'd traveled for a while, stumbling over fields of grass in Askund until I'd come across a path. There, I'd made the mistake and learned the lesson of telling people I was Covan. Turns out, people stop caring so much about the lost little boy with blood on his face once they know where he's from.

So I'd found my own way. All the way to Silva. It was nice because I could hear the trees, and I wanted someplace like that; someplace with a lot of sound. I was afraid of silence, afraid of what it meant. Afraid of the quiet that came after one breath and before the next, the silence that stretched out when the next one never came.

Walking along the forest floor quickly became frightening to me — some ingrained sense informing me that it was *dark*, almost *Darkness* dark, and so I'd began climbing the trees, because I was pretty sure I'd heard that the Silvans did that. I'd climbed and climbed and climbed, until I'd come across a civilization. And then I'd settled down not too far from it; close enough to steal food every once in a while, but far enough that I wouldn't be bothered.

Or so I'd thought.

Theodore had found me, of course, and the rest was history. I'd never told him about any of it. Not my past nor my experiences, though I think he might have some sort of inkling about my parents. I can't be sure, and it's not like I want to bring it up. Plus, I feel like it's too late now — like I'd be trying to piggyback off his own parents' death or something.

It's not like it really matters, anyway. What *does* matter, and what I'm endlessly grateful for, is the fact that I was so distrustful back then. I'd thought that Theodore would never believe me about the Darkness, about any of it, and so I'd never brought it up, thank the Stars. I can't imagine if I had, if he knew everything I do, right now. He'd already be clamoring to go to Cova, so much closer to the answers he needed, to the knowledge that Restoring the Light was intrinsically tied with my old home. Sure, I have no idea how it's actually supposed to be *done*, but I do know what my mother told me — we can't Restore the Light. Not without dooming my people.

And somehow it's just my luck that now I'm on the mission to do exactly that. Just my luck that I had to experience the Darkness all over again — the uncomfortable, unsettling sensation of it all around me; the air vaguely heavier than usual, the creatures surrounding me in abundance. Just thinking about it has my arms exploding in goosebumps, and I'm not even doing anything out of the ordinary.

Eleanor wandered off a little while ago, her explanation of leaving in search of roots and vegetables just barely making itself known in my mind. Now, I'm sitting with my back against the tree, and at some point during my musings, during the onslaught of my own memories, Theodore managed to maneuver his head into my lap. I can tell he's asleep by the sound of his breathing, and it's with that information secure in my mind that I let my fingers venture into his hair.

"What am I going to do, Theodore?" I say quietly.

I hate myself for touching his hair, because now I know I'll never want to stop. It's soft between my fingers, thick, and even though it feels a little tangled right now, I bet his curls look perfect. They certainly *feel* perfect.

It's a nice enough distraction, I guess. From the doom I'm facing. Because I *can't* let Theodore Restore the Light. I know I can't.

"You'd understand, wouldn't you?" I sigh. I want to think he would. That he'd fall silent that way he always does when he's thinking, and then tell me I'm right. That we can't doom my people just so that he can get back to his brother, that we'll have to find another way.

But a bigger part of me thinks that he'd be wrapped up in anger. That he'd hear me suggesting to not do the one task he'd been given in order to return home and explode.

I feel like this is all so selfish of me. I *love* Hector. Of course I want to get Theodore back to him and keep him safe, but I just can't do it in good conscious. There has to be another way, but I have to figure it out on my own. Only then can I tell Theodore; only when I can curb his hurt and anger with the immediate suggestion of another solution.

Suddenly, Theodore groans in my lap. He always groans before he wakes up — I can hear it from across the house. But this time, instead of pushing himself up and yawning loudly, he just groans again, quieter. It sounds like he's in pain.

"Theodore?" I say gently, and my hand falls on his shoulder. I don't think he realizes it was just in his hair.

He reaches up and grabs my hand, his palm clammy, and he gasps, his fingers tightening around mine. "Ren?" he says. His voice is weak. "I'm — my leg hurts, Ren."

I'm panicking now, though I try not to show it. Eleanor needs to get back here. She needs to look at Theodore's wound and figure out if it's infected and then decide how the hell we're going to fix it, because Theodore's not dying of a stupid infection on my watch.

"What does it feel like?" I ask him.

"Hot," Theodore says. "*Hurts.*"

"Eleanor's coming, okay?" I promise him, even though I'm not entirely sure. How long has it been since she left? My mind scrambles for an answer but I have absolutely no clue, having been sitting here uselessly zoned out all the while. What if something happened to her? What if she decided dealing with Theodore's injury was too much and took off without us? What if she *stole Icarus?*

I shake my head. There's no way she could've managed that. Icarus loves Theodore too much, it's obvious. She's probably napping somewhere down by the lake while Eleanor gathers fresh roots from the plants growing along the bank. I need to calm down, because everything's going to be all right. Theodore's going to be fine.

"Ren?" Theodore says.

"Yeah?"

"Can you make Hec's dinner tonight? I don't really feel up for it."

Aaaand I'm panicking again. Fuck, is he hallucinating? What does it mean when you can't remember what's going on? Has the infection made its way into his *brain*?

I don't want to remind him of where we are, though. I don't want to remind him that he's hurt and that Hector's all alone back home — that we have an impossible mission before us. So I just start petting his hair again, because no way is he going to be able to remember this anyway, and I assure him that yes, I can take care of dinner tonight.

He keeps rambling like that, almost never completely lucid. He talks about his parents and Silva and me. Sometimes he gasps and his head rolls back and he tells me it hurts, Ren, it hurts, when will it stop hurting? And I tell him soon, because what the hell else am I supposed to say? But Stars, I hope I'm right.

And then, miraculously, Eleanor returns. The canteens slosh as she carries them up the hill — apparently she took it upon herself to refill our waters, too — and she pants a bit as she starts to greet me, but I'm already talking over her.

"Something's wrong with Theodore," I say. "I think he's infected."

Eleanor obviously doesn't like that idea, and she drops down beside the two of us. I hear the unbuckling of Theodore's belt, which is completely necessary but fills me with an irrational rage anyway, and then Theodore's pants are being tugged down, his bandages undone, and Eleanor sucks in a breath.

"Is it bad?" I ask.

"Do Silvans normally turn green and ooze when they heal?" she asks weakly.

"Oh no," I moan, and I curl over Theodore, my hand clutching his shirt as my forehead rests against his feverish one. "What are we going to do?" The nearest town is far from us, and I don't think we have enough money left for any medicine. Eleanor's not the best at haggling, surprisingly, and she spent an absurd amount on those bandages she bought.

"There's a little forest down by the lake — maybe there's some plants that can help us heal him," Eleanor suggests, and it's better than sitting here and crying over Theodore, so I agree to it. Eleanor knows jack all about plants and I know even less about seeing, so we team up to go into the forest together where she'll describe every plant she lays her eyes on until I think she's found one with healing abilities. It's certainly not the best of plans, but it'll have to do.

We'll have to leave Theodore behind, too. Carrying him around for that long would just aggravate his injury even more, and apparently Icarus is too big to fit in the tiny forest, Eleanor says. So we position him down by the lake, in case he wakes up and needs more water than is in the flask we leave him, and we tell Icarus to watch over him for good measure.

With that, the two of us walk toward the forest, and I concentrate on Theodore's breathing for as long as I can hear it. When I'm too far away and all that's behind me is silence, I have to remind myself that this is Theodore, not Mom, and that he's still back there, breathing.

CHAPTER 7

WILL

It's dark down here.

Then again, it's always relatively dark at the bottom of a lake. The only indication that it's daytime is the light dancing across the lake's surface, filtering down through the water until it just stops, letting the darkness take over. I watch the bubbles stream out of my nose and toward the surface, knowing I don't have much time left. This water tablet's almost out, and I really don't have many of them left — I'm just so used to spending time underwater.

This is all pretty pathetic of me, I'm aware. I've only been living on my own for a week, and even then I can barely leave this little lake I found. It's not like we actually live like this in Ilma — we have actual buildings and stuff, they just happen to be underwater. You never have to get wet if you don't want to, but many Ilmans prefer it. Most of us take a water tablet every morning for an assured day of easy breathing.

It was stupid of me to grab so many of them in my desperate scramble to escape my house. I was panicking, though, definitely not thinking properly about what I needed. That's why I have more shirts than pants and more pants than underwear. That's why I have only a few more water tablets, a couple truth tablets, and a stupid amount of indigestion tablets.

My chest tightens, and I know that's the tablet's built-in mechanism warning me that I'm about to choke on one of my next breaths of water, so I start to get a move on. I make sure I haven't left anything down here at the bottom of the lake, but all I have is my bag anyway, and that's on my back. It's lined on the inside to protect everything from the water, and the outside of it and me will dry pretty quickly otherwise. It's not just our medical technology that's advanced these days.

I burst out of the lake with a gasp, having been forced to hold my breath since about halfway up, and I swim until my feet can touch the ground, at which point I trudge through the mud until I reach the bank, shaking water out of my hair. I'm about to duck down and go through my supplies — it's all I'm really good for these days, organizing and reorganizing my shit — when I freeze. Behind me, there's a loud squawk, and I slowly turn my head to see the biggest fucking bird in the entire world looming over me.

I'm in the midst of debating whether I'll be able to shove another tablet in my mouth and dive back into the lake before it can eat me when it cocks its head and chitters innocently. Things that want to kill you don't normally sound like that, right?

I slowly straighten up, hefting my bag onto my back, and the bird steps out of the way, revealing a person — its rider? — laying on the ground behind it. It's a guy, and he's not in good shape. There's sweat beading his forehead, but despite that, he's shivering. And despite *that*, he's sitting up on his elbows, looking at me with wide eyes.

"Dude, you just come outta that lake?" he says. I blink.

"Um," I say, looking back toward the lake. I guess that would be strange to see if you weren't used to it. "Yes."

The guy flops back onto the ground with a groan. "Tha's cool," he slurs, and I can't just not look into it. I know it's pretty stereotypical of me, but back home I was studying medicine. Not like officially or in school or anything, but just in my mom's old books. She was a doctor.

I kneel next to the guy, who for some reason is totally unfazed by the killer-looking bird hovering over us, and I try to figure out what's wrong with him. It's not hard, because he's not wearing pants, so the sloppily bandaged injury on his thigh jumps out at me.

"What happened to you?" I ask, scooting closer.

"Got sliced," he sighs sadly. "Where's Ren?"

"I don't know," I tell him. "Is it okay if I give this a closer look?"

"Mhm," says the guy, but I was going to do it anyway, because I'm the closest thing he has to a doctor and I don't think he really understands doctor-consent formality right now anyway.

His bandage is too tight. It's cutting off his circulation, which might be needed if he was actually bleeding through the bandages, but he's not, for some reason — although that reason soon becomes terribly clear. Underneath the bandage is a sloppy line of stitches. It looks like this guy could've done them himself, maybe right after he got injured. I hope he at least cleaned the needle first.

"You have an infection," I inform him, and he groans, turning his head to the side.

"'M gonna die?" he asks.

"No," I say, and to prove it, I walk back toward the lake and pull some roots up from just under the water. This dude is lucky lemluck grows in abundance around here. It won't heal him completely, but it'll definitely take the edge off his pain, and it's good for cleaning the wound, too.

I walk back over and take my knife out of my belt, and then I slice cleanly through the root. Inside is a thick gel, which I smear carefully over his wound. It's an unsettling green and leaking some sort of pus, but hopefully the lemluck will clear all of that out.

The boy hums moments after I put it on, and his eyes open. "Wow, much better," he says, and already his voice doesn't sound so weak. He should feel more lucid as the lemluck makes its way into his system. "What's your name, again?" he asks.

I hesitate. Back home, everybody knows my name. The one I was given, anyway. But the one I *want* roves around in the back of my head, the one that I've been harboring and holding close and hoping people would call me for the longest time now. I open my mouth and it rolls off my tongue much easier than I ever thought it would. "Will," I tell him. "I'm Will."

He smiles. "I'm Theo," he says. And then, lifting a finger at the bird, "and this is Icarus. She's an Avis."

Alright, so Theo's insane. He stole an Avis from Volant. Whatever, I can work with that.

But then, "Get away from him!" someone shouts, and I look up. Two people are running toward me, the girl looking furious and the guy looking… well, he's kind of expressionless, actually. They're both carrying armfuls of plants, which makes their gait look disjointed and awkward.

It's obvious they're talking to me, though, so I back away from Theo. They come to a stop in front of me moments later, both panting.

"What did you do to him?" the girl demands, glaring at me.

"Nothing," I say.

"Then why's his bandage undone?"

"Okay, I was helping him," I admit.

The girl doesn't look thankful or relieved to hear this, just angrier still.

"We don't need your help," the guy cuts in. He was hovering back, closer to Theo, but now he steps forward.

"Really?" I say plainly, eyeing the plants in their arms.

"Yeah!" the girl says. "We're healing him just fine, so–"

"Sure," I interrupt, and I take an exaggerated step back. "But just to make sure, 'healing' *does* mean 'poisoning' where you come from, right?"

They both pause. I look down at their plants again. Poison, poison, poison — it's literally *all* poison. They're just going to make Theo's condition worse.

"Eleanor!" the guy exclaims, rounding on her now. "I said small, round leaves that grow close to the ground!"

"They're *all* like that!" Eleanor snaps, and then the two of them are arguing back and forth. Behind them, Theo has managed to sit up, looking much better than he did when I first arrived.

"Ren," he says, and I only hear it because I'm looking at him. Ren, on the other hand, is in the middle of a loud argument, and yet he shuts up and turns to face Theo anyway, somehow having managed to hear him.

"Yeah?" he says.

"He helped me," Theo says. "He wasn't trying to hurt me or anything, I swear."

"We can't just trust some random guy," Eleanor says, and even though she's insulting me, I feel giddy anyway. *Some guy.*

"Sure, we can," Theo argues. "We trusted you."

Eleanor's mouth falls open, and then promptly clamps back shut. She crosses her arms and huffs, giving me a side-eye. I try to come off as un-intimidating as possible, which honestly shouldn't be hard. I don't think I've intimidated a single person in my entire life.

"How do you know all this stuff about plants, anyway?" Ren asks me. He's not glaring like Eleanor was, but I get the feeling he's just as angry underneath his cool exterior.

"It's basic education back in Ilma," I say, and both Ren and Eleanor stiffen. Stars, these guys are ridiculous.

"*Ilma?*" Ren says, and he turns back to Theo. "Theodore, come on. He could have all kinds of secrets or ulterior motives—"

Theo bursts into laughter, bending over his knees as his body shakes. I have no idea what's so funny, but after a moment or two, I realize that Theo's not actually amused. "You're not seriously telling me you're judging someone because of where they're *from*, are you?" he says.

And for some reason, that shuts Ren up.

"Look, I can prove to you that I'm trustworthy, if it's such a big deal," I say. And I don't really know why I'm doing this. I did these guys a favor by helping their friend, I don't owe them anything. I don't need to stick with them just to make sure Theo actually gets better.

But that doesn't change the fact that I *want* to stick with them. I can't live on my own — that's becoming more and more apparent with every passing day — and I've never actually been close with anyone my own age before. The fact that these people see me as I really am makes excitement thrum through me, and I have this stupid, childish desire for them to like me.

"But you guys have to prove that I can trust you too," I add suddenly. An eye for an eye, right?

"How?" Ren says. He looks on guard. I dig my medicine pouch out of my bag.

"Truth tablets," I say. "We all take one and tell a secret that nobody here knows. If you manage to do so, the effects of the tablet will wear off. Sound trustworthy to you guys?"

"The effects?" Eleanor says, and I just nod. No need to tell her before it happens.

"I don't know if this is a good idea…" Ren says.

"I think it's a great idea!" says Theo, and with that, I dump out the pills. It's easy to tell which ones the truth tablets are, because they're bright blue, and I pass them around to everyone in the group.

"Are we really about to take a pill handed to us by a stranger?" Ren mutters, and Theo scoffs.

"I'll take it first if you're so scared," he says, and promptly pops it in his mouth. I follow suit, as does Eleanor, and Ren's the last one to take the pill. Immediately, I can feel the effects taking place. I hate these things. They remind me of school and the assholes that inhabit it.

I look down, and sure enough, my hands are blue. My whole body's blue, actually, as is everyone else's. We'll go back to normal once we've told a significant truth, but until then, we'll look like this. Although surprisingly enough, even *this* makes me miss home, just a little. Occasionally, you'll see someone walking around with their skin akin to that of a blueberry, and you just know that they're in trouble, or that they were playing some dumb game with their friends.

"Woah!" It's Theodore who says it, and he's looking right at me. Then he looks down at his own hands, and between his friends.

"What? What is it?" Ren demands inexplicably.

"We're blue!" Theo explains. Maybe Ren's colorblind. Either way, I step forward to intervene.

"We'll look normal again once we tell the truth," I say. "It has to be something significant, and something no one here but you knows, as we agreed upon."

Eleanor looks intrigued, her eyebrows having climbed way up her forehead as she listened. Finally, she turns to me. "How about you start us off, Will?" she says. I can't help smiling at the sound of my name.

"Sure," I say. And this'll be easy, because none of these people know anything about me. I tell them, "I ran away from home. I have nowhere to go and no one to help me."

My skin returns to normal. I can tell none of them know what to say, and the atmosphere is quickly growing awkward, so I gesture to Theo. "Your turn," I tell him. He nods. Clears his throat.

"Okay, um…" He looks down at his feet, thinking. "Okay," he says again, and then his voice lowers. "It's my fault that my parents are dead."

It's a heavy statement, so I expect silence to fall, but Ren doesn't let it. "*Theodore*," he says roughly. "You know that's not true." Except Theo doesn't know that, apparently, because the blue in his skin fades. He looks normal again.

"Ren?" I prompt, because otherwise I think he's going to keep waiting and waiting for Theo to agree with him, even though it's obvious he can't. Not when the effects of the truth tablet have already faded.

Inexplicably, Ren's cheek pinken. "I don't have any secrets," he says, except that's a lie, because if it weren't he would look normal again by now.

"Nice try," I say, and then I sit down. I have a feeling this might take a while. Back home, we call people like Ren *Atalasi*. It means someone who suffers under the weight of the secrets they bear — oftentimes, it takes a while for *Atalasi* to open up. Rarely do they realize just how much better off they would be without their secrets weighing them down.

Eleanor and Ren follow in my wake, joining me and Theo on the ground, and I lean back on my hands, assessing Ren. Now that he's sitting, it's even easier to see how distinctly uncomfortable he is. He was fidgeting a little when he was standing, sure, but now that he's sitting it's not some subtle side-to-side swaying, it's full on foot tapping and thumb twiddling.

"I'll go first," Eleanor says suddenly, and Ren's body deflates in relief, though not for long, I suspect. "Before Askund, I lived like royalty," Eleanor says, and her blue skin disappears. Theo whistles.

"That's lucky," he says, looking extremely interested. His leg no longer seems to be bothering him, though I should probably find some more lemluck soon. Then I'll need to venture into the forest and see if there's anything else around that could help speed up his healing process.

But not right now.

Right now, everyone's looking at Ren, waiting. He knows this. Sucks in a breath. Lets it back out. His whole body is a coil of tension, twisting and fidgeting as if that might fight off the coming revelation. Time slows down and circles around us, around Ren. His hair flutters in the breeze, but besides that, not a single part of him moves — he's gone completely still. Everything falls silent. The sound of the lake's waves against its shores, the wind through the grass and the trees, even the insects chirping — it's all gone.

When Ren speaks, head bent toward his lap, he doesn't move a muscle. "I love Theodore," he admits.

Theo laughs. "I already know that," he snorts, elbowing Ren in the side. "I mean, we've been best friends for years, dude!"

Ren's blue skin is fading, though, and Theo's watches on in confusion. Then he turns to me, frowning. "I thought you said no one here could know the secret?" he demands. "Were the tablets faulty?"

"Um," I say, because *holy shit*. I can't stop looking at Ren — his head is still bent toward the ground and I can't see any of his face, but the tips of his ears are bright red. Eleanor looks as shocked as I feel, and as I glance between Ren and Theo in astonishment, she reaches out and rubs Ren on the back. His shoulders hike up toward his ears.

Eleanor cuts in, trying to save the situation. "Maybe, subconsciously, you *didn't* know that," she suggests, and Theo turns his confusion on her, already shaking his head.

"But I did!" he insists. "Who doesn't love their best friend?" he adds. And then he turns on me. "So was it the pill? Were my friends right about you?"

"No! I—" I start to say, but my words stutter to a stop. Ren's already told his secret, sure, but Theo didn't understand it. Doesn't he deserve a second chance, then? All my life, I've been told that *Atalasi* are suffering, but is this really my choice to make? Will Ren just suffer more, if Theo doesn't love him back?

Theo scoffs. "I can't believe you!" he yells, and it looks like he wants to get to his feet, but his leg still can't handle that kind of pressure. "I defended you, and you just — you just!" he can't wrap his mouth around the words he wants to say, but I get it. He thinks I've betrayed him, somehow. Lied about the pills and tried to get one over on him. He looks hurt, and I don't know what to do.

"Theodore," says Ren.

"These pills are faulty," Theo seethes, looking around at all of us in turn — me in anger, his friends in support.

This is it, huh? I came this close to having a friend group, this close to having people who might finally understand me, and I'm not going to get it. Something I've chased for all my life, hand always extended toward, fingers constantly reaching for, only to fall short just before I could grab and hold on.

"Theodore," Ren says again, louder, and this time he looks up from his lap. This finally garners Theo's attention, and my throat goes dry. I realize what's going to happen moments before it occurs, and I don't know what to think. Ren clearly doesn't like me, and yet, perhaps out of righteousness...

"What?" Theo says, impatient.

A pause.

"I'm *in* love with you," Ren clarifies, and this time he doesn't shrink in on himself. He doesn't even move. He just sits there, completely still, waiting. I'm not sure if he's even breathing anymore.

And then Theo says, "No you're not."

Now Ren moves. He reels back like he's been delivered a physical blow, and I hear him suck in a breath before he stumbles to his feet, managing to get a few steps away from Theo.

"Wait," Theo says almost immediately, but Ren's not waiting. He's backing away, turning around, and Theo tries to get to his feet to follow him but he lets out a cry of pain when he's reminded of his injury. Ren falters, his foot actually catching against the dirt at the sound of Theo's pain, but he only waits a second before he's moving again, walking purposefully toward the forest.

"Oh no…" Theo says lowly, and I can't help but agree.

CHAPTER 8

THEO

I'm an idiot. I don't even know how this happened — not really.

What I *do* know is that it's all my fault. I can't wrap my head around why I said it. *No you're not.*

I think I was just surprised. I mean, who wouldn't be? Your best friend's in love with you — you don't just take that in stride. You need a moment to process! A moment long enough so that you don't blurt out the first stupid thing that comes across your mind.

It's still going across my mind, actually. *Ren.* In *love* with me. That just *sounds* ridiculous! He's my best friend! How could he possibly be spending all this time as my best friend while also harboring feelings for me? Wouldn't that just be exhausting?

It doesn't matter, though. Because despite all of this, I hurt Ren's feelings, and I need to do something about it.

Unfortunately, there's not a lot of *doing* that I can do, right now. Although my leg no longer throbs with my every heartbeat and those feverish chills are gone, there's still no hope of me being able to stand. The second I tried to put weight on my leg my entire body viciously reminded me of that fact, so I sent both Eleanor and Will into the forest after Ren.

They were gone for what felt like forever, and yet they still came back empty handed. Or, Eleanor had. Will had had a bunch of plants in hand, and he'd spent the better part of an hour boiling and crushing them into a paste for my leg. A whole bunch of it was now slathered under my bandage.

Ren still hasn't returned, though. The moon is steadily rising and both Eleanor and Will have assured me that he'll be okay, that he probably just wants some space and seems perfectly capable of fending for himself, but they're idiots if they really think that that's what I'm worried about.

So once they fall asleep, both having taken out their sleeping bags after helping me set up mine, I crawl away from the camp. It's exhausting and painful work, mostly because I have to drag myself with my arms as my leg trails uselessly behind me, but I do it anyway, panting and working up a sweat in my determination. I continue like this until I'm a good distance from where my companions are sleeping, and then I call Icarus over to me.

She comes immediately, and I know she's worried about me. For the past several hours, she's scarcely wanted to leave my side, more often than not bumping up against me as she lays down, scared of venturing too far from me. Plus, she keeps nudging my leg with her beak, surprisingly gentle for her size, while chirping at me lowly in concern. She doesn't like that I'm hurt, which just makes me want to get better even faster, for her sake.

Now, I take the time to pat her head and rub her beak, murmuring to her before I ask her for a favor. It sounds crazy, but she can totally understand me. Talking to her is calming, and I think if I weren't so determined to go and find Ren, I'd just lay on the ground and tell her all about everything that'd happened.

Unfortunately, Icarus is too big to fit in this little forest out in the middle of Askund, looking absolutely nothing like Silva. The trees are *tiny*. I mean, sure, they're still like, way taller than *me*, but compared to the trees of my home they look like teensy little toothpicks. They grow so close together, and their branches look all thin and spindly, like the more dangerous branches I venture up toward when I'm bored. This forest is completely unsettling to look at, wrong in an innumerable amount of ways, but I can understand Ren wanting to disappear into there of all places.

I look up when Icarus returns, having wandered toward the forest on my request. She has a few branches clutched carefully in her beak like I asked, and I praise her for being the smartest Avis in the entire world. She lays down next to me as I arrange the branches on my lap, the extra bandages from my bag in the grass next to me. Then I set to work.

It takes more bandages than I would've liked — especially since I need them for my leg — and *much* longer than I wanted it to, but eventually I manage to break and tie the series of branches together into two makeshift crutches. One's accidentally taller than the other, and they're both covered in bark and bound to give me splinters, but they'll have to do.

Icarus helps me stand without me even having to ask, nudging her beak under my armpit as I get to my feet, and then I steady myself on my crutches and head to the forest, Icarus shadowing me for as long as she's able to. I shoot her a smile when I slip between the trees, though the way she croons sadly at me almost has me turning right back around.

None of this is easy. My branch-crutches keep sinking into the soft dirt of the forest floor, and despite the fact that I'm not putting my leg on the ground, it's starting to ache again from all this movement. I wish I could climb up into the trees and walk along the branches, but I know that's impossible right now. In order to find Ren, I'll just have to use my eyes and my instincts.

I don't call out to him. That would just drive him further away, when he's feeling like this. He'd realize that I'm out here looking for him and climb higher and farther away in order to avoid the coming interaction.

Unless… he wouldn't. What if I don't know Ren as well as I think I do? I mean, how well *can* I know him when I never even realized he was in love with me?

Ignore it. I have to ignore it. All that matters right now is finding Ren. Plus, I *do* know him, despite how my anxiety-ridden thoughts are trying to say otherwise. He might've hidden his feelings from me, sure, but there's still plenty else that I know about him. Like how he'll yell at me for singing the same song all day long only to start humming it to himself for the rest of the week. Or how he's too stubborn to ask for help when he can't find something and will spend hours retracing his steps, running his fingers over every possible surface he can find. Or how when he's upset, he tries to find the loudest place possible — a place where he can just drown himself in noise.

It's with that in mind that I continue my search. Deeper into the forest, through more difficult terrain, where my crutches slip over roots and get tangled in grass. I'm exhausted. My body aches and I'm covered in sweat, but I forge onward, listening intently. And then I hear it.

Cicadas.

They get louder as I keep walking, and I can't help picking up the pace. Ren's around here somewhere, I know it.

And sure enough — up there. He's climbed one of these tiny trees and wedged himself into a fork in the branches. It looks horribly uncomfortable compared to the usual branches we get to lounge on.

As I stare up at Ren, his body lax and his head tipped back, comfortable in the knowledge that he's alone, I realize that I've sneaked up on him. Possibly for the first time ever. Not because I'm moving especially stealthily, or even because the cicadas are that loud, but because of how lost in thought Ren looks. One of his legs dangles out of the tree and swings lightly through the open air, his arms folded against his chest. I stand directly underneath him, breathless, my arms shaking from the effort of using my crutches, and say, "Ren."

His whole body stiffens. It's so different from what I'm used to — normally, he relaxes in my presence — and because of it something pangs in my chest. He shouldn't have to feel uncomfortable around me.

"Theodore," he sighs. "How'd you get out here?"

"I built crutches," I tell him.

For a second, I think Ren will laugh — I swear his lips twitch — but he just shakes his head. "Do you really think that's a good idea for your leg?" he asks, head still tilted away from me. It looks like his fingers have tightened against the skin of arms, starkly white where they dig in. No doubt his arms are cold in the chill of the night, a stark difference from the heat of the day. Of course, he wasn't thinking about the temperature when he stormed off without his jacket.

"I feel fine," I lie. My leg is throbbing with every heartbeat again, but Ren doesn't need to know that. I can make it back to the camp like this. Probably.

Ren doesn't believe me. He sighs before swinging expertly out of the tree. His face shows a whole lot of nothing and he doesn't say anything to me as he turns and starts walking back the way we came. I crutch after him.

We've only been walking for a minute before Ren huffs and turns around. "You're in pain," he announces.

"No, I'm not," I say, struggling to breathe.

"Just get on my back," Ren says gruffly, and I try not to show how thankful I am when I wrap my arms around his neck and situate myself on his back, abandoning my crutches on the ground. *Thank you for your service, shitty crutches.*

We're moving at a much faster pace now, and the pain in my leg is slowly fading again.

"I'm sorry," I say, after less than a minute of silence. I've never been good with silence, I'll admit it. I like to fill it with sound, words and conversation. Although usually, silence with Ren doesn't feel like this — uncomfortable, that is. Normally with him, I can pass hours in silence, just spending time in his company without needing to say a word.

Now, the silence feels thick and tangible, and I want to squash it underfoot.

"What are you apologizing for?" Ren says, except it sounds like a warning. Like a, *don't even say it, Theodore.*

"For the way I reacted," I say anyway. *Sorry, Ren.* "It doesn't matter if you feel that way about me. I mean — it, like… for *you* it matters, um—"

"Theodore."

"—but it doesn't *change anything.* Like, you're still my best friend, you know? And I'm flattered, honestly! I've just never really thought about any of that before—"

"Theodore."

"I mean obviously, I'm thinking about it *now*, 'cause how can I not? But—"

"*Theodore*," Ren says, sounding embarrassed, and I remember how to close my mouth and cease my endless torrent of words. Ren's fingers are digging painfully into my thighs.

"Yeah?" I manage.

"Thanks," he says, and he bounces me up higher on his back even though I wasn't slipping. I rest my chin on his shoulder and close my eyes.

"Just don't run away into a random forest again," I sigh. "I was really worried, you know. And my leg fucking *hurts*."

Ren snorts, and I think he says something, but I'm not quite sure. I'm quickly slipping into sleep, though my arms remain locked firmly around Ren's neck, because even in my sleep I don't want to let go.

When I wake up in the morning, Ren's already awake. In fact, he's sitting up and glaring in Will's direction.

"What are you doing," I ask him, except it's not really a question.

"Will talks in his sleep," Ren mutters.

"By the Stars!" I gasp dramatically. "Let's have him arrested!"

Ren huffs, and for a second, I panic — *did that make him fall out of love with me?* — but then I wonder why that's even a cause for panic in the first place. It'd probably just make our lives easier.

"I'm just suspicious," Ren says lowly. "Like, he spent the whole night with us. And made you that healing stuff. When is he going to leave?"

I stretch my leg out to kick Ren, tapping him on the side of the thigh with my foot. "I don't think he will," I say casually. Ren splutters.

"What do you mean?" he demands. "Of course he's going to leave!"

"You heard him, yesterday," I say. "He said he has nowhere to go and no one to help him. I think he'll want to stay with us, and honestly, I don't think it's a bad idea. It'd be nice to have his help in Ilma."

"We can't take on *another* stranger," Ren says desperately, although I get the feeling he and Eleanor don't dislike each other anymore. I guess someone almost dying really brings people together. That or they're suspicious enough of Will to trust each other. The devil you know, and all that.

"Sure we can!" I say happily, enjoying the increasing look of frustration Ren gets about him. Barely noticeable, but there. His shoulders tightening. His jaw clenching. "Besides, I don't think you hate him as much as you pretend to."

I can see the internal struggle Ren has with himself — whether to claim he doesn't care enough to hate him or say that he really doesn't like him any more than he appears to. Finally, he just settles on, "What do you mean?"

"You stepped in when I was yelling at him," I say carefully, broaching the whole topic of *yesterday*. I don't get angry like that very often. Usually, I'm pretty forgiving and laid back, but when I do get mad, it tends to explode out of me in a whirlwind of emotions. For a second there, I really did think Will was pulling some sort of trick on us with the pills.

"I didn't do that for *him*," Ren argues, and he can deny it all he wants, but I know he's got a big, soft heart. He couldn't bear me turning my undeserved anger on Will. "Besides, if we're going to talk about yesterday, we're going to talk about you."

I freeze.

This whole time, I've been sitting up, having joined Ren in his upright position once I woke up, but at these words I plop right back down in my sleeping back and turn away from him. Eleanor's on the other side of me, but our conversation hasn't woken her. She's a deep sleeper if I've ever met one, and right now her mouth is hanging open, drool crusted on her chin.

I thought I'd be able to get away with it. That in the aftermath of Ren's colossal secret, mine would get brushed under the rug.

Apparently not.

"Theodore," Ren says, exasperated. "Why do you think your parents' death is your fault?"

Because it is, I want to say. I try not to think about it much. At all, if I can help it. But sometimes it creeps up on me when I least expect it, and I want to jump into the past and punch myself for not doing anything sooner.

When my parents died, everyone mourned for them. They were well liked, in Silva, and for a while, before I was pegged as a delinquent, people mourned for me too. *Poor boy*, they would say. *I hear he was there when it happened. He must be so messed up.*

I'd put up a strong front. Hector needed me, after all. I was almost an adult, but he was still just a little kid. A little kid who'd lost his parents. I had to be there for him.

The days after it happened are a blur. I don't think I was even the one to tell Ren — he was just there, somehow. He found out and came without me having to get him. There was a funeral and a wake and lots and lots of papers, things I'd signed that I'd hardly understood. And through it all, though I'd kept up a strong front for Hector, I'd felt like a shell of a person. *It's my fault*, I'd thought to myself, day in and day out, each night as I'd fallen asleep. *It's my fault, it's my fault, it's my fault.*

"It wasn't your fault," Ren says now, his hand landing on my arm. He squeezes. Shakes. "You hear me, Theodore?"

"Yeah," I say gruffly, even though he's wrong. He'll never understand. He wasn't there that night, when it started storming without any prior warning. When the branches grew slick with water as lightning danced across the sky and thunder shook the very earth our home was rooted in.

Mom and Dad had started hurrying. My dinner had suddenly felt much less satisfying, roiling around in my stomach like that, and distantly, I'd felt glad that Hector had complained about dinner enough that he'd been allowed to stay home. No one had said anything, but I could tell we were all worried about how hard it was storming, how the wind was shaking the trees and the water was making it hard to walk as quickly as we wanted to.

My parents had been arguing that night. Tensions were high when we'd left the house, my mom annoyed that Dad had conceded to letting Hector stay home during what was supposed to be our nice dinner out. In the end, the meal wasn't very nice, full of snippy comments here and there that they both kept making to me, as if I'd wanted to be part of their argument in any way. It'd annoyed me to no end, and always had. My parents had never argued a lot, but whenever they did, they'd acted like it was impossible to keep me out of it.

Even the walk back home had been electrified — and not just after the storm started.

I remember wishing they would stop arguing as we'd walked home in the storm. A fleeting thought had darted through my head, a thought that I'm still convinced is what jinxed everything. What killed them.

This storm is insane, I'd thought fervently. *What if we fall?*

And then, like a righteous god had heard the words in my head and taken it as a dare, lightning had stricken the branch in front of us. It was loud and hot and blinding, and I didn't even realize it'd happened until my dad cried out, "Theo!"

My eyes had shot open. Before me, the branch had been split down the middle, a section of it holding on by twigs. On the other side had been my mother, holding desperately onto Dad's

124

hands as the branch had tipped terrifyingly below her. Dad had been on the very edge, the branch beneath him blackened and smoking, sizzling in the rain.

"Theo, take my hand," Dad had ordered, and he'd held one hand out to me, the other still gripping my mother's. All three of us had been soaked, and I remember the feeling of my fingers on my face, trembling, as I'd pushed my sopping hair out of my eyes.

My legs had felt like jello, and I'd inched closer to the two of them, my arm extended toward my dad. And then, thunder — loud and overwhelming and shaking me to my core, making me flinch back into myself.

"Theodore," my dad had said, stern but not unkind, "Don't be afraid." I'd come closer, closer. The branch had felt weaker there, just on the precipice of breaking. Again, I'd reached out a hand, flinching when lightning lit the sky.

And then, before Dad could utter my name a fourth time, a loud *crack* rent the air. It was in no way louder than the thunder, and yet that was the sound that'd been deafening. I don't remember screaming out, don't remember scrambling along the broken branch, don't remember sobbing or begging the universe to bring them back. I just remember that in one moment, they'd been right there, my dad's fingers a handbreadth from mine. In my fear, I'd hesitated, and in the next moment, they were gone.

It was all my fault.

"Ugh, he's waking up," Ren whispers to me. I sit up, embracing the distraction fully.

"Can you stop being so skeptical of him?" I say.

"No," Ren says. And then, "Tell me what he looks like."

I sigh. Ren does this sometimes. I have no clue how he decides which things he wants to know the appearances of, but I always humor him. A few years after we'd met, I'd told him about my dark skin, my brown hair, my brown eyes. And before he could ask, I'd told him about himself, too: pale skin, black hair, slanted eyes.

Will doesn't seem too awake yet, though he's shifting around in his sleeping bag, so I figure it's safe to whisper about him without him overhearing.

"Okay he has... brown, choppy hair," I say, and Ren nods beside me, his own hair falling in front of his eyes. "He's pretty short and skinny. I think he's injured, too, 'cause he has these massive bandages on his chest."

"He does?" Ren says, confused.

"Yeah. I mean, you can only really see it through the arms of his tank-top, but I think he must've gotten in a fight or something."

"So he could be dangerous?" Ren concludes.

"You're impossible."

The day starts out slowly. When Eleanor wakes, she pats herself on the back for knowing Ren so well — *I told you he'd come back!* — and promptly begins foraging for food, all of which she shows to Will before throwing into a pile for a breakfast stew she plans on making. Will changes my bandages, commenting on how well my injury seems to be coming along, and generally gives Ren a wide berth. I think he can tell Ren doesn't like him.

Speaking of Ren, he's avoiding everyone a little bit. Except for me, 'cause we already had our heart to heart last night. But I'd be embarrassed too if everyone suddenly knew who I was in love with, so I can understand. I'm just glad he can't see the pitying looks Eleanor keeps shooting him, nor the analyzing ones from Will.

Eventually, though, Eleanor demands that Ren help her with some sort of harness she's trying to make for Icarus, and that leaves just me and Will in the general vicinity, though I can tell Ren's trying his hardest to eavesdrop on us from where he's ventured off with Eleanor and Icarus.

I can't help rolling my eyes at his antics. It's ridiculous that he's so distrustful of Will, especially after he went through all that trouble to help with my leg. And even if Will were a problem, I could totally take him. And even if I *couldn't* take him, I could for sure outrun him. If my running abilities weren't currently compromised, that is.

"How's your leg?" Will asks, taking a seat by my side. He seems most comfortable around me, which I don't blame him for. It's not exactly the easiest of tasks to get on Ren's good side, and Eleanor can be intimidating too.

"Feels good, Doc," I joke. "How's your chest?"

"I — my what?" Will stutters, looking stricken.

"Your… chest?" I say, and I gesture to my own for clarification. Do they call it something different in Ilma? "I just noticed you have bandages, too," I explain. "Did you get hurt?"

"Oh!" Will says, and he sounds relieved. "I'm — yeah, yeah. Getting better though," he says, laughing nervously. And then, "So… Ren's really in love with you, huh?"

I glance over at Ren, and he's stiffened suddenly. Eleanor's saying something to him, surely having noticed this, but he's not answering her. It doesn't look like he's trying to listen to mine and Will's conversation with every fiber of his being anymore.

"Yeah," I say. "I mean, we haven't really talked about it, but… Now that I know about it, yeah. I can see it." And I *can*. A bunch of little things that never meant anything to me suddenly add up. The way Ren's never really seemed to like anyone touching him, yet never protested when it was me. The way he always listens to me when I get some inane idea in my head and lets me ramble until I realize just how crazy I'm being — or joins me when I don't. The way he left Silva for me, because… he's in love with me.

"And do you… with him…?" Will asks, trailing off expectantly. The way he says it isn't all that clear, but I know what he's asking. *Do you love him, too?*

I don't even think about it. "No," I say with a laugh, my voice lowered even more so I know Ren can't hear it. "I mean, he's my best friend."

128

"Aren't you his best friend, too?" Will asks. And that just throws me through a loop. Too many gears are trying to spin in my brain, at different speeds and in different directions, and I feel like my head's going to explode. I don't have time to think about this right now. It's too much — I just need to Restore the Light and get back to Hector. Then I can think about everything that's confusing.

Thankfully, Will saves me from having to answer. He asks me what we're all out here for, anyway, so I tell him everything. I tell him about finding Icarus and getting exiled and Ren following me. About running into Eleanor and going to Udula and the strange lack of information about the Darkness' origin. Hell, I even tell him that Ren's Covan so we won't have to go through that whole fiasco again, and that if he has a problem with it, he can just go ahead and leave us now. Luckily, he doesn't.

"Ilma's definitely the way to go if you're looking for information," Will tells me. "They're not kidding when they say we're the land of secrets. We trade in them just as much as actual currency."

"That's insane," I say.

"It's home," Will sighs, and I can't tell whether he sounds homesick or not. And then, "I can take you guys there, if you want," he offers. "You won't make it a day in the markets without me."

I laugh. "Sounds like you're bribing me."

"I think I am," Will admits. "Your friends don't seem to like me very much. I wouldn't be surprised if they tried to get rid of me."

"Eleanor likes you just fine," I say. I haven't talked to her about it explicitly or anything, but I like to think I'm pretty good at reading people. You know, when they're feeling anything but in love with me. "And you'll grow on Ren. He's just stubborn."

"I guess we'll see," Will sighs, and I lean over and bump my shoulder into his. Will shoots me a smile.

Across from us, I can see Ren sitting on Icarus, and it looks like he's holding something for Eleanor as she walks around her, measuring the leather she secretly bought for her grand harness idea at some point when I was passed out. (Ren says that's where all our money went.)

Just then, Eleanor pulls the leather a little too tight and Icarus screeches, making Ren clamp his hands over his ears. But then Icarus rears back and Ren buries his hands in her feathers instead, mere moments before she takes off into the air with another angry screech, Ren's yells following in her wake.

Eleanor collapses on the ground, cackling, and I keep my eyes trained on Ren, unsure what to make of the growing warm feeling in my stomach.

I think I'm scared of it.

CHAPTER 9

ELEANOR

"I thought you said full grown Avi could carry *four* people?"
Theo complains, not that he really has the right to. I mean, at
least he gets to *sit* on Icarus. The rest of us are just walking along
beside her.

"Maybe she's not full grown," I say, my temper starting
to get on the short side. That's what happens when your feet hurt
and you're hungry and you still aren't sure if you're even heading
in the right direction.

"I think she's faking," Ren grumbles. He's convinced it's
my fault, that Icarus isn't flying us anywhere because she's

dissatisfied with her new harness, but I think he's still just upset about being dragged through the air for an impromptu joyride. He's glaring at me as he says it — or, in my direction, I guess.

I'm still getting used to the fact that Ren is blind. That he's Covan. Admittedly, when I first heard it, it freaked me out. Or actually, I'd already been freaking out, considering we were being chased by monsters in the dark. But afterwards, as we'd divided and got to figuring out just how we were going to save Theo, I'd had a lot of time to think about it. A lot of time to stare at him and realize he had no idea I was staring. A lot of time to ruminate over the fact that Ren was *Covan*, the people we all grew up hearing about.

Except now I'm starting to realize just how bullshit everything we heard about them was. It's what I believed for so long, though. When it wasn't politics, stuff about guarding the border and being prepared in case of invasion, it was prejudice. People offhandedly making remarks about them, dumb jokes and comments. It was a whole institution of racism, and only since meeting Ren do I feel like I've seen the light, funnily enough.

Because Theo was right.

I brought it up to him when I was still a little uneasy after learning Ren was Covan and he'd talked some sense into me. And I could pretend that I don't trust either of them for as long as I want, but it's just easier to admit that not only do I trust them, I *like* them. Plus, Ren being blind puts a few things into perspective. Like the fact that he always refused to look at me. Or how he couldn't find the right books in the library.

I'm still curious about how he figured out my scam, though.

Besides, if there's anyone here I'd have to decide not to trust, it'd be Will — simply because I know him the least — but I can't even do that. Partly because I think Theo's a good judge of character, and partly because Will just seems like a good guy. He healed Theo all on his own, after all, and though he seems pretty quiet, I think he knows a lot. I guess that would make sense, seeing as he's Ilman. He's probably bought and sold his fair share of secrets, too.

"What if she's hurt?" Theo frets, and he's leaning forward on Icarus now, peering into her face. "Or what if she's hungry?"

"She ate a ton of fish from that lake," I say. "I don't think she's hungry."

"What's wrong, Icarus?" Theo says to her. I wish she would answer. It was frustrating, all of us having piled onto her back and waited for a good few minutes while Theo tried to coax her into the air. With Icarus' stubborn refusal, we were forced to climb off and go on foot.

What makes this worse is I feel like flying on Icarus would establish a bit of normal into our routine again, which we're in desperate need of after that whole secret-sharing fiasco last night. Ren hasn't been the same since. He's more reserved, and not just with me. He barely speaks without being spoken to, and he doesn't really act the way he used to with Theo. It's like he's doing his best to avoid everyone when avoiding anyone is impossible.

I think Theo is noticing the distance, too. When we woke up, finding Ren with us again, it seemed like everything would be just fine. But throughout the day Ren had just drifted further and further away — and not necessarily physically, either. Any of their conversations that I overheard sounded stilted and strange, nothing like the easy banter they'd shared before. I wish I could help them sort it out somehow, but I know it's not my place to intervene, and I don't even have any bright ideas to begin with, anyway.

"Has she done anything like this before?" Will asks, looking up at Icarus. He still seems uneasy around her, and he skitters to the side whenever she gets too close.

"No, she hasn't," Ren says dryly. "Funny." He's insinuating something between Will's presence and Icarus' sudden inability to fly. Theo catches it too, and he sends Ren a look, which of course goes unnoticed, but if Will recognizes the hostility, he doesn't say anything about it.

I think Ren's being ridiculous. Will's done nothing to garner this much distrust. It makes me wonder if Ren's just trying to channel all his feelings elsewhere.

And I really can't force myself to pay attention to any of this anymore. Theo snaps something at Ren, and Ren returns it, and Will's placating tone crescendos and I just shut it all out, completely over it by now. If the bird doesn't want to fly, she doesn't want to fly. There's nothing more we can do about it.

At the very least we can appreciate the view. I know Askund has a bad rep, what with it being what it is, a place of nothing and nobodies, but it really is quite beautiful. There's hardly anyone out here, and aside from the few towns scattered around, there are no structures either. Just nature, rolling fields and bouts of trees. Occasionally, a lake.

Of course, obstructing this beautiful view is the wall of Darkness rising up in the distance, but we're all just neglecting to mention it.

I've never seen the Darkness before. I mean, I was in it, sure, but I didn't really see what it looked like from the outside. And the whole time we were flying away from it I was just panicking over the blood covering Theo's leg and dripping through the open air.

From here, though, I can see that it's nothing like I ever expected. It's not uniform, or still, or at all planned-looking. It's *moving*, roiling in the air and curling around itself, like a thick smog contained to the area it already fills. It almost looks like it's alive, terrifyingly enough, and looking at it for too long gives me the creeps.

So I avert my gaze and forge onward, really hoping we're getting closer to Ilma now, which is when I see something *else* rising in the air. Dust?

"Guys," I say, still squinting at it. It's just a little plume, gathering in the distance right along the path we're on, and it almost looks like it's getting closer.

"—well have you thought that *maybe* she doesn't like your *attitude*—"

"*Guys*," I say louder, interrupting Theo, and then I point. "What is that?"

Everyone shuts up, thank the Stars.

"I assume you're referring to something you can see," Ren says snidely.

And despite the fact Theo was just arguing him, he answers immediately, like he's done it a thousand times and will do it a thousand more. "There's some sort of dust rising in the distance," he explains.

"Like a sandstorm?" Ren asks.

"Nah, it's not that intense. It's almost like—"

"I hear it!" Ren interrupts.

"The dust?" Will says incredulously.

"No, the *hooves*," Ren bites. "They're on horses."

For a second, we all just stand there, curious and for some reason unafraid of random strangers riding toward us in Askund. But then we remember we're in *Askund*, the land of criminals and thieves, and we all scramble to get off the path.

The grass is tall all around the path, so I dive to one side, dragging Ren with me. Will darts into the grass opposite us, and Icarus follows him at Theo's urging. She doesn't really manage the best job of hiding, seeing as she's so big, but it'll have to do. Hopefully the strangers will ride right past us and we can avoid any type of conflict.

The galloping gets louder, finally audible for the rest of us, and I lay there anxiously, Ren looking just as tense as I am, as they get closer and closer…

And then, dread it all, they stop.

"What the hell is *that*?" one of them says. I peek through the grass and see the guy peering straight down at the ground. He looks like an actual cowboy. His feet, secure in his saddle stirrups, are fitted in tall, leather boots — complete with spurs — and he's wearing a cowboy hat on his head. I bet Icarus left some sort of weird tracks when she scurried off into the grass with Theo, which would explain why Mr. Fancy Boots over there is scrutinizing the path so hard. This can't end well.

"Leave it alone," says the cowboy's companion. "Probably some sort of wild animal."

"That look like an animal track you've seen before?" the cowboy scoffs, and I pray for him to just listen to his friend, *please*.

He doesn't.

"Let's check it out," he continues, and they dismount. I can hear them walking away from us, thanks to the cowboy's boots. *Ca-chink, ca-chink, ca-chink.* It's all I can do to stay still and silent, waiting anxiously, listening with all my might.

"Woah! What *is* that?" says the one that doesn't look like a carbon copy cowboy, and then there's a deafening squawk followed by the sound of wings beating. I see Icarus take off into the air, Theo still clinging to her back, and maybe the bandits won't notice the rest of us, maybe they'll just move on and leave us alone and later we can meet back up with—

"Theodore!" Ren cries, launching up and out of the grass. I don't even bother to muffle my groan. I just get to my feet too, because I might as well with our cover blown.

I watch as Will pops up on the other side of the path, looking up at where Icarus is carting off with Theo into the distance. He's waving his arms wildly, trying to get her to turn around, I think, but she's not listening to him, for once.

My attention is quickly drawn away from Theo, however, because unfortunately, the bandits aren't just interested in Icarus. They're interested in us too, and for a second, I swear their eyes are locked on me — wide and full of recognition — but there's no way of knowing for sure because in between one moment and the next, they start trying to kidnap us.

And I know. It's three against two — we should totally be able to take them, right? Except we weren't really anticipating getting kidnapped today, and these dudes are way bigger than us. Like, they're *adult* adults. Meanwhile the rest of us are just a bunch of teenagers, none of us particularly trained in the art of fighting. Sure, I know a bit of fencing, but that's about the only type of combat I know, and even then, I'm pretty sure the royal guards were going easy on me. Plus, while I do have a knife, it's not on me. It's in my bag, currently being toted somewhere far away by Icarus.

So yeah, I scream and fight and even try to bite the cowboy when he puts me in a headlock, but none of it does me any good. The next thing I know, I've been elbowed in the head and the ground's swaying viciously under my feet. My hands are tied together and a blindfold is fixed over my eyes. A length of rope connects me to Ren and Will, both of whom were similarly defeated, and I stumble when we're tugged, bumping into Ren, who's in front of me.

"Cooperate and your friend will find you alive, when he comes back for you," one of our captors promises us. His voice *sounds* like grease. Don't ask me how.

We're led out of the field, me and Will stumbling along and Ren walking perfectly fine — I would laugh at the idea of Ren being blindfolded if I weren't so scared right now — and the men climb back onto their horses. My head is still throbbing. I want to sit down, but we're not given a chance. We start walking when the horses do, heading in the opposite direction than we were trying to go, I'm pretty sure, and with every passing moment I'm beginning to feel more and more hopeless. At the very least, I suppose it could be worse. It seems like I was just being paranoid back there, that they didn't really recognize me as the Lost Princess after all.

I can't hear Icarus anymore. There's no telling where she might've flown in her panicked state, and it's not like Theo can do anything if she won't listen to him. Even if he managed to get her to land, he couldn't come running after us on that leg of his.

"That was an Avis, right Hal?" says one of our kidnappers. It sounds like the cowboy. He then tugs on our rope, just to be cruel, and I stumble into Ren while Will crashes into me. The three of us huff angrily but don't say anything, straightening up and falling in line again.

"Sure looked like one to me," says Hal. "How much you think we can get for Avi meat?"

I gasp — I can't help it. The thought is insane. You don't *eat* Avi! They're militaristic creatures! Everyone respects them, honors them. Hell, some researchers say they're even smarter than we are!

"You got a problem with that, little lady?" says the cowboy.

"You're cruel," I say through gritted teeth.

The two men laugh, and they yank the rope again, and my anger melts. I'm scared. What are they going to do to us? Where are we even going?

We walk for what feels like an hour. None of us dare talk to each other, too scared of the consequences, and then we take a detour off the dirt path we're used to traveling on, the bandits leading us directly through a field, which isn't easy to navigate even when you aren't blindfolded.

We trip and stumble through the field a while longer before we're on a dirt path again, and then we enter some sort of town. I can tell because I can hear all the voices as we approach, and then we're in the thick of it. It's times like this when I truly despise Askund, when not a single person protests to three people obviously being kidnapped. In fact, a few people make jeering comments, obviously familiar with our captors, and I want to break out of my bindings just so I can punch each and every one of them in the face.

The noise of the town dies down as we enter some sort of building. The floors are wooden and creaky and every nerve in my body ignites with fear as we're led down a set of stairs. There, the three of us are fastened to chairs.

"Your buddy better come for you quick," says Hal. "Otherwise you three will pay the price."

On that note, our captors leave us, murmuring to each other as the sound of their footsteps disappear back up the stairs. Barely a moment passes before Ren speaks up.

"They're lying," he says.

"What?" says Will.

"They were talking as they went up the stairs. One of them said, *'Think they believe we're really after the bird?'*, and the other guy said, *'No doubt. We'll leave before sundown, make sure the damned thing can't really find them. The Sorceress will be pleased'*."

"Sorceress?" Will scoffs, and I don't blame him. He's a man of science, coming from Ilma, so it makes sense that he wouldn't believe in magic. Most people don't — my family included — so I've never given it much thought either. Besides, those who actually believe in magic have always seemed kind of cult-ish, to me.

"That's what he said," says Ren.

"Will," I feel inclined to say. "I swear our travels aren't usually like this."

Ren snorts, and even Will huffs out a tentative laugh. "That's reassuring," he says. "Those guys are idiots, though. They didn't even pat us down."

With that, I can feel Will shifting on the left of me. He wiggles around a whole lot, his shoulder bumping into mine several times, and he grunts doing whatever it is he's doing. Finally, though, he goes still, having made a triumphant sound.

"What is that supposed to mean?" Ren finally asks, clearly as confused as I am.

"They don't know I have a knife," says Will, triumphant. I feel my face break out into a grin, relief coursing through me, but Ren clearly doesn't share this feeling.

"You've had a knife this whole time and you're *just now* using it?" he demands.

"You're right, I'm sure they wouldn't have noticed me taking it out of my boot as we were walking. I'll be sure to do that next time," Will says snarkily, and Ren bristles while I laugh. I have no idea how Will managed to retrieve his knife with his hands tied behind his back like this, but I have to give him props. Dude must be flexible.

He cuts off his own bindings first, and it takes a while because his hands are still tied together, but once he gets them, he lets out a pleased noise. Then he's moving, his presence disappearing as he circles behind the chairs before crouching down behind me. He holds my wrists steady as he cuts through the bindings, his hands surprisingly soft, and when I'm free I let my arms fall away from the uncomfortable position they've been held in for so long now, rubbing my wrists. The next thing to go is my blindfold, which I yank viciously off my head.

"Don't you dare come near me with that knife," Ren says when Will takes a step toward him.

"What?" says Will.

"No offense, but I don't really trust you to do something you'd normally do when you can see."

"Dude, I took off my blindfold the second I was free. It's not even that dark down here."

That shuts Ren up. I think he forgot that we could just take off our blindfolds and see again, and I have a feeling he's embarrassed. He doesn't say anything this time when Will moves toward him.

While they're doing that, I take the time to examine our surroundings. Though there's no electricity down here, natural light seeps through the cracks of the floorboards above us, along with under the door at the top of the stairs. It isn't much, but it's enough to see by.

The three of us aren't the only things down here — not by a long shot. Our chairs are clumped together near the wall, and the rest of the room is chock full of junk. Old furniture shoved against the walls and endless knick-knacks scattered around the room. There doesn't seem to be any sort of organizational system to it.

When Ren's free, he stands up and takes off his blindfold, though it seems like an afterthought.

"Should we go?" Will says, turning to look at the door we came in through.

"No," says Ren. "They're still up there. I can hear them."

"Well what do we do?" I say.

"I think there might be another way out," says Ren, and he raises a finger and points across the room. He's pointing at a wardrobe.

"Yeah, that's a wardrobe," says Will.

"What? But—" Ren's cuts himself off after taking a step forward because he trips over a stack of plates, and they clash loudly as they hit the ground. We all freeze.

"Crap! They're coming!" Ren says, and we all scramble back to our chairs. I pull my blindfold back over my eyes and drop into my seat with my arms held behind my back, breathing heavily. The door to the basement opens and footsteps thunder down, accompanied by the sound of spurs.

"What the fuck was that?" the cowboy shouts. We're all silent, tense. And then, his voice low again, "How the hell did you take off your blindfold?"

Oh no.

Ren sucks in a breath. "I—" he says, but he doesn't get a chance to explain himself before a sharp *smack* rings out in the room, making me gasp.

"You got a problem with that?" the captor demands, and realizing he's talking to me, I shake my head hastily. I can hear Ren breathing faster, and I don't doubt for a second that he just got slapped across the face. "You lot better start praying," the man growls, "'cause I'm not sure how much longer you've got."

And then his footsteps retreat. He's going up the stairs again — maybe to get his companion — and panic fuels me into action.

I rip off my blindfold and crouch in front of Ren, tilting his face toward mine. He looks shell-shocked, his eyes still blown wide, and the left side of his face feels hot to the touch. It looks a little swollen, even.

"Are you alright?" I ask him, and he blinks. Shakes his head.

"I'm fine," he says, and then he stands up. His hand makes an aborted movement toward his face before he clenches his fist and keeps it by his side. "Just — lead me to that wardrobe. I think there's some sort of entrance behind it."

We don't have any better options, so with a glance toward Will I grab Ren's arm and lead him through the junk. We have to squeeze through all types of furniture, but then we finally come to a stop in front of the wardrobe. I reach out and open the doors.

"Oh no," I say.

"What?"

"It's just a wardrobe." I can hear footsteps above us — loud, angry — and I know they're coming.

Will shoves his way between me and Ren and steps into the wardrobe. "You really think this is an exit?" he says.

The door to the basement opens, and our captors come racing down the stairs. We're not where they left us, so they're already shouting, furious and confused, though it only takes them seconds to scan the room and find us.

"Yes!" Ren decides, just as our captors start shoving their way through the obstacles. Will backs up, takes a deep breath, and kicks the back wall of the wardrobe. Surprisingly, the wall falls backwards, and it keeps falling, because behind the wardrobe isn't another wall, but a tunnel.

"Thank the Stars," Ren murmurs, but we haven't escaped yet. Will reaches out and tugs Ren into the tunnel after him, and I know I should follow, but instead I just stand there, watching as our captors race toward us. The cowboy's in the lead, his face twisted into a mask of pure fury, and I feel my own emotions morph into something similar. I remember the *crack* of his hand connecting with Ren's face, the shocked expression Ren had worn when he normally wears no expression at all, and the fiery heat under my fingers as I'd touched his cheek. I remember their words that Ren overheard, something about taking us somewhere else and turning us over to a higher power.

"Eleanor let's go!" Will snaps, but anger has its claws in me and right as the cowboy nears, shoving aside an entire end table to get to me, I lunge forward. I know I can't take him, not really, which is why my foot lands in his stomach, making him double over with a groan. And then, with him bent over like that, I snatch the hat off his head. I don't know why I do it, but it feels appropriate. I hope he loves this stupid hat.

Then I turn around and sprint into the tunnel, Will and Ren waiting impatiently for me, and we take off. Almost immediately, I can't see a thing. It's pitch black in here, but I can hear our captors voices as they chase after us.

Both Will and I have slowed down, afraid of tripping in the complete darkness, but Ren keeps sprinting on ahead of us.

"Uh, Ren," I call, making the sound of his footsteps falter. "We can't see down here."

"Oh," says Ren, and then he doubles back and grabs my hand. I think he grabs Will's too, based on the surprised sound he makes, but neither of them say anything about it. Ren just starts running again.

Soon enough, I can't hear the sound of pursuers anymore. I think they've given up, or maybe gone back for flashlights.

But Ren doesn't hear them either, he tells us shortly after, and with that, we start walking, catching our breaths. I'm hoping this tunnel isn't too long, because walking in the dark is unsettling, and it reminds me of that dark patch we were in. I'm still clutching that guy's hat, and with nothing better to do with it, I reach up and plop it on Ren's head. He makes a surprised sound.

"Did you just put a hat on me?" he says, incredulous.

"Yeah," I say. "I stole it off that guy with the spurs."

I think Ren's going to say something about the hat, probably demand I take it back, but then he just scoffs. "What is the point of having loud shoes?" he demands. "It just tells everyone exactly where you are."

I find myself smiling in amusement. Of course Ren would have a passionate opinion about something like that.

We continue to walk in relative silence, Ren occasionally taking us around a turn that we wouldn't have known was there otherwise. It smells like dirt and earth — we're truly underground — and I wonder how this tunnel even got here in the first place.

And then, suddenly, Ren gasps.

"What? What is it?" I say.

Ren doesn't answer, but I can feel his hand shaking in mine. I squeeze it harder. "What is it, Ren?"

He whispers something, but it's too quiet and I don't catch it.

"What?"

"We're in Cova," Ren realizes, still standing frozen, his hand still shaking in mine.

"How is that possible?" Will demands.

"There are secret entrances and exits everywhere," Ren explains. "Cova expanded after we were pushed underground."

Neither Will nor I know what to say to that. We all just stand there, silent, until Ren lets out an unsteady breath. "I'll find the nearest exit," he promises, and I can't shake the feeling that he sounds *scared*. But why would he be scared of his own home?

The further we walk into Cova, the more uneasy I start to feel. I think it's because of how uncomfortable Ren clearly is. Even so, he continues to navigate just fine, though sometimes he sucks in a breath and squeezes my hand, speeding up or turning abruptly.

I think Will feels it too, because he's the one to break the silence. Create a distraction. "So," he says. "How long have you loved Theo for?"

Ren actually stumbles. "*What?*" he says, and I think I must have misheard him too, because he can't honestly be that tactless. It doesn't take a genius to see that Ren wants us all to forget we even heard that little fact in the first place.

"In Ilma, we talk about the secrets we learn from the truth tablets," Will explains. "The more you talk about them, the less like a secret they feel, and the easier it is to do something about them."

"Okay, well in the rest of the world, we don't even share our secrets in the first place," Ren snaps. "And we certainly don't talk about them." He starts walking again, pulling us at a faster pace this time.

"It's nothing to be ashamed of," Will tries to reason, only making Ren speed up even more. "Plus, what if he feels the same way?"

Ren scoffs. He doesn't slow down. "He doesn't," he says.

"Why are you so sure?"

"Because I am."

"But why?"

149

"Because Theodore's not like me!" Ren snaps, breath heaving. He's stopped again, and I listen in silence, still holding onto his hand tightly. "He's not stupid enough to fall in love with his best friend. Okay?"

"But—" Will says.

"*Okay?*"

And Will concedes. "Okay," he says softly.

Without talking, Ren takes one final turn. Here, the ground starts to slope upward. It takes a while, but eventually, I can see light spilling toward us. The uneasy feeling goes away.

"Can you see the exit?" Ren says, sounding anxious.

"Yeah," I say, and Ren breathes a sigh of relief.

"Good," he says, and he walks just a little bit faster. I turn to look behind us, peering back into the tunnel. The dark is unnerving.

CHAPTER 10

VELOREN

I should be thinking about everything that just happened. I should be thinking about getting kidnapped and tied up and uselessly blindfolded. About our captors' strange words — their mention of a Sorceress. About the heat of that man's hand connecting with my face. I should be thinking about Cova, about stepping foot in the place I used to call home for the first time since I was nine.

I should be thinking about all the creatures we walked past, the ones that didn't attack us because they thought we were Covans, unlike the ones we encountered aboveground. I should be thinking about how lucky I am that the exit I found wasn't one with Darkness escaping into the abovelands, about how the information I know is still just mine, my secret still safe for now.

I should be thinking about how horrible I felt down there, my mother's warning echoing through my head on repeat. *You leave and don't ever come back. Hear me? Escape this Darkness, Veloren.*

And instead, I'm thinking about Theodore. We were the ones who were kidnapped, the ones who were dragged across Askund and shoved into some musty basement and forced to escape through the tunnels of Cova — and yet *I'm* worried about *him.*

It's always been like this. When I was thirteen, I'd tripped and twisted my ankle on the way to Theodore's house. I'd sat down on the branch and cried, unable to put any weight on it, and thought about how I wasn't going to be able to make it for dinner. How I was imposing on Theodore and his family and how they would probably postpone their meal waiting for me.

I can't help it, though. Where did Icarus take him? And *why* did she take him? Right now, I wish I could see. Wish that I could scan the skies for him myself, even though I know Will and Eleanor are already looking, keeping a constant eye out.

"What should we do now?" Will says. The sound of his voice makes my body stiffen. It's *grating* on my nerves — I can't help it.

And I know it's horrible of me. I know Theodore doesn't like that I don't like him, and that's enough to make me want to try harder, but I *can't*. His very presence is a constant reminder of the secret that I'd kept under lock and key for *years* now being common knowledge. Plus, I feel like it's only a matter of time until he realizes that that isn't the only secret I have.

Just thinking about last night — Stars, was it really only last night? — makes me want to shrivel up until I stop existing. It was horrible. Sitting there, my skin blue, apparently, and waiting. Knowing it was coming.

Because what secrets did I have that Theodore didn't already know about? It was either tell him I love him or tell him I'm not going to let him Restore the Light — the answer was obvious.

And so I'd told him. I'd felt hot and cold all over, numb to the bone. I don't even remember saying the words, couldn't tell you how they sounded coming out of my mouth. I just remember the awful silence that had followed them, seconds that'd stretched into centuries, and then, finally, Theodore's voice.

No you're not.

Only seconds had passed before I was ensconced in the forest. Getting to my feet and escaping the suddenly suffocating atmosphere was a blur but plunging into the forest and following the same path Eleanor and I had traveled along earlier that day was not. The tension and panic had slowly drained out of me, until I'd just felt tired. And partially convinced that everything that had just happened wasn't real.

Of course Theodore had come after me — that's just the kind of person he is. I don't know why I was surprised. Back when I twisted my ankle, I was sure I'd sit there all night, until Theodore eventually came to find me in the morning. Instead, he'd come looking for me rather than eating his dinner, and instead of going back to get his parents for help, he'd insisted on helping me hop all the way to the hospital. I hadn't had the heart to tell him that it would be faster and less painful if he could just go get his parents to carry me.

At least it's over now, though. I mean, mostly. There's still the problem with people (*cough, Will*) thinking they can casually mention my feelings for Theodore, and the horrifying knowledge that creeps up on me occasionally that *Theodore knows.* He *knows* that I'm in love with him and remembering that fact makes my breath catch in my throat, my heart skip several beats.

But besides that, it's over. And I got to keep my second secret to myself, which I can definitely count as a win.

"Guys?" Will says, and I realize I've ignored him. I guess Eleanor did too. "What are we going to do?" he repeats.

"Where are we?" I say in lieu of an answer. I reach up to touch my hair — a nervous habit — but my hand bumps into the hat Eleanor put on my head. I don't know why I'm still wearing it, but I don't know what I would do with it if I took it off, so I just let my hand fall back to my side.

"Um, in the middle of a field?" Will says. "There's nothing around."

"Good," I say, and then I sit down. "We'll wait here."

"Is that really a good idea?" Will asks.

"Icarus is smart. She was able to find a lake," I say. "Hopefully she'll be able to find us, too." Eleanor, apparently in agreement with this being our best plan of action, throws herself to the ground beside me. I jump when something touches my thigh, and then I realize it's just Eleanor's head. She sighs as she moves around a bit, shifting until she's comfortable.

I don't know what to say, so I say nothing at all. I just lay back on the ground, my arms folded behind my head, which makes the hat slant down over my face. Will sits down somewhere beside us.

Night's falling.

I don't mention it, and neither do the others, but we all know it's coming. It's cooler out than it was earlier, so I assume the sun's beginning to set. Will Icarus be able to find us in the dark? Will she even listen to Theodore when she wasn't bothering to do so earlier?

Hours pass. We spend most of the time sitting in silence, though occasional conversation crops up. Eleanor realizes she has a bag of almonds in her jacket pocket and we descend on it like vultures. After that, we all lay back down. Eleanor's by my side again and I let her press in close; ever since the sun set it's grown cold. I lay there with my eyes open and struggle to stay awake — I'm uneasy and high-strung after the day we've had — but I'm exhausted, and Eleanor is so warm against my side…

It's not until I'm jerking awake that I realize I even fell asleep. It's the thud of something on the ground that does it, and I sit there for a second, my heart pounding, as I listen with all my might.

And then — the rustle of feathers. The sound of feet hitting the ground followed by a quiet, "*Shit.*" Footsteps running toward us, sounding disjointed, as if the owner has some sort of limp.

I've rolled out from under Eleanor and gotten to my feet before I've even processed that Theodore is here and running toward us on his injured leg. I sweep him into a hug the second he's in reach, pulling him close and tight and burying my face in his shoulder as he laughs, arms wound around my back.

Let go of him, I tell myself as I continue to stand there, holding onto him as tight as possible. *Let go of him. He knows you're in love with him. It's weird.*

I finally manage to peel myself away, but I don't go far. Just half a step away.

"Are you alright?" I ask him.

"Am *I* alright?" Theodore scoffs, his hands landing on my shoulders and shaking me. "You're the ones that got kidnapped!" And then, "Are you... wearing a hat?"

My hand flies up to the rim of the hat still perched on my head. "Oh," I say. "Yeah."

"You stole that guy's hat," Theodore states. He's trying to process this information.

"Eleanor did."

"Then why are you wearing it?"

My mouth opens, but I realize I don't have an answer. "I don't know," I say.

"It's 'cause it makes him look so spiffy!" Eleanor says suddenly, and I almost jump in surprise. I forgot she was here. "We're fine, by the way," she adds. "Got away with all our limbs intact."

"How did you get Icarus to listen to you?" Will pipes up, proving that he, too, was awoken by Theodore's arrival.

"Well, she didn't really want to, so I threatened to jump off."

"And that *worked?*" says Eleanor.

"Yeah, no, not at all," says Theodore. "So then I *did* jump off. She took me straight to you guys, after that."

"I hate you," I groan, because the thought of Theodore doing that makes me want to hold onto him and never let go, just so he can't get himself killed.

But, "That's not what you said yesterday," he jokes, and I freeze. "Oh, Stars," Theodore splutters. "I'm not — I didn't mean... I don't know why I said that, fuck. I'm sorry."

"It's fine," I say, even though I don't really know if it is and everything inside me feels strung so tight I think I might snap and fall apart any second. I can't tell if he's making fun of me. Or if I'm making him uncomfortable by having feelings for him. I can feel myself shrinking inward, my face wiped clean of emotion, my posture straight and orderly and hopefully expressing absolutely nothing. I wonder how different my life would be right now if I'd just stayed behind with Hector like Theodore wanted me to.

"Well!" Eleanor says too loudly, clearly trying to get rid of the tension. "We should probably just stay here for the rest of the night, right? And head to Ilma in the morning?"

Murmurs of agreement follow her suggestion and everyone starts arranging themselves on the ground again, this time with our sleeping bags. I pretend to busy myself, digging through my bag with some made up purpose, simply to avoid going and laying down beside the rest of them. I know there's a space left open next to Theodore — the place where I always sleep — but I'm avoiding it for all I'm worth, listening as everyone's breathing slowly evens out into the rhythm of sleep.

All except for one, anyway. But that's Theodore's fault for waiting up for me. I'm not going to make either one of us more uncomfortable than we have to be, anymore. So I stand up and walk over to Icarus. She stirs when I near her, but she doesn't make any noises that make me think she wants me to go away, so I sit down and lean against her. She's definitely Theodore's bird, there's no doubt about that, but maybe that's why I'm sleeping next to her. She's the next best thing. Plus, I think loving Theodore is something we have in common.

Speaking of Theodore, he doesn't say anything when I lay down next to his bird. I know he's looking though, if not by the shifting sounds of his sleeping bag then by the heat I swear I can feel from his gaze. I ignore it and close my eyes, telling myself it's better this way.

Icarus doesn't want to go to Ilma. It's the only answer left, seeing as she's well-fed and well-rested and can't possibly have anything else wrong with her. And yet still she doesn't want to fly us anywhere. She wouldn't even move with Theodore riding on her back today, meaning he now has to walk on the ground with the rest of us. It's not as bad as it could be since Theodore's leg is doing much better after Will's ministrations, but I'm sure it would be even more beneficial for him if he could keep off it and continue to rest.

"Why wouldn't she want to go to Ilma?" Theodore says after I share my theory. He's wearing the hat now. I woke up this morning to him plucking it off my head and plopping breakfast onto my chest.

"I don't know. Maybe she can sense something inherently bad about it," I say, and it's not really another theory so much as a jab at Will. By the sound of his scoff, I think he understands the true meaning.

"That can't be it," Theodore says, oblivious. "What if she's scared of the water?"

"But she played in the lake," Eleanor points out.

"Maybe it's a sign that we shouldn't go," I say. It's a weak attempt to turn this trip around and keep us from getting any closer to discovering the truth about the Darkness, but I wasn't really expecting it to work when I said it.

"I don't think so," Theodore says. "I really feel like we're supposed to go to Ilma. I think we'll find answers there."

"Well then maybe she's scared of you leaving her," I suggest. "Ilma *is* underwater. Plus, the last time she was away from you, you got hurt."

And Stars, do I wish that just *sometimes* I could be wrong. Because I'm not wrong, and in her excitement, obviously satisfied that I could figure out what she wanted and demonstrating just how creepily aware she is of human language, Icarus squawks and leaps forward, snatching me in her talon as she takes off into the air. I scream the whole time, demanding to be put down even though she's never let me fall to my death before. I still hate it though, and I fall to shaky knees when she finally sets me on the ground again.

Someone pulls me to my feet and I thank them absently, assuming it's Theodore, until I hear his voice over to my right.

"Aww, Icarus!" he's saying. "You don't want to leave me? Is that it?"

Icarus is chirping in excitement — a sound that really shouldn't come out of an elephant-sized bird — and I turn toward the person on my left. "Eleanor?" I question.

"Will," he corrects me. I nod and hold in whatever shitty comment wants to escape me.

"Icarus, we're gonna be fine," Theodore says seriously. "I swear, I won't let us get in any danger at all."

Icarus squawks indignantly. I wish I couldn't understand the sounds she makes so well.

"Would an Avis whistle make you feel any better?" Eleanor says.

"Woah, how long have you had that?" Theodore says. Presumably, Eleanor is now holding a whistle.

"All my life."

"They just *give* everyone in Volant Avis whistles?" Theodore says incredulously.

"Uhh… Yep!" says Eleanor. "We all carry 'em around in our pockets." And then she blows the whistle. I know because the sound is so piercing it feels like it's stabbing into my very brain, and I collapse back to my knees with my hands over my ears as I groan, my head throbbing. Finally, it stops.

"Let's never blow that again," I say weakly.

"It didn't even make any sound," Theodore protests.

"It did, it's just a higher pitch," Eleanor corrects him. "I guess Covans can hear more pitches than us."

"Ugh," I groan, pitching to the side and laying down completely. Icarus comes over and nuzzles me sympathetically, and I wonder if that sound hurt her as much as it hurt me. It must not have, though, because equipped with the knowledge that we have the whistle — something that she'll apparently be able to hear as long as we're within a few miles of her — she complies with taking us to Ilma.

I'm the least happy with this outcome out of everyone, although I suppose that's because I don't want to Restore the Light and hate flying. Still, we pile onto her back, and there's this weird moment where I try to sit in the back row before Theodore pulls me up front beside him. I concede and grab onto the harness — Eleanor actually did a bang-up job with it, apparently — and then Icarus takes off. I have to admit that it's a little bit less scary than when we only have her to hold onto.

Even still, I close my eyes and try to ignore where we are. Try to ignore that the rushing wind around us means I can't hear the things I usually can, like someone breathing or clothes shifting or a hushed conversation. I ignore the crisp cold of the wind and the continuous movement of Icarus' body and the looming terror of the knowledge that Theodore might really learn how to Restore the Light. And when his hand bumps against mine on the harness, I ignore that too.

CHAPTER 11

THEO

Ilma is beautiful.

    Kind of terrifying too, with all the water everywhere, but it's impossible to deny the beauty of it all — even when I'm dripping wet and standing in the middle of the domed path, still finding it hard to believe that I just *breathed water* thanks to Will's funny little pills.

    Icarus is tucked away in the belly of a field a mile away from here and Eleanor's Avis whistle presses against my thigh where it rests in my pocket. It's almost hard to believe we're finally here.

"Where to now?" Ren says, standing stiffly beside me with his arms crossed. He really hadn't liked swimming down here, completely disoriented in the water, so I'd grabbed his hand and pulled him along with the rest of us. He looks so grumpy that I want to put the hat back on him, just to see what expression he would make, but I restrain myself. It's sopping and heavy on my head right now anyway, so I don't think he'd appreciate it.

"Our best bet is the trading market," Will says, shoving his hair out of his eyes. Wet like this, his tank top clings to his torso like a second skin and I can see the bandages on his chest underneath. I wonder if he's been changing them.

We follow as Will leads us through Ilma. The city is bustling with people, but not in the loud way that Udula was. Here, the majority of the Ilmans are outside the glass bubble we're walking in, swimming from place to place in clothes instead of swimwear. I even see a guy with a briefcase go by.

Instead of stepping into one of the exit ports — areas of encased glass where people both leave and arrive, the water in there filling and draining appropriately — we stick to the streets, the entire world around us drowning in soft, flickering blue light from the water. I see as many fish swim by as humans, all intermingling like they belong there, and I guess they do. I can't help examining all the buildings we pass, their entrances embedded in the oxygen-filled streets while the rest of their exteriors extend into the water.

"We can buy you some healing tablets while we're here," Will says, gesturing to my leg. "You'll be healed in minutes, considering how much better your leg is already."

"You guys sure do have a lot of tablets," Eleanor comments.

"The healing technology was the hardest to create," Will explains. "After that, our scientists had an easy time creating tablets that can do things other than heal, like make you tell the truth."

When we arrive at the market, it's more like what you would expect a city to look like. Here, the majority of the people are on this side of the glass. All around, people are talking and bartering, items in bags being handed over counters and pouches of coins being dumped on them. Additionally, unlike most markets, there's several cases of people leaning close to others, a hand held up protectively as they whisper into someone else's ear. They're trading in secrets.

Will doesn't give us much time to ogle, obviously all too familiar with this unfamiliar sight, because he just plows through the crowds, heading directly for a vendor with a sign above them that reads *Remy's Remedies.*

"Morning, Remy," says Will, and Remy looks away from the bag of coins he was peering into to look up at him.

"Pipsqueak!" he greets, and I realize the nickname fits. Ilmans seem like a different breed, almost all of them towering over us, but especially over Will, who's even shorter in stature.

"What are you doing here? Word around town is that you up and left."

Will shrugs, neither confirming nor denying this claim, which I realize is deliberate. Any information he has is an advantage. I notice Remy observing the rest of us curiously, but he doesn't say anything.

"I'm just here to buy a healing tablet," Will tells him.

"Yeah? That'll be nine silvers unless you've got anything interesting for me."

Will's face splits into a grin. He looks like a different person, totally in his element, which I suppose makes sense. He did grow up here, after all.

"Have you heard about the Zolands' divorce?" he says.

Remy scoffs. "Hasn't everybody?"

"Well did you know that…" Will leans in close, a hand over his mouth, and Remy leans down, his eyes widening as Will relays the information.

"Is that so?!"

"Yes," says Will. "*And*—" he leans in again, and I find myself frowning, inexplicably curious about these people I don't even know. Ilmans are a bunch of gossips, apparently.

Remy laughs, clapping his hands together suddenly as he leans back. "That was good, Pipsqueak," he says, and he grabs a paper bag, rummaging through his wares before putting a green pill in there. "You know what? Have a couple of these too. You've earned it." Remy throws a few more pills of a different color in the bag and Will takes it from him, grinning.

He digs out the green pill when we're barely three steps from the stand, holding it out for me to take.

"How come you only got one?" I say, pinching it carefully between my fingers.

"Huh?" Will says, his eyebrows drawn inward in confusion.

"What about you?" I say, gesturing to his chest. Will clears his throat.

"I'm fine," he assures me. "Just take the pill."

"Why don't you want to heal?" Ren suddenly asks, and I nearly jump. Both he and Eleanor had been so silent — likely observing that whole interaction as intently as I had — that I'd nearly forgotten they were here.

"Because I'm *fine*," Will says, shutting down the conversation.

There's a pause.

And then Eleanor's curiosity bubbles up. "How did that guy know you weren't lying?" she asks. "I mean, he just believed you."

"Well, yeah," says Will. "The oxygen in the market is infused with a vaporized form of the truth tablet. A kind that doesn't make your turn blue, anyway."

I gape. We can't even *lie* here?! Not that I was really planning on it, but...

"Just take the pill, Theo," says Will.

Eleanor hands me her flask of water and I swallow the green pill. It feels cold in my throat and then in my stomach, and for a second, I feel lightheaded. Then, in between one step and the next, the pain in my leg that I'd been only dully aware of disappears.

"Woah!" I say, stumbling because of the sudden change. I can't see my leg through my pants, thanks to Will stitching together the holes left behind from that creature's claws, but I'm still gaping down at it. "It doesn't hurt anymore!"

"The stitches will have fallen out," Will says proudly. "Though you'll still have a pretty brutal scar, unfortunately." I'm grinning in excitement, only now realizing just how much my leg had been bothering me.

"I don't mind," I claim. I don't think anything could deter my current excitement. "Hector's gonna be so impressed."

Eleanor punches me in the shoulder — a way she shows affection, funnily enough — but my smile finally begins to slip away as I realize where we are. We've walked further into the market, and no one here seems to be selling anything physical anymore. It's all whispers. Some vendors hang back in the shadows, others even going so far as to hide their faces.

Ren's head is whipping back and forth, and I realize there's a possibility he can hear some of these conversations. He looks unsettled, so I think I'm right.

"What are we doing back here?" Eleanor murmurs, as aware as I am that we've entered some sort of separate section of the market. Its underbelly.

"This is where the serious secret trading occurs," Will tells us. "Hopefully someone down here will be able to tell us about the Darkness."

And boy, do we talk to a lot of people. Most vendors end up sending us to someone else, someone who they say will be more likely to know about the Darkness. Except no one seems to know more than we do, and these vendors aren't interested in gossip like Remy was. Will is getting more and more frustrated with the more people we talk to, especially whenever one of them suggests we visit Alaric Endring.

"Why can't we just talk to this Endring guy?" Ren says after the sixth person directs us to him. "Is he here?"

"No," Will says gruffly. "He'll be at his house."

"What's so bad about him?" Eleanor says. "Why don't you want to see him?"

"I just don't," Will grunts. He's become impatient and annoyed, but he takes a deep breath and continues. "He's the High Secret Keeper of Ilma. If you want to go see him, I'll wait around until you're done."

Will looks at us, waiting.

"Well…" I venture slowly. "It seems like no one else has any answers…"

"Right," Will says, and he lets out a sigh, his shoulders slumping. "Okay. Yeah, I'll take you guys there."

It's a relief to get out of the dark and creepy part of the market, and then we leave the area entirely. Will coaches us as we walk, telling us not to give away any information we don't need to and to never give away our best secret first, et cetera, et cetera. He stops suddenly, gesturing to a house at the end of the street. "We're here."

I was expecting something similar to the dark section of the market, gloomy and creepy in general, but this just looks like a regular house along a regular street. Granted, it's a little bigger than I'm used to.

"He's not gonna, like, hurt us or anything, is he?" I ask, suddenly nervous.

"Not at all," Will says. "Everyone knows he's a good guy." Except this he says with a different tone, and his eyes seem far away. I don't know what to make of it, and I don't get the time, because Eleanor's speaking next.

"We'll meet you back here when we're done," she promises, and with a nod from Will, the three of us turn and head toward the house, ready to divulge its owner's secrets.

We crowd together on the front stoop despite the abundance of room up it provides, having drawn closer to each other instinctively. The door is bright red, a silver knocker hanging from the middle of it. It's far taller than it needs to be, making the house look all the grander.

It's Eleanor who does it. She leans past me and grabs the knocker, rapping it against the door before leaning back again and crossing her arms. We all stand there, still, silent.

And then the door swings open.

Behind it is a man. The door is too tall for him, too, but less so. He squints down at us — not because he's *that* tall, but out of confusion. He obviously wasn't expecting anybody.

"Can I help you?" he asks.

"Yes," I say immediately, taking a step forward (as the unofficial but clear leader of the group). "We're here to see Alaric Endring?"

"That'd be me," says Endring, leaning against the doorframe. He crosses his arms, now looking at us suspiciously.

"We want information," I say. Endring's squint turns into a glare.

"I told those guys down at the market that I'm not selling anymore. Not after what happened last time." Endring steps backward and reaches for the door, swinging it shut. Before I even know what I'm doing, I've stepped forward and shoved my foot in the crack.

"Please," I say. "I *need* this information. My brother's depending on me."

"That's your problem, not mine," he says, still holding the door firmly (almost) shut.

"Isn't there anyone you would do absolutely anything for?" I try, desperate. "A sibling or a — a kid?"

Endring stands there, looking at me but still not *at* me. As if he's seeing something else. And then, slowly, he opens the door and steps to the side of it. "We'll make this quick."

The inside of Endring's home is nice. Very different from Silva, but nice. Mostly, it's different because it's not made out of a tree. The floors are wood, sure, but they're polished smooth and completely flat, not a ridge to be seen. Inside, there's furniture of all kinds, but they're made from a million different materials. He has large shelves brimming with books and table lamps on every surface. Also decorating nearly every surface are photo frames.

Pictured are any combination of him, some older woman, and a girl, though the woman and girl aren't in any pictures together once the girl's older than an infant. The daughter looks oddly familiar, probably because she bears a resemblance to Ilma's High Secret Keeper.

"Can I get you anything to drink?" Endring offers politely, and I open my mouth to accept when Ren cuts in.

"No thank you," he says. I roll my eyes because Ren's always been overly suspicious like that, but I don't make a big deal out of it. Just smile and nod politely.

"Well, you all know my name," Endring says, and he sits down on a big leather armchair in his living room. Ren, Eleanor, and I pile onto the couch opposite him.

"Right," I say, and remembering how Eleanor made us use fake names the last time we introduced ourselves, I say, "I'm Will."

I'll admit it. I'm not the *best* at coming up with names.

Following my lead, however, Eleanor introduces herself as Catara, and Ren sits there for a second before saying, "I'm Red."

It takes everything in me not to bury my face in my knees, laughing.

"Right," says Endring, letting his gaze linger on Ren, like, *poor soul, he must've had some crazy parents.* "You three know information around here comes at a price, correct?"

"Yes," I say firmly.

"Then what is it you'd like to know?"

"How did the Darkness originate?" I say, plunging forward. "And do you know anything about Restoring the Light?"

"My knowledge on this topic is spotty at best," Endring warns us. "But even then, it's going to cost you some real information."

"I can tell you where a few entrances to Cova are," Ren says, his arms crossed over his chest and his face impassive. Endring looks impressed.

"What else?" he says.

"I know quite a bit about Volant's royalty," Eleanor says. "And about the Lost Princess." I turn to look at her, surprised, but she doesn't meet my gaze.

Endring's eyes light up with excitement. "That'll definitely do it," he says, and then he stands. "I'm going to get us some water. We'll each drink a mild version of the truth serum so we can know our information isn't false. Everyone agreed?"

We nod. I really hope Eleanor wasn't lying about the information she knows.

Endring leaves and returns with a pitcher of water which he pours into four glasses. Just in case I come up with a secret, I guess.

"You first," he says, after we've all downed our water.

"And you promise to give us our information afterward?" Eleanor prompts him.

"Yes," he says.

With that, Ren lists off three entrances to Cova, failing to divulge exactly how he knows this information. Endring nods and asks questions to clarify exactly where they are, and then he turns to face Eleanor.

First, Eleanor tells him about some boring royalty stuff that she must've learned from her time in Volant. You'd think that hearing about how stuff works with royalty would be interesting, but it's totally not. Eleanor drones on and on and I realize I can't even tell what she's talking about, and Endring looks similarly bored. I wonder if he's retaining this information any better than I am.

"And the Lost Princess?" Endring finally prompts her, once she's fallen silent long enough to clue us in to the fact that she's done talking.

"She's only lost because her fiancé tried to kill her," Eleanor says, and refuses to say anything more. I realize I'm gaping, but that's because I've never heard this information before.

When Volant's princess went missing, everybody knew about it. The information spread between the kingdoms like a wildfire, igniting everyone's interest and confusion. What happened to her? Where did she go?

Half the people speculated that she ran away, tired of the pressures of the kingdom, leaving her beloved to be her father's successor in her place. The other half claimed she must've been kidnapped, her love for her people too strong for her to have willingly abandoned them.

No one had ever suggested that her disappearance could've been the doing of her betrothed.

I can tell Endring wants more information, but he doesn't ask. Instead, he partakes in his part of the deal.

"The true origin of the Darkness is buried in legend," he says, leaning forward and resting his elbows on his knees. "How much of that legend is true, I couldn't tell you. But this is what the legend says:

"The Darkness was once contained. It was a curse on the daughter of Night. When she had a child, the Darkness left her, but she soon realized she could see its presence in the eyes of her baby. Disgusted, she buried her son alive, hoping the Darkness in him would die too.

"No one knows for sure, but people say where the Darkness first cropped up was where she buried her son, and that the Darkness grew from him like a tree. The areas of Darkness that continue to grow today are his saplings, seeds spread from him by the wind."

I frown. "So… the Darkness is a baby?"

Endring shrugs. "It's just a legend," he says. "But most legends have some amount of truth in them. I've heard it said that the entirety of the Darkness is an actual, living being."

And that's just... unsettling. "So how do we Restore the Light?" I ask.

"That is also buried within the legend," Endring says. "It says that Night's sister, Day, also had a daughter. Instead of being cursed, however, she was blessed — she had the gift of Eternal Light. And when Day's daughter had a child, instead of burying him, she raised him. It is said that his light still runs through his descendants today, and only those that share his blood can Restore the Light."

"Well who's descended from him?" I demand, eager. "Which nation?" I feel like we're finally getting somewhere, closer to the answer.

Endring laughs. "It won't be an entire nation, Will," he says, and I abruptly remember the alias I gave him. "Only a select few within it."

"Which one?" Eleanor presses him. "And what do they have to do to Restore the Light?"

"That, I don't know," Endring says. "I've heard nothing about how it must be done, but I know that only the Light's descendants can do it. Unfortunately for you three, it is said that descendants of the Light reside in Cova alone." I try not to let a grin spread across my face, because that *should* be something unfortunate. Most people have never even met a Covan. "Those with the Light's blood in their veins are said to be dominated by their emotions. Still, I can confirm none of this for certain. That's all I have."

"Thank you," Eleanor says, because I'm too lost in my thoughts to say it myself. *What if Ren's one of the descendants of the Light?*

We all stand up, Endring ushering us out of his house, and we walk back down the hall toward the entryway, past all those picture frames again. I don't know what makes me say it. Maybe I feel like I need some sort of closure. Maybe that's why I open my big mouth.

"Your daughter," I say, pointing to one of the picture frames. "Is she why you let us come in?"

Endring's face hardens. "My daughter is dead," he says, before opening the door for us. We all pile out onto the porch, shocked. "But yes," he says, his voice softer, right before he closes the door in our faces.

CHAPTER 12

WILL

Being back here is weird. Seeing people I've seen before, living the way I've always lived — it's creeping me out.

I know it shouldn't. I mean, I've lived here my whole life and I've only been on my own for a week, but in that time I managed to convince myself that this was really it. That I'd never be able to come back. Now, I'm starting to wonder if instead of running away from Ilma, I should've just run across town.

Except I'm tired of secrets. I'm tired of keeping them and I'm tired of watching them ruin my life.

I accidentally came out to one person, and then steadily more and more people found out, until even the last person I was ready to tell knew. The only good that's come of it is getting to finally feel like myself, no more lying and no more pretending.

And... I guess the people I've met since then aren't so bad either.

Speaking of, where are they? I crane my neck down the street, certainly not for the first time, but the front door of my old house remains firmly shut.

With nothing better to do, I pull that paper bag Remy gave me out and open it up. There are four calming tablets in there, which definitely cost more than the gossip I gave him, but he's always had a soft spot for me. I smile looking at them, and then I close up the bag again, tucking it away safely.

Remy knows that I have a tendency to let myself get too stressed out. I've definitely spent entire nights lying awake before, letting my mind run and run until suddenly it's morning and still none of my problems are fixed. Often times he's managed to slip me a few extra tablets I don't really need, just because he likes me like that. I was afraid things would be different today. I definitely didn't expect him to give me anything extra. I was afraid that I'd get up there and he'd ignore me or turn me away. Hell, I was even afraid he might not recognize me, that I'd have to stutter my way through some sort of explanation.

Instead, he'd known exactly who I was, and nothing had changed. Come to think of it, I'm not surprised by his lack of surprise, either. Information spreads quickly in Ilma, so the second my secret was out, it was really only a matter of time until everyone knew.

"—just had to go and say that, didn't you?"

"How was I supposed to know?!"

I stand up when I hear their voices, finally seeing them coming up the street toward me. Theo and Eleanor are arguing, Theo gesticulating wildly as they do, but Ren's completely silent beside them. He looks lost in thought.

"How'd it go?" I interrupt, making both Eleanor and Theo jump in surprise. Apparently they hadn't noticed me approaching.

"Good!" Theo says, immediately brightening. "At least, I think so... I'm still kind of confused, actually."

"We know how the Darkness began, but we only really have an idea of how to Restore the Light," Eleanor explains.

"I think it's a load of crap," Ren interjects. "It's all based on legends and myths."

"Those don't come from nothing," I point out. "They're usually just true stories that've been distorted over time."

Ren grits his teeth and turns his head. I want to think he doesn't like the words I'm saying, but that doesn't make any sense. Besides, it's obvious I'm the one he doesn't like. I don't know what it is I've done, or how I haven't managed to convince him to trust me yet, but I'm on the verge of giving up. Maybe you don't need to be on good terms with everybody in a group to still be in that group.

"I think we should head toward the nearest area of Darkness," Theo proclaims.

Ren makes a sound like he's choking on his spit. "Are you kidding?" he says. "You nearly died the last time we were in there—" Wait, they've been *in* the Darkness? "—and we don't even have any serious leads!"

"Sure we do!" Theo says. "We know that only a descendant of the Light can stop the Darkness."

"And where are we gonna find one of those?"

Theo puffs his cheeks. Blows the air out of his mouth. "Well..." he draws out the word, letting it sing through his lips as his eyes wander toward the sky. "I kind of think that... you might be one."

I'm not entirely sure what this descendant of the Light business is, but based off Eleanor and Ren's reactions, I can assume this is a pretty wild claim for Theo to make.

"Theodore, you have no way of knowing that," Ren says.

"Yeah, I'm with Ren on this one," Eleanor says gently.

"Come on, it makes sense!" Theo says. "I mean, the descendants are in Cova!"

"And I'm just *one*—" Ren lowers his voice, and even though he can't see, his eyes shift around, as if he's searching for onlookers. "—*Covan*," he hisses. "Besides, Endring said he didn't even know if any of that was true."

"I think it is," Theo says with conviction. "*And* he said the descendants are dominated by their emotions. Ren, it makes sense! I mean — you're in love with me!"

Ren freezes. He says, quietly, "I'm not in love with you because of some ancient ancestor, Theodore." Then, "And can everyone stop bringing that up?" He looks furious, except I think he's just embarrassed.

"Sorry," Theo says, cowed. And then he lowers his voice too, as if he can make this conversation any more private when Eleanor and I are both standing right here. "Um. You don't have to be embarrassed, though."

Ren ignores him. "And even if I was a descendant — which I'm not — what would you have me do once we got to the Darkness?"

"I don't know," Theo says, and he waves his hands around a bit. I wonder if Ren knows how much Theo talks with his hands, considering how he never actually sees it. "I was hoping it would just come to you when we got there."

Ren scoffs. "Like how it 'came to me' last time?"

Theo groans, frustrated. Eleanor is worrying her lip beside him, and Ren lets his impassive expression slip. He's glaring at Theo, now. "What you're asking me to do is going to get us all killed," he decides. "And aren't we supposed to take Eleanor back to Volant now, anyway?"

That puts a pause to the conversation. I know Eleanor's from Volant because we all got to talking as we flew on Icarus, but I didn't know her time with us had an expiration date.

"Oh, yeah," Theo says softly. "Eleanor — I'm so sorry, I totally forgot. We can take you back first."

Eleanor looks just as surprised as Theo, though. "No, I — I forgot too," she admits, looking embarrassed. "I think for the first time since I've been in Askund, I forgot. You guys are the first real friends I've ever had." And she looks between all of us as she says that — even me.

Theo's looking at her with the biggest, happiest eyes, and he cries out, "*Aw*, Eleanor!" Then he pulls her into a hug, his face buried in her wild, curly hair, and she wraps her arms around him too, grinning. And then she reaches out and yanks me and Ren into the hug too, and I'm laughing. I think even Ren isn't cringing at the fact that he happens to be touching me.

"I'm glad I met you," Theo says, and then I propose staying in Ilma for lunch — my favorite noodle place ("How about sandwiches?" says Theo) — so we go to my favorite sandwich place. Ren no longer seems so stressed out, now that conversation of shoving him into the Darkness to somehow Restore the Light has ceased.

I recognize our server in Supremo Sandwiches, but I don't think she recognizes me — not like this — so I don't say anything. Eleanor asks me what I like to get here, so I start listing off all my favorites, and then I realize Ren's listening too. I list off a couple more options, ones that I don't get that often, just in case. When our server comes back for our orders, Ren orders one of the things I suggested, and I feel like I did a good thing.

"I'm sorry," our server — I think her name might be Isabel, but she's not wearing a name tag — says to me. "I just… do I know you?"

For some reason, I don't know what to do. It's like my brain just stops working. "Um," I say.

"Sorry," she says again, and laughs. "I just feel like I recognize your face."

"You might," I say, and I can't be entirely sure why I say it. Admitting to her who I am means having to admit to my friends who I am, too.

Isabel gasps. "Wait," she says suddenly, excited. "You're—"

"Will," I interrupt her, before she can suggest anything else. And I tack a smile on too, hoping she'll take the hint.

"Of course," she says, smiling. "Will Endring! I thought you left?"

"I did," I say. "I'm just… visiting."

"Well I'm glad things seem to be working out for you," she says. It seems like she really means it. "Let me go put these orders in!" she adds, and with that, she spins on her heel and walks away, ponytail bouncing from side to side behind her. I turn back to my friends only to find them gaping at me. Theo's eyes are bugging out of his head.

"What?" I say.

"Will *Endring*?" he says. "Like, as in Alaric's son, Will Endring?"

I smile. "The one and only."

"But that doesn't make sense," Ren points out, frowning. I feel my smile grow stiff. My shoulders taut. Eleanor looks like she's caught on, and Theo's gears are definitely turning, but Ren just seems confused. "Endring never mentioned having a son, and he said his daughter was dead."

Just like that, my entire good mood shatters. My heart sinks through my body and the booth beneath me, burying itself into the earth and waiting for the rest of me to join it. He really said that?

I swallow. I want to say something, anything, but I can't seem to get my mouth to work. My tongue feels heavy, like concrete, and suddenly I'm holding tears at bay.

I know I'm not messed up. I'm not the only person like me out there — a boy who wasn't born as such — but I've never *met* anyone else like me, and I never knew how to bring it up. I didn't even realize that's what it was, for a long time. Growing up, I just felt *uncomfortable*. Like my skin was stretched thin, my body made wrong.

I'd thought I wasn't happy with my weight. And then I'd thought I wasn't happy with my hair. I'd tried to change things — tried to work out and eat healthy and cut off all my hair, just to see if I'd like myself better that way. Everyone else seemed so happy with themselves and I never knew how to bring it up, how to broach the subject of my own unhappiness.

So I'd kept it a secret. Only one of the thousands of secrets in Ilma. And like any good Ilman would, I set out to get more information. I'd eavesdropped on Dad's conversations, traded his secrets like they were my own, anything to get my hands on some knowledge that might clear things up for me.

And at thirteen, I did. I'd learned about people just like me, and it was like a blast of fire was shot right through my brain, lighting up everything about me that'd ever seemed off and connecting them like a puzzle. Everything had clicked, and I'd felt better than I had in all my life.

There was still the problem that I hadn't exactly *looked* how I'd wanted, but fixing that seemed feasible in the grand scheme of things when I at least understood. Since then, my plan had always been to move out as soon as I was old enough. I'd go to a distant town in Ilma where nobody knew me, and there everything would be different. *I* would be different. I'd planned on working up the courage to tell my dad, to be myself.

I used to have a whole lot of plans.

That changed when I made the mistake of telling someone at school. It's so stupid, looking back on it. All of this happening because of some dumb girl I know I'll never talk to again. But at the time, I'd had a huge crush on her, and I wasn't as discreet about it as I'd hoped to be. She'd tried to let me down gently.

"I'm sorry," she'd said. "And I'm flattered, really, but I'm just not into girls."

"But I'm not a girl!" I'd blurted. I remember her looking at me like I was insane. "No, I mean — I'm trans. I'm a guy."

That hadn't cleared things up for her at all. And she still hadn't liked me back, go figure.

It was stupid of me. You don't just go blurting your biggest secret like that to people in Ilma. Especially not when your dad is the High Secret Keeper. I don't doubt someone out there got a buttload of information out of him with my secret.

And not even a month after that fateful day, my secret got back to Dad. I'd just gotten home from school, exhausted and stressed out because everything was stressful now, and he'd been waiting for me in the foyer.

"Dad," I'd said, immediately spotting him. We never hung out in the foyer. "Why are you sitting there?"

For some reason, the bad grade I'd just gotten on an essay had weighed heavily in my backpack. Of all things, that was the first to come to mind.

"I had a busy day, today," he'd said, staring at me, his fingers laced together in his lap. "I learned some things about you, actually."

My blood had run cold. I'm sure I turned as white as a sheet, and I'd started stammering some kind of answer immediately.

"Is it true?" he'd said, interrupting me. He'd known it was true. We both had. Nothing that got said to him by his clients was false, not with the measures he was always sure to take.

So I'd panicked. I'd bolted up the stairs, slamming my bedroom door behind me, and my entire body had shaken as I'd heard his footsteps following me up the stairs. It'd felt like a dream, when you try to do anything except nothing goes right, your fingers the wrong length and your legs too heavy and you brain disorganized. I'd thrown a random assortment of clothing into my backpack, having dumped all my school supplies right there in the middle of my floor, and snatched the case of tablets off my desk.

Dad had reached the top of the stairs, and he'd started knocking on my door — I'd managed to lock it in my hysterical state — but I'd ignored him, not even realizing there were tears streaming down my face. All I'd known was that everything was different now that he knew, and that every inch of me was ingrained with a fine-tuned sense of panic. My entire body was itching with adrenaline, fight-or-flight, and I'd known I couldn't fight. Couldn't open that door and explain myself and look at my father's face. Couldn't tell him that I wasn't the daughter he wanted me to be, his perfect little girl so like my mother, everything good I'd ever done always reminding him of her, of my dead, late, never-coming-back *mother*.

I'd failed him. Just like Mom's health had failed her. And there I was, the final straw that broke my father's heart. The piece of the puzzle with all the wrong edges, one that would never fit flat and perfect into the puzzle, not if you wanted it to look right.

So I'd fled. Bag on my back, I'd thrown open my bedroom window and slid down the roof, jumping from its lowest edge and swearing that I'd never face my dad again, never have to witness his disappointment.

"Will?"

I suck in a breath and look up. I don't know how long I've been zoned out. Our food's in front of us, but nobody's touched any of it. I realize there are tears on my cheeks and I hastily wipe them away, feeling like an idiot.

I clear my throat. "Yeah?" I say.

"You know this doesn't change anything, right?" Eleanor says gently. "I mean, we all love you the way you are."

"Yeah," I say, nodding stiffly. "Yeah, I know." Except I didn't know. I've never known. And now my heart is beating faster. I wish we were doing that group hug thing again.

"Hey," Theo says, and by the tone of his voice I can tell he's caught on now, too. "If it makes you feel any better, your dad let us in because of you," he says. "He said he doesn't sell secrets anymore, but I told him about Hector, and asked if there was someone he'd do anything for, too." Theo smiles at me, and I return a watery one back at him.

I don't know what else to say, so I pick up my sandwich and take a bite. It's just as good as it always it.

Everyone else starts eating too, though none of us talk for a while. Surprisingly, it's Ren who breaks the silence.

"Hey, Will," he says, and when I look up, he's looking at me. Or — not really *looking* at me, per se, but he's facing me. If I didn't know he was blind, I'd think we were making eye contact.

"Yeah?"

Ren holds up his half-eaten sandwich and his mouth quirks up. "This is delicious," he says. It feels like a peace offering.

CHAPTER 13

VELOREN

Something isn't right.

The idea slips through my mind absently, between one sleep fuzzed thought and the next. My mind has been all over the place lately, brought to the brink of panic again and again with how quickly everything has been happening. With the new information about the Darkness' origin (and the not-so-new information about Night's baby being buried — it certainly explains why the Darkness was waiting for us Covans down there) and Theodore thinking I might be a descendant of the Light… it's too much.

So when we all settled down to sleep, having left Ilma and its horrible water and delicious sandwiches behind, I welcomed the ease of unconsciousness with open arms. Anything to get my mind away from my tumultuous thoughts for a little while.

Now, though… *Something isn't right.* The thought nudges at me again, and my eyes fly open, though that doesn't do anything for me other than kickstart my brain into wakefulness. Still, it worked. I'm awake now, aware, and I can feel this weight pressing down on my chest, making me breathe faster as I begin to panic, start to wonder *what the hell is on me*—

"Mmmgh," says Theodore, asleep, and all the stiffness and panic in my body fades away. I want to say that it comes back, that I'm shocked and confused by the fact that Theodore is for some reason cuddling me, but I'm not. Knowing that it's him pressed up against me, that it's his head on my chest and his fingers curled in my shirt… it just makes me feel good, my decision to distance myself from him be damned.

And I *did* decide to distance myself. It seemed like what I should do — give Theodore more space so he wouldn't have to feel crowded and overwhelmed by the fact that his best friend is in love with him. And yet now he's pressed up against my side and I can feel his each and every breath through my shirt.

I don't cuddle him back. I don't wrap my arm around his waist or press my face into his hair. I just lay there, still, knowing I'll pretend to be asleep if he happens to stir. It has to be this way, because otherwise I'll just seem weird. Creepy. Like I'm trying to force my feelings on him.

Even though it feels like he's the one forcing my feelings on *me.* I know that sounds dumb, but every time I think about him knowing how I feel, every time I remember him saying, *"Ren, it makes sense! I mean — you're in love with me!"* I feel so embarrassed that I swear my stomach starts trying to escape through my throat.

I'm still laying stock still when Eleanor wakes up. I'm planning on pretending to be asleep for her too, but somehow I forget my stupid eyes are open. The next thing I know she's stepping closer to me, and then she crouches down. "Morning, Ren," she whispers, quietly enough that it won't wake Theodore. She sounds *delighted*.

I don't answer her, because I'm afraid if I speak he'll feel it and jolt awake.

"I was gonna ask you to help me get some vegetables for breakfast, but I think I'll wake up Will instead," she continues. I nod minutely so she knows I'm listening. "You'll be fine alone?" she asks, and I nod again.

When Eleanor goes to wake up Will, I really do pretend to be asleep, not wanting him to question me about this unfortunate cuddling situation as well. The two of them head off together, and they're whispering to each other, but I don't try to listen in on them. I have a feeling I know what it's about.

It's a while longer before Theodore wakes up. He does it slowly, his fingers twitching against my chest before his breath escapes his lungs in one long exhale. Finally, he starts to become aware of himself, and he pushes himself up with the hand resting on my chest, as if that wouldn't awaken any actually sleeping person, the idiot. Seeming to realize what he's done, Theodore absently pats my chest before getting to his feet with a yawn. I'm debating pretending to wake up now that Theodore's up, but then Theodore pulls the sleeping bag up to my shoulders and his hand briefly brushes through my hair.

It takes everything in me not to stiffen. I'm holding back a blush through will alone. Stars, I'm ridiculous. This is nothing to get flustered about. Friends do this kind of thing for each other all the time.

I lay there for another ten minutes at least, too overwhelmed to even think about pretending to wake up, but then Icarus starts chirping at whatever Theodore's doing with her and I sit up without thinking about it.

"Morning Ren!" Theodore calls almost immediately. The sleeping bag slides down from my shoulders.

"Morning," I say, and I get to my feet and start walking toward him. "What are you doing?"

"I'm teaching Icarus to catch," Theodore says. "Or at least, I'm trying to. Most of my peanuts are just hitting her in the beak. I don't think she really gets what I want her to do."

I'm smiling a big, ridiculous smile. I can feel it. My insides go warm because Theodore's so cute and stupid and I *love* him. I never used to think about it this much.

"Hey," Theodore says suddenly, and it sounds different. Strange.

"What?" I say. Maybe he's about to blame me for the cuddling. Maybe he'll just straight up tell me that he's uncomfortable and needs time away from me.

"How come you never told me?" he says, wrenching me out of my quickly spiraling thoughts. "About... you know."

I sigh. I think I'm getting used to this feeling — the debilitating shock, the flash of panic, the resignation that comes with my love for Theodore being casually mentioned.

"Remember when I said I didn't want to talk about this?"

"Yes," says Theodore. "But... come on," he pleads. "What if I was in love with you?" My heart clenches, the blood in my body coming to a halt as everything hangs suspended. "Wouldn't you want to talk about it?"

I exhale. "No," I say, crossing my arms.

"Liar," Theodore says, and he steps closer, drumming his fingers on the skin exposed by my jacket sleeves, which are pushed up to my elbows. "You always cross your arms when you lie to me."

I huff, throwing my head back. At least we're alone, finally. I can't remember the last time I spoke to Theodore without one of our friends present. "It's embarrassing," I say to the sky. "Would you want to talk about it, if it were you?"

"I wouldn't be embarrassed," Theodore claims. "You can't control your feelings, and it's not like love is a bad one."

Just hearing the word 'love' out of his mouth makes me want to throw up.

"Please?" Theodore says, and he grabs my hand, tugging it so that my arms uncross. And this just isn't fair at all. His fingers are playing with mine, squeezing them. They're warm.

Evil.

"Fine," I whisper, but I cross my arms again, escaping Theodore's touch. "What do you want to know?"

"How long?" Theodore says immediately, like he's been thinking about it for a while. "Have you loved me, I mean?"

I hate him. Shift my weight from foot to foot. Shrug.

"You don't know?"

"Theodore," I try to say sternly, except it comes out sounding like a whine. I can *hear* him grinning.

"Just tell me!" he begs. "I'm your *best friend* — you're *supposed* to tell me this kind of stuff."

So I huff. And then I reach out and shove him. "A long time, okay?! Practically always."

Theodore was in the midst of shoving me back — I've already stumbled half a step away from him — but then he latches onto my arms and drags me back. He holds me there, still.

"Really?" he says.

"Are we done now?" I say in lieu of an actual answer.

"Maybe you just need to kiss me," says Theodore. And then the clouds fall out of the sky and the earth splits in two and Icarus turns into a cat. Or at least, that's what *should* happen. All of it is just a plausible as Theodore actually saying that to me.

Still, I squeak, "What?" even though I'm sure I hallucinated it.

"It could help!" Theodore says. "You know, like, get it out of your system. Maybe then you'll be able to move on."

But I don't want to move on, I think to myself. I want to say that Theodore's pulling my leg, that he's just making some kind of elaborate joke, but he wouldn't do that to me, which means he's completely serious.

I think that might be worse.

Because Theodore's weird like that. To him, things that are supposed to be big deals — *like first kisses* — aren't. But then he'll meet a war-bird from another nation and uproot all his beliefs in order to ride it.

I can't kiss him. It would just make things worse, right? I'd have this intimate knowledge of what kissing him feels like only to have to deal with the fact that I'm never going to get to experience it again.

But if I don't, I'll never know what it's like. What's worse? Knowing what a kiss from Theodore feels like — the pressure of his mouth against mine, the texture of his lips, their warmth — and never getting to feel that again, or never even knowing at all?

"Ren?" Theodore says, and I can't remember if he's said my name more than once.

"Are you being serious?" I blurt out.

"Of course I am," Theodore says. "You're my best friend. If you want to know what it's like, and it'll make you happy... I'll do it."

"Okay," I say weakly.

"Okay you want to?" Theodore prompts me. My head's spinning, my mind whirling desperately. Do I want to? Will I regret it? Will I regret *not* doing it?

I open my mouth. I think I've known my answer the whole time. Because I'm weak. And desperate. And my whole body feels high-strung and light and tight at the idea of Theodore's hands on my body, of his lips on mine.

"Yes," I say. My voice shakes.

I expect Theodore to step closer. I expect him to reach out for me, his hands careful and tentative against my skin. I expect for it to last a second, maybe two.

I expect *wrong*.

He grabs me and yanks me forward, making me stumble into him. One of his arms wraps around the small of my back, the other coming up to cup the side of my face, hot against my skin. Theodore's doing all of this like he's done it before, except he hasn't. Right?

I can't breathe.

"You still sure?" Theodore says, except he whispers it, and I can feel his breath against my lips. It's unfair of him to expect me to be able to respond right now.

"Just kiss me, Theodore," I say, after I've managed to remember how to speak. Theodore's thumb presses against my chin just a little bit harder and my whole body seizes up, goes completely still as I stand there, waiting. For a second, I wonder if his eyes are closed, and then I abruptly close mine, just in case.

I don't know if he was waiting for that or if it's just a coincidence, but in the next moment, our lips meet.

My breath punches out of me as Theodore's lips move against mine, soft and insistent. I realize that I've reached out for him, that my hands are clutching his elbows.

All of the sudden, I realize that this is *happening*. Like, *really happening*. Stars, what am I even doing right now?!

Theodore has taken full initiative. He draws me in, stealing the breath from my lungs and lighting my insides on fire. He doesn't even seem to realize he's doing it, not as he sucks my lip between his and not as he swipes his tongue against mine. I'm melting against him, clutching him as hard as I can because otherwise I think I'll just collapse to the ground entirely.

He pulls away from me for a second and I think that that's it, it's over, but then he comes back in, his lips slotted against mine a little bit differently, and I want him to stay like this forever. This is where he belongs, obviously. Can't he feel it too? The electricity flooding his veins, the heat creeping over his skin, the goosebumps all along his body despite the heat?

But then Theodore pulls away again, coming back for one more quick press, and then another. And then he's not kissing me at all anymore. He slowly steps away. My face is cold where his hand just was.

"Ren?" Theodore says.

"Yeah?" I say, but it comes out as a whisper. I feel dizzy. And like that didn't just happen. And like it should still be happening right now.

"You can let go of me now," Theodore says, amused. I suck in a breath through my nose, wrenching my hands away from him and pressing them against my sides. Then I take a step back.

"Sorry," I say hastily.

"Don't be," Theodore says. And then he pulls me into a hug and for some reason I'm more embarrassed about this than the fact that our lips were just touching. "Do you want me to find us something for breakfast?" he says after pulling away.

"Eleanor and Will are getting breakfast," I say, not thinking about how I would've had to be awake before him in order to know that. My brain's too scrambled to comprehend anything other than how to get words from my head to my mouth. "I need to go… do something," I tell him, and then I turn around abruptly. Theodore laughs once, sharply, like it was surprised out of him, but I ignore it. I stalk off, and I walk around Icarus for a sense of privacy.

She's laying on the ground, and she chirps when I circle in front of her face. Wind whooshes past me as she lifts her wing up, a few feathers brushing my face, so I walk right under it and plop down against her body. She's warm, and I tug my knees up to my chest, wrapping my arms around them. Her wing falls back down, then, blocking the warmth of the sun from my skin.

I just kissed Theodore, I think to myself. His mouth was on my mouth. *His tongue was on my tongue.*

Theodore offered to kiss me — some kind of monumental act as a best friend — and I agreed. I ignored every instinct I should've had and said yes.

Things should feel weird between us now, right? That's just what happens. You kiss your best friend and everything changes. It becomes awkward.

Except I don't feel awkward. I feel enlightened, which is stupid, but I can't help it. I feel like I want to kiss him again, and like I don't regret kissing him, and like I never will. I feel like this wasn't a huge mistake. Like I'm glad I took the chance when it came to me.

And like I need to convince Theodore to kiss me again.

That can happen, right? Maybe one kiss isn't enough. Maybe one more will help me 'get over him'. Maybe he'll kiss me again if I tell him that. Maybe I can convince him that kissing your best friend isn't so weird, and then we can just do it all the time.

"Ugh," I say, and I lean my head back. It collides with Icarus and my whole body moves every time she breathes. I'm being ridiculous. Theodore doesn't like me like that, so no more kisses will be forthcoming. End of story. "Hear that, Icarus?" I tell her, and I reach a hand up, burying it in the fur of her underbelly — no feathers anywhere to be found down here. "I'm not gonna kiss him again."

Icarus squawks, except it sounds like a laugh. I feel my cheeks heat up.

Oh, what does she know? She's just a stupid bird.

CHAPTER 14

THEO

I'm staring at Ren.

I wouldn't normally, because I think it's rude to just stare at him when he's totally unaware, but right now I can hardly help it. All I can think about is the feeling of our lips pressed together, and I think that's pretty weird of me. I shouldn't be dwelling on it like this.

For a first kiss, though, Ren was good. His first kiss, by the way. Not mine. My first kiss was a secret, and it was with Emily Haze behind the gymnasium. She told me my lips were chapped and that I was a bad kisser, but now I think she's the one that was bad. I remember her lips being weirdly cold, nothing like Ren's. And even though that was his first kiss, he totally did it right. Our mouths fit perfectly together, like we were meant to use them for that exact purpose. Maybe that's just what happens when you've been friends for as long as we have — even something as unfamiliar as kissing is easy.

I never told Ren about my first kiss. I'd had this feeling that he would be upset, for some reason, though I hadn't been able to put my finger on it at the time. Now, I wonder if some subconscious part of my mind had realized that Ren was in love with me, had known that telling him would only upset him. Or maybe I just hadn't wanted to tell him that I was a bad kisser, apparently. Who knows?

Anyway, now I can't stop thinking about him. About *it*, I mean. He's sitting against Icarus, his mouth moving as he talks to her, though I'm nowhere near close enough to hear what he's saying. And for the first time, I realize that I've never really seen him when he's on his own before — when he thinks nobody's watching.

He's different. I guess that makes sense, because everyone's different when they're by themselves. There's no need to put on a show or hide behind walls or even pay attention to anyone else. It's just you, and that means you can relax.

Ren *has* relaxed. His emotions are completely on display, for one thing, and his body has lost that line of tension that usually runs between his shoulders. He has his hair pushed away from his face, and as I watch, he brings his thumb to his mouth and starts biting on the edge of it. I had no idea Ren bit his nails.

He says something then that makes Icarus squawk and he reaches up and slaps her side playfully. She jumps to her feet and towers over him. The sight is terrifying, except I know Icarus, so I'm not scared, and Ren can't see it, so he's not scared either. Icarus flaps her wings and assaults Ren with a barrage of wind while he lays on his back and holds his hands up in front of his face, laughing and telling Icarus to stop.

I realize I'm grinning. Ren is too, not too far from me, and some traitorous voice in the back of my mind goes, *I want to kiss that smile.*

Uh oh.

My good mood jumps off a cliff and I'm left standing there, reeling at the thought that'd just slipped through my head and danced out of reach. Because *what?* Since when do I want to do that?

Since when do you offer to kiss your best friend? that same voice counters, and I cringe. That wasn't weird, was it? I mean, I was just being a good friend. I'd do it for anyone! Like if Eleanor suddenly fell in love with me, I'd just do the good deed and plant one on her, you know?

"Oh Stars," I whisper to myself, because it feels like there's an army of caterpillars in my stomach just waiting to turn into butterflies. It doesn't matter if I want to kiss Ren again, because I can't. That'd just be toying with his feelings, and I can't do that to him. I love him way too much to risk hurting him.

So I force myself to get it together, turning away from the adorable sight and squatting near our supplies. Our sleeping bags are still in a pile together, waiting to be put away, so I start rolling them up. I don't think about how I woke up on top of Ren, or how I could hardly bring myself to actually get up — not when Ren felt that warm, that comfortable.

It's not much longer before Will and Eleanor return. Eleanor's holding an array of plants, the majority of them piled on top of the cowboy hat, held like a bowl, and Will's just straight up holding a couple of fish. They must've found a river nearby. The two of them are talking and laughing and all my problems are momentarily put on hold as I feel a smile creep across my face. I like it when everyone gets along.

"Theo!" Eleanor says once she sees me. "You're awake! We got breakfast!"

I put together a fire while Will prepares the fish, and Eleanor has no idea what she's doing with the plants so she enlists the help of Ren. We're all starving by the time it's ready and we dig in with barely a word to each other. Icarus keeps pestering me for our fish, but she seems as satisfied with eating the bones as the actual meat, so I keep giving her our leftovers instead.

"Ugh," Will announces, plopping backwards on the ground and throwing an arm over his eyes. His other hand pats his stomach, currently full of probably more fish than he should've eaten. He tugs his shirt up above his stomach and I can see the bandages on his chest peeking out from under it.

He's not actually injured, I know now. Not because I was rude enough to ask, but because I put two and two together. He never actually seemed like he was in any pain, and in the market he'd said that he didn't need a healing tablet, so it must be true.

"Hey," Eleanor says suddenly, picking a piece of a stringy vegetable out of her teeth. "We never decided what we're going to do."

"We're taking you back to Volant, aren't we?" Ren says quickly.

"Well, the thing is," Eleanor says, and I realize she's staring at me, looking anxious. "I kind of don't want to go back yet."

"*What?*" Ren says.

Eleanor hastens to explain. "I like you guys!" she says. "Plus, my life back home's totally boring. And I've been gone this long, right? It can wait a little longer."

"Can it?" Ren says, sounding desperate now. I frown at him, because his desperation sounds kind of rude from my point of view, but of course this does nothing to deter him, seeing as he doesn't realize it's happening.

"Yes," Eleanor says excitedly, Ren's tone not affecting her in the slightest.

"Great!" Will says, looking genuinely enthusiastic. "It would've been sad to say goodbye so soon."

"Right?!"

"And this means we can go to the Darkness!" I interject. Silence immediately falls.

"Yeah, I'm still not doing that," Ren scoffs. He's leaning back on his hands, eyelids lowered enough that it almost seems like his eyes are closed. He gets like this, sometimes. Stubborn. Except I know that I'm more stubborn, because I almost always get what I want with Ren.

Wait... *am* I more stubborn? Or is it just because he's in love with me that I usually get my way?

Stars, everything is so confusing nowadays.

"Come on, Ren," I say, and I turn sideways so that I'm facing him completely. He's ignoring me, or at least pretending to. "This is our only lead so far!"

"Yeah, and it's leading us straight to our deaths," Ren says. "Eleanor? Will? Back me up here."

I turn to them, ready to feel betrayed.

"It does sound dangerous," Eleanor hazards. There is it. The betrayal. "But it *is* our only lead."

"Maybe we could just get close to it," Will suggests. "And we could try just sticking a hand in or something."

"Or we could try going in at night!" Eleanor says suddenly. "Remember last time? We didn't even know we were in it until morning!"

"See, Ren?" I say. "We could study it at night — there weren't any of the creatures there, then."

"Creatures?" Will pipes up.

"Yeah, they have massive claws and make clicking sounds," I say flippantly. "Ren? What do you say?"

Ren's hugging his knees to his chest. "I don't know why you even think I'm a descendant."

"*Because*," I say, scooting closer on my knees, and then I grab him by the shoulders. "It would *click*. You're on a mission to Restore the Light with me — it makes *sense* that you would be a descendant! Don't you believe in fate?"

Something funny passes over Ren's face, and then he shakes his head. "No, Theodore," he says. "I don't."

And we don't have the time to pick *that* depressing statement apart. "Well I do," I say fiercely. "Our destinies are intertwined, Ren, and there's nothing you can do to change that."

"Fine," Ren finally says, his voice quiet. His eyes are looking straight at mine, even if he doesn't know it.

It's probably my fault for letting myself think that this part of our mission would go smoothly. I mean, when has anything ever gone smoothly for us? Something insane happens around every corner — it figures that even when we're headed to the Darkness to do something crazy completely of our own volition the universe *still* decides to fuck us over.

We're in the first town in Askund to have a name. We came across it by accident, the town tucked away in a little dip between rolling hills, and we ended up landing after we were spotted. Below, there'd been so many people waving so urgently that we'd assumed they were in some kind of danger. Instead, they were just really excited to see an Avis. So excited, in fact, that they insisted on pampering us.

Everyone here calls the town 'Sudbina', something that we'd been informed of as we were ushered through the streets. Sudbina's residents are not only weirdly interested in Icarus, but Eleanor too, a few of them having reached out and touched her hair or her clothes when near enough. It was all kind of flattering at first — if extremely creepy — but now it's becoming alarming. See, these people won't let us *leave*.

First, they sat us down for lunch, and when we tried to wrap things up, they offered to bathe Icarus, refusing to take no for an answer. Yet to see her since then, I thought I'd go check up on her and make sure she was doing okay. Eleanor, Ren, and Will hung behind, still not quite sure if we were supposed to pay for our lunch or not ("I know a great way to get a free meal out of people, if they try to make us pay," Eleanor had said alarmingly), and I'd made my way out onto the street on my own. Except no matter who I asked — and I swear the majority of these people had been cheering along the streets as we'd been ushered toward the fancy restaurant — no one could tell me where Icarus was. Or… they *wouldn't* tell me where she was.

I spent hours looking for her, eventually giving up on asking any of the unhelpful strangers in favor of trying to locate her on my own. Except she was nowhere to be found, and I hadn't been able to shake the uncomfortable feeling of being watched, even along completely empty streets. I swear I'd seen a curtain or two twitch as I'd walked by, my skin itching with unease.

Finally, I'd ended up going back to the restaurant, coming to the realization that I'd never find Icarus on my own.

Walking through the doors now, I can see my friends still seated at the table, looking increasingly uncomfortable at the still growing amount of food before them. Ignoring them, I turn toward the host stand, where a woman I recognize from earlier is standing. I can tell I've met her before, because I remember feeling distinctly unsettled at the fact that she didn't blink once.

"Hi," I say, coming to a stop in front of her. She's grinning, too many of her teeth showing, and I try to ignore my unease.

"Hello, Theo!" she says. "What can I do for you? Still hungry?"

"No, I'm good, thanks," I say slowly. "Actually, I was wondering if we could get the check? We really need to be heading out soon."

She laughs. "Nonsense!" she says. "This meal is free!" Then she reaches out and pats me on the shoulder. "But we couldn't possibly let you and your friends travel on such weary feet. Please, rest in Sudbina for the night. You will be well taken care of."

A million alarm bells go off in my head. I smile weakly. "Your generosity is appreciated," I say, "but really, we need to get going…"

The woman cocks her head. It looks alarmingly inhuman. "You would regret not staying the night with us, Theodore," she says, and that's it for me. I know my name's pretty obviously short for Theodore, but only Ren calls me that, and I can only stand up against creepy people who I'm pretty sure are threatening me for so long.

So I say, "You're right!" and I try not to laugh nervously when her smile stretches even thinner. I turn around and join my friends at our table, shoulders hiked to my ears and feeling distinctly uncomfortable. Suddenly, I realize there are people staring at us no matter where I look.

"Did you find Icarus?" Ren asks. He tries to put his elbow on the table and immediately bumps into a heaping plate of what looks like something that shouldn't be fried, so he sits back again.

"No," I huff. "Also, we can't leave."

"What do you mean, we can't leave?" Will says. His hands come up to clutch anxiously at the brim of the hat on his head. I swear Eleanor was wearing it when I left.

"I mean that very creepy woman just said we can't leave, and so we're staying the night," I say, jerking my head toward said creepy woman.

"*She's looking at us,*" Eleanor hisses.

"She *doesn't blink*," I inform everyone importantly.

We don't get any longer to discuss, because the next thing we know several of the people that have been staring at us come over, and they offer to escort us to our hotel. Unable to run away with them passively surrounding us, we agree, letting them lead us out of the restaurant and further down the street to an opulent hotel. It's strange. Most towns in Askund are totally run down, and yet this place has it all together.

The creepy restaurant people leave us with some creepy hotel people, and then we're taken to our rooms. Our guides split off, heading in two different directions at a fork in the hallway, and all of us exchange panicked glances before splitting up appropriately. Me and Ren turn left, and Eleanor and Will go right.

"Here you are," says the man before us. His name tag says Chancey.

"Thanks," I say with none of my usual polite inflection, and Ren and I step into the room after he opens the door for us. The second he's gone, the door closed after him, I turn to Ren. "We're gonna die here," I inform him.

"No, we're not," says Ren. "We just need to find wherever Eleanor and Will are staying and sneak out in the night." With that stellar plan in mind, Ren turns and reaches for the door handle. Tugs. It doesn't open. "Yeah, this is locked from the outside," he says.

"We're gonna die here," I repeat, and Ren reaches out and shoves me.

"Maybe they're just *really* hospitable," Ren says.

"You don't understand," I say. "You've never seen a smile like this. That woman has serious ulterior motives."

"I've never seen any smile," Ren points out, and I mock him, repeating his words in a higher pitch. "Look, we might as well make the best of this," Ren says. "I mean, we're in a hotel! We can take advantage of the shower and beds."

And, well… we may be trapped in here and facing our doom, but Ren's not wrong. I'd rather die freshly showered, given the choice.

Ren showers first. He comes out with a towel wrapped around his waist and his hair dripping water on his shoulders, which slide down his chest, and then soak into the fabric of his towel…

"Theodore?"

"What!" I jump, eyes shooting guilty up to his own before remembering it doesn't even matter. I mean, beyond it being a total invasion of privacy.

"I said the bathroom's all yours now. Are you okay?"

"Me?" I laugh. "I'm fine. Time to shower! Goodbye!" I can't get to the bathroom fast enough, slamming the door shut behind me. I can hardly even appreciate the comforting warmth or the pressure of the water because my thoughts are so wrapped up around Ren. I think I'm going insane. I think I caught something from that kiss — something contagious.

When I come out of the shower, having accidentally washed my hair twice (one of the times being with body wash), Ren is dressed in clothes that aren't his. It seems the Sudbinians left clothing for us, and I follow Ren's lead, because even if they are probably trying to kill us, you really can't be choosey with your clothing when you've been wearing the same underwear for as long as we have.

"Check for bugs," Ren says to me. I blink. I don't think he's ever said that to me before.

"What?" I say.

"Under the mattresses?" Ren says. "It's what you're supposed to do in hotels."

"How would you know?" I ask, but I do it anyway, lifting up the first mattress and scanning its underside for bugs of any sort. There's nothing.

"Because my mom and I traveled a lot when I was little," Ren says, and I straighten up so fast I get dizzy. Ren never talks about his parents. Or about any of his life before Silva, really. So I'm trying not to freak out, and I'm trying not to let Ren realize that I'm failing at not freaking out, but my whole body's going haywire with surprise right now. "We liked to visit the lands under Ilma for their hot springs," he continues, unprompted. "Of course, Mom always checked for bugs with her hands, but I figure using your eyes is more efficient."

"Yeah," I say, my voice sounding faraway. "Definitely more efficient. Cova has lands under Ilma?"

Ren flushes. I wonder if he even meant to talk about any of this stuff or if it just slipped out somehow. But, "Yeah," he says. "It's kind of everywhere."

I take that in stride as I go and check under the second mattress, also bug free, before plopping down onto my own. "Do you miss it?" I ask. I expect Ren to climb onto the second bed, to turn away from me and pull the blanket up over his head and put an end to this conversation. Instead, he comes closer and climbs onto my bed, slowly, as if giving me time to object or maybe just to make sure he doesn't accidentally climb onto me. He ends up leaning against the pillows beside me as I wait for him to say something.

"No," he says finally, and I'm surprised. I always imagined he would miss it — deep down, at least. He lived there for the whole beginning of his life. I still don't know the exact reason why Ren left Cova, but I always imagined it was because he had crappy parents — abusive or something. I assumed he was abandoned and that it was thanks to pure luck that he ended up in Silva.

Now, I don't really know what to think. The way Ren's talking about his mom… it sounds so nostalgic. Not like how you'd talk about someone who'd failed you as a parent.

"No?" I question him. "Not even a little?"

Ren just shakes his head and it puts a frown on my lips. Is Cova as bad as everyone says it is?

"I miss Silva, though," Ren says quietly, redirecting the conversation. "And Hector."

I sigh loudly, throwing a leg over Ren's dramatically. "Hector's not prepared for how hard I'm gonna hug him," I say.

"He might be a little prepared," Ren tells me. "Remember when he killed that spider for you? He screamed because of how hard you hugged him."

I huff out a laugh, grinning as I shake my head and get lost in the memory. I know it hasn't really been long since I last saw Hector, but I miss him a ridiculous amount. And it's because of that pang in my chest that I desperately push my thoughts away, needing to concentrate on something else for my own sanity.

Maybe idiotically, my thoughts turn to Ren. I could think about Eleanor and Will, wonder if they're locked in their room like we are, but I don't. I just think about Ren because it's easy, because I've already been doing it all day.

I'm facing him, now. He's facing me too, but I don't think it feels the same for him, because he's not staring at me like it's the first time he's ever seen me, like he's suddenly desperate to drink me in.

That's how I feel. Like maybe I'm an idiot for never realizing how Ren felt about me. And maybe I'm an idiot for not knowing if I feel the same way.

Looking at him like this... it feels surreal, for some reason. His hair's still wet from the shower, the side of his face damp because of it. His eyelashes are unnaturally long, it seems like, and every time he blinks I watch them brush over his cheeks. He looks so soft and peaceful and open, when normally he's so tough and closed off.

I want to touch him.

I want to tug him into my arms, or lay my head on his chest, or brush my fingers through his hair. Why? Why do I feel like this now?

Neither of us have said anything in a long time, and I can't even remember what the last thing we talked about was. Ren blinks again and my eyes follow the movement down to his cheeks, and from there my eyes continue, past his flat nose and the freckle on the side of it, past the tiny mole right above his lip, until I'm just staring at his mouth. Small and pink, smooth despite the fact I know he's never owned his own tube of chapstick in his life.

I *know* his lips are soft. I know what they feel like against mine, what the inside his mouth tastes like, how it feels to have him gasp into my mouth. Ren doesn't know that I'm staring at his mouth, that all I can think about is being able to kiss it again, so there's really no need to give myself away. Despite this fact, I do it anyway.

"Have you thought about our kiss?" I say. My face is only inches from Ren's, so I'm privy to all the minuscule emotions that flit across his face before he shuts them down.

"Yes, Theodore," Ren says, and he sounds resigned, almost like he thinks I'm just being nosy. Except I'm not, because obviously I was thinking about our kiss first to have even brought it up. I don't think he realizes that though, probably too busy feeling embarrassed again, so I know I'm gonna have to prompt him further.

"Well I was thinking…"

"Dangerous," Ren interrupts, and I kick him in the shin.

"I was *thinking*," I continue with a huff. "That it's not really fair for you, you know? I mean, that was your first kiss and you have nothing to compare it to, so you have no way of knowing if you even liked it."

Ren frowns. "I'm not going to kiss anyone else," he says, and I want to smack him upside the head. He's really not making this any easier for me.

"*No*, I'm not suggesting—" I say, and groan. "I'm saying I can kiss you again, if you want. You know. For the learning experience."

I don't know what I'm expecting. For Ren to gasp in surprise, maybe. Or for him to call me out — *why are you so willing to kiss me, anyway?* Instead he just nods, almost immediately, and says, "Okay."

"Right now?" I prompt, and he nods again.

I don't know what I'm doing. This is a horrible idea. I mean, we could totally screw up our friendship with whatever the hell we're doing. Plus, I have no *reason* to kiss Ren.

And yet I scoot closer anyway. Ren is completely still, laying there with bated breath, and I can't talk any sense into myself at all. I just reach forward and cup his cheek, cataloguing the way his eyes flutter, and then I lean in.

Ren tastes familiar. It's only the second time we've done this, yet it feels like the hundredth. I know the shape of his face, the curve of his waist, the way his hair parts — and now I know how his tongue feels in my mouth. It's no longer slow and tentative like our kiss before. It's turned determined, the two of us moving faster, gasping into each other's mouths as our hands touch and grab and pull one another.

Ren's more reserved about this than me. He'll take control of the kiss, deepening it, angling his head, and then it's like he remembers himself and he backs off a little, a couple times even pulling away completely, face still close as he pants. I just go right back in though, and with no objection from Ren, we continue.

I think it's because he's in love with me. Like he's afraid he's gonna creep me out by being too into this or something. Except there's nothing Ren could do to creep me out, and I'm enjoying myself way too much to even give it as much thought as Ren must be.

I learn a lot about him. Like how he gasps when I drag my teeth across his lip, or how pliant he turns when I've got him like this, his body melting into the bed when I clamber on top of him and kiss him from above. Or how he says my name when I kiss down his throat and learn the taste of his jugular — Theo*dooore*.

It feels like we kiss for hours, though I know it hasn't been that long. The sheets are rumpled and Ren's hair is a mess, courtesy of me, and the two of us lay panting beside each other. Ren's facing the ceiling, looking kind of shell-shocked and dazed, and I'm still just *staring* at him, unable to get enough of him.

"That was," Ren says slowly, "...*very* educational."

I snort, and then I grab a pillow and hug it to my body. My eyes slip closed, and I know I should probably be thinking about everything we've done, about whether I've ruined our friendship, but I can't. I just think about Ren and the way he smells and every unrestricted expression I saw on his face tonight. I fall asleep with a smile on my face.

BANG BANG BANG.

I jolt awake with a gasp. The lights are still on from last night and Ren's hand is dangling off the bed, probably feeling all prickly and horrible right about now.

"Theo? Ren?!" comes Eleanor's voice from outside the door, followed by more banging, and I shake Ren until he groans and slaps my hand away.

"Coming!" I yell back. Ren sits up, blinking sleepily.

"What?" he says, unprompted.

"Oh no," I say.

"What?" he says again, this time prompted.

I can't think though, can't formulate words — I'm just staring at him, and at his *neck*. When did I do *that*? There's a dark bruise gracing the side of it, evidence of last night's activities, and I can't do anything other than gape at it.

"Theodore?" he says.

"Guys!" Will shouts, and there's more banging.

"*What's 'oh no'?*" Ren demands, punching me for good measure. I punch him back.

"There's a hickey on your neck!" I whisper-yell. Ren jolts backward in surprise.

"Is it noticeable?"

"Only for everyone who's not blind!"

Eleanor and Will start banging with every hand they have available, I'm pretty sure, so I get up and march over to the door, flinging it open.

"Good morning," I say pointedly. The two of them look exhausted, both sporting dark bags under their eyes.

"You guys were locked in your room too, right?" Eleanor says, ignoring me.

"Yeah," I say.

"Oh, good," she sighs. "Will and I were really panicked. We stayed up all night trying to get to you guys."

Just then, Ren coughs loudly, probably feeling as awkward and guilty as I do, hearing that. "Us too!" I say quickly. "Yeah, couldn't sleep a wink. We were really freaked out."

"Ren, what the hell happened to you?" Will says suddenly. I turn around, face burning hot, in time to see Ren slap his hand over the wrong side of his neck.

"Nothing!" he says unconvincingly.

I laugh loudly. "Don't be embarrassed, Ren!" I say, and Ren shoots me the most confused look imaginable. Luckily, both Will and Eleanor are looking at me now instead of him. "He fell over and hit his neck in the shower last night," I inform them. Across the room, Ren's look of confusion turns into a glare. I'm glad I'm not any closer to him, considering how angry he looks. I think he might punch me again.

"Esteemed guests," a voice that's not any of ours says, and I jump in surprise before turning around, seeing Chancey from last night standing in our doorway. "I see you have already reunited. Please, follow me for our breakfast special."

"Actually, it's about time for us to leave," I say. "Where is Icarus being kept?"

Chancey's eyes dart to the side. "Icarus can be brought to you while you enjoy breakfast," he says uneasily — probably because I'm glaring at him. It's just that I know this isn't going to be made any less difficult for us. They're clearly still trying to keep us here for whatever reason and I'm sick of it. I just want to be on our way again.

I don't know what else to do, though, so I start following Chancey, and everyone else follows as well. Chancey starts going on and on about all the kinds of food and specials they have this morning but none of us are listening. We're all trying to communicate silently, aside from Ren, who doesn't know about the non-verbal conversation we're having without him.

Eleanor looks at me with wide eyes, pointing toward Chancey and throwing her hands up in the air. I assume she means something along the lines of, *what the hell are we going to do about this?!*

Considering I have no idea what we're going to do about it, I give her an exaggerated shrug. Will looks between the two of us and puts his thumb and forefinger against his lips. Unsure what that means — and kind of afraid he's trying to convince us to smoke something — I look at him in confusion. He repeats the gesture, which clarifies nothing. Eleanor doesn't seem to understand what he's trying to say either.

"Does that sound good?" Chancey says, turning around, and the three of us abruptly stop gesturing, arms snapping to our sides like soldiers.

"Yep. Splendid," I say quickly, and Chancey smiles, satisfied, before opening the hotel doors for us. We're out on the streets again, so close to being free and yet still so far, and he begins to lead us away, presumably to whatever breakfast place has these millions of specials.

Will does the gesture again, more urgently this time. I ignore him, because he should really get better at making gestures that don't look like he's suggesting we try drugs as a solution to our problems, and instead try to silently convey the question of: *how are we going to get Icarus back?* When my attempt at making a bird out of my hands goes unanswered, I just pretend to be Icarus entirely, and Will huffs loudly, briefly drawing Ren's attention.

The next thing I know, Will's yanking me close and shoving his hand into the front pocket of my pants. He pulls out the Avis whistle and presses it demonstratively against his lips, his eyebrows raised in overt annoyance. *Oh.* So that's what he was trying to say.

Still looking annoyed, Will blows the whistle, and Ren immediately cries out.

I forgot that Ren could hear the silent whistle, as did Will, apparently. He stops blowing it immediately, hiding it in his hand as Chancey turns around in alarm, looking at Ren who's fallen to his knees.

"What's wrong with him?" he demands as Eleanor helps him back to his feet, Ren holding a hand to his head.

"He has frequent migraines," Will says quickly. "Nothing to be done about it."

"It'll pass soon," Ren grunts, playing along. Apparently satisfied with that, Chancey nods and continues on. Ren turns on us with a growl.

"A little warning would've been nice!"

"Sorry!" Will answers.

And even though I felt a burst of hope at Will's idea, it's already dissipated. Icarus doesn't suddenly appear over the horizon, and as more time passes, the more uneasy I become. She's probably just locked up somewhere and unable to escape, but terrifying thoughts keep invading my mind. What if they hurt her so badly that she can't fly anymore? What if they killed her?!

By the time we make it to the restaurant I've already worked myself into a panic. I barely notice the people already seated at the table we're being led to until I'm sitting across from them, staring directly at the creepy unblinking woman from yesterday. Several masked people — what look like guards — sit beside her.

"Good morning," she says, her voice oddly lilting.

"Where's Icarus?" I demand, getting straight to the point.

"Well taken care of," she promises. "However, I must ask you not to rile her however you did some minutes ago again. She could hurt herself trying so hard to escape, you know."

I push myself to my feet, hands splayed on the table as I lean over it, glaring at the woman before me.

"We're leaving," I tell her. "Right now. And I'll only ask this once more — *where is Icarus?*"

Instead of looking intimidated by my threat, the woman just smiles at me pleasantly. Then she raises her hand in the air and does this little motion and the next thing I know my hands are being yanked behind my back. There's a guard standing behind me, restraining me, and another stands in front of me with a knife to my throat.

"You're not the one making the decisions here," she informs me. "However, I *will* allow you to leave — with your stolen Avis, even."

"She's not stolen," I interject.

She ignores me.

"I only ask that you leave the girl with us."

I'm silent. Not because I'm actually debating it or anything, but because I'm shocked. She wants us to *leave* Eleanor?

"That's not an option," I say. I look over at Eleanor, bewildered, but Eleanor doesn't look nearly as confused as I do. She looks like she's realized something, like some sort of answer just clicked into place for her.

"That is your only option," the woman tells me. "Either you leave without her, or you won't leave at all."

"What, you'll just keep us here?" Will scoffs.

"Something like that," the woman says, and I have a feeling our stay won't be nearly as pleasant as it's been so far. Considering the knife still at my throat, I'm thinking it won't be much of a *'stay'* at all.

"What do you want with Eleanor?" I demand.

The woman laughs. "It's your own fault for not realizing who you were traveling with," she says.

"What have you done?" Eleanor says. "Who have you told?"

Wait, so she knows what this woman is talking about?

"All will be revealed soon enough, Princess," the woman says. "Until then, please, enjoy our breakfast specials."

CHAPTER 15

ELEANOR

"You guys should go," I say preemptively. We've been left alone at our table but the people who were previously sitting with us stand at attention around the room, staring at us. To make matters worse, there are regular people sitting around at all the tables who clearly have no idea what is secretly going on in their society.

"Did she say 'Princess'?" Theo says, frowning at me. I ignore him.

"Just stand up and accept her offer. I'll be fine here alone," I say, even though I'm not so sure. These people know who I am, obviously, but I have no way of knowing who they're going to end up handing me over to. They could be turning me in to my family for whatever reward is surely out there or they could just as easily be selling me to our enemies, exiles of Volant looking for a bargaining chip or rebels who want some sort of leverage in order to rise up. There's no telling what's going to happen to me after this.

"We're not going to leave you," Ren says abruptly, and I have to ignore how oddly touched I am. I can remember how long it took for him to warm up to me. Who'd have thought he'd be standing up for me now?

"What did she mean when she said 'Princess'?" Theo says.

"We just need to think of a way out of here…" Will murmurs.

"Um, *hello*?!" says Theo. "'Princess'?! Did anybody else hear that?"

"I'm assuming it's because she's a princess, Theodore," Ren says calmly.

"Yeah, I am," I say. "I'm the Lost Princess."

Theo gapes at me like his entire worldview has changed. Ren looks expressionless, but that's normal for him, although I figure he really isn't too surprised — it seems like it's hard to shock him. Will, on the other hand, just looks thoughtful. I guess it's not that out of the ordinary for him to hear major secrets.

Finally, Theo gets his mouth to work, and he starts stuttering a bunch of questions out at me. *Why didn't you tell us?*

Don't you want to go back? You know we definitely *can't leave you with them now, right?* His voice just fades into the background.

Everything's going wrong. Theo's freaking out about me being a princess, I'm probably about to be sold into slavery or something similar, and Ren has the biggest hickey I've ever seen in my life adorning his neck. Seriously, who thought *that* was a good idea?

"Everyone be quiet," I snap, even though it's really only Theo talking (coupled with Ren's interjections of his name, sounding exasperated). Still, Theo shuts up immediately and I wonder if I really sounded that harsh or if it's the fact that he knows I'm a princess now. This is exactly why I didn't want to tell them (you know, after I knew I could actually trust them and all). "It's time for you guys to leave."

Finally, Theo gets ahold of himself, and he shakes his head, eyebrows furrowed. He's the one I have to convince if I really want them to get out of here. Not that I'd ever tell Theo for fear of inflating his ego, but he's kind of the unofficial leader of our group. It's thanks to him that we're even together right now — it's *his* mission we're helping to complete, after all. So it makes sense that we usually defer to him when decisions need to be made, although this time I'm going to need him to step down.

But, "No," Theo says, crossing his arms. "We're not leaving you here."

"You have to," I say. "We don't know what these people are capable of, and we don't know what they plan to do with me, much less you guys, if you disobey them. We've already wasted too much time here — you could've made it to the Darkness hours ago."

"Eleanor—" says Theo.

"I don't need you treating me differently now that you know I'm a princess," I huff. I feel unsettlingly like I'm talking to my guards. That's also part of the reason I didn't feel quite ready to go back to Volant.

For the first time in my life, I've had true freedom. And *friends*. Going back means more people pretending to like me and having my every move watched, guards constantly posted by my side. I can't imagine what security will be like when I get back after having been gone for so long.

If I get back.

"I'm not unwilling to leave you because you're a princess," Theo says. "I'm unwilling to leave you because you're my *friend*. Plus, these guys are creeps — we couldn't possibly abandon you with them."

"Well, you'll have to," I say, because I saw that woman's eyes when she was threatening them, and I know these people aren't above killing a bunch of innocent teenagers in order to get what they want. So I wave down the woman from earlier. She starts walking over as I ignore the protests of my friends. Will's practically shouting in my ear and even Ren has reached over and grabbed my wrist, but I have to do this.

All my life, I've learned to protect people. *My* people, the ones that my family is responsible for leading. And I've protected my family, who nefarious nobles have countless times tried to unseat with made up lies, desperate for power themselves. And now I have to protect my friends — it's just the duty of a princess.

"Eleanor, *don't do this—*"

"They're ready to go now," I inform the woman, who has come to a stop beside our table, her hands linked behind her back.

"No, we're *not*," Theo snaps, but the woman has already made some motion with her hand and her guards are rushing forward, pulling my friends to their feet. Outside, there's a loud thump followed by a deafening screech, and through the window, I can see Icarus' lower half. I can also see the chains restraining her, pulled taut and trailing out of view toward their handlers.

"Icarus!" Theo gasps, attention momentarily drawn toward her, before he's yanked to his feet. He's distracted now, and the amount of noise in the restaurant has risen considerably, enough so that I can tell Ren's having trouble orienting himself.

Only Will is still paying attention to me.

"Stop this," he pleads. "We can escape somehow else, I know it."

I squeeze his hand. "Just get out of here," I tell him, before he, too, is yanked to his feet. I watch as my friends are dragged from the restaurant, Icarus screeching so loudly it hurts my ears, before her wings beat, shaking the glass of the buildings around her. She snatches Ren in her beak before jumping into the air and grabbing both Theo and Will with her talons. That's the last glimpse I get of them, and distantly, I wonder if it'll be the last I ever have.

"We thank you for your cooperation," the woman says. Since my friends left, I've heard the guards call her 'Sorceress', which sends chills all the way down my spine. It dredges up memories of a dark basement, the clink of spurs and the sharp crack of Ren being struck. *The Sorceress will be pleased,* one of those men had said. Could this be the same Sorceress that they were talking about?

If magic really *is* real and this woman can actually conduct it, I might be in more danger than I thought. I've been in plenty of scary situations in the past year — Askund really isn't the safest place — but I've always managed to get out of them. You learn a lot of skills, being a princess, and not just from the countless teachers. If you ever want any sort of freedom, you have to learn to think outside the box. You have to be a fast learner, which is how I started scamming people out here in the first place.

Not that I think I have any chance of scamming these people. They're no longer treating me all nice and pampered like they were earlier, before they revealed their whole plot to hand me off to whoever. No more luxurious restaurants or hotels or services. Now, we're somewhere underground, a select few of the guards having accompanied us to the room I'm now being kept in. The walls and floor are unfinished, some kind of cold, gray concrete, but they haven't chained me up. I'm just sitting on an old couch that's been brought down here, the springs poking uncomfortably out of it, while the Sorceress stands before me, looking annoyingly triumphant.

"Are you going to tell me what you plan to do with me now?" I demand. It doesn't follow the Princess Protocol — basically what I've been instructed to do should I ever get captured. *Always tell them you'll pay the ransom,* my father had said. He was adamant about that, and about how we can always, always top an enemy's price.

"Seeing as you have no chance of escape? Sure, why not," she says. I cross my arms and wait.

"You might have noticed that our little town in Askund is unlike the others," the Sorceress begins. It's true. I haven't been anywhere in Askund nearly as nice as this place. Plus, there doesn't really seem to be any crime. The streets are clean and I haven't seen a single person getting dragged around with their hands tied or with a knife to their throat. "Well that's because we have a sponsor," she continues loftily. And then, "You might know him — his name is Warren." She grins at this, her smile stretched thin and terrifying, her entire body leaning forward as she studies me, obviously waiting for my reaction.

I don't give her the pleasure of having one, forcing myself to sit still and impassive despite the fact that my lungs have been squeezed free of air. Warren was my fiancé. Still is, technically.

"Word of the Lost Princess began to arise recently," the Sorceress continues. "Some librarian thought she saw you, apparently, which was inspiring for some, but for others…" she trails off. "Well, you were supposed to be dead."

I swallow, my throat barely cooperating. I've known it for a long time, but deep down, I always wondered if maybe I was wrong. If maybe it wasn't exactly like I expected. But no. Warren really did mean to kill me.

"Naturally, Warren got in touch with us," the Sorceress says. "We've done him a few odd favors in the past, no questions asked, so we sent out scouts immediately after he contacted us. Doubled the amount, when one pair happened to find you, and tripled it when a nasty rumor began to spread, something about the Lost Princess' disappearance being the result of her fiancé.

"Funny how you ended up coming to us all on your own, huh? Flew right in on that Avis of yours. I still can't figure out how you called it out of Volant from so far away, but no matter." The Sorceress shakes her head, clearly coming to the conclusion of her speech. I can't wait for it to be over, for her to stop talking so I can think about everything she's said and try to stop freaking out.

The Sorceress steps closer to me and grabs my face with one hand, her long nails digging into the soft flesh of my cheek. When she speaks, her voice comes out low and falsely apologetic. "You didn't *really* think you were going to make it back to Volant, did you, Princess?" she croons.

And I feel cold all over. I feel like an *idiot*. I should've accepted Theo's offer to fly me back to Volant when I had the chance. What did it matter if I was enjoying my time with them? My people needed me and I decided to be selfish, and because of that I'm going to get myself killed.

Because she is going to kill me. I know that, now. Not only am I not going to make it to Volant, I'm not going to make it out of this *basement*.

"My father will pay you more," I blurt out. I don't want to beg — it's embarrassing — but I can't help it. I want to live.

The Sorceress laughs. "Warren's giving us something your father never could," she says. And then she snaps her fingers and flames ignite around the room, throwing the basement into stark light. "*Power*."

I barely even register her voice. I'm too busy observing the room I'm in. There are cuffs on the walls and chains on the floors. Unsettling splotches of dried blood decorate the room here and there and I feel my shoulders shrink into myself. I don't want to be here. I'm starting to regret sending my friends away, even though I know it was the right thing to do. Better me than all of them, right?

The Sorceress continues. "Your royal family wishes they had the guts to do what Warren's doing. He'll unite the nations and lead them as one — with *us* along with him! Once everyone assimilates, there will be no more outsiders, no more *Askund*. And what better way to do it than by harnessing the power of the Darkness?"

234

My mouth goes dry. That doesn't even make *sense*.

"You're insane, just like him," I bite out. What she's talking about... would Warren really do all that? Uniting the nations is crazy-talk. They're separate because they want to be, because they value their differences. We learned this centuries ago, when the Covans tried to do the same thing!

And harnessing the Darkness? There's no way that's possible, right?

"Of course it's possible," the Sorceress snaps, and I realize I was talking out loud. "Or it will be, soon. Warren has all kinds of people conducting research. It's only a matter of time until he can control it. Too bad you won't get to stick around to see it..."

I've had enough. I'm shaken to my core, scared and unsettled and desperate to escape. The flames around the room had risen as she'd spoken, throwing the horrors within it into even starker clarity. I need to get out of here.

So I jump to my feet, heart pounding away in my chest, and sprint toward the door.

"Get her!" the Sorceress yells. I've only taken three steps but I'm breathing like I've run a marathon. Someone before me grabs my wrist and I yank it out of their grasp so hard I end up punching myself in the stomach.

Hands reach for me and spears try to trip me but I lunge my way through all of them, sheer panic forcing me forwards. The stairs leading upward are wooden. I barely remember how we got down here in the first place, but I start scrambling up the steps toward the door anyway. They creak and groan under my weight but that hardly registers. All that I'm aware of is the exit getting closer and the strip of light beneath it, the pounding on the stairs behind me, the people yelling and the awareness that they're close.

I'm almost there. I reach for the handle, my fingers brushing the brass, and then someone grabs my ankle and *yanks*. My feet are pulled out from under me and the stairs fly up to meet my face. Heat blooms in my head and I curl in on myself as I'm dragged, my body thunking down every step.

"No," I say, my voice lost in the cacophony of everyone shouting, and I reach out, fingers scrabbling against the steps. Finally, I catch onto one, and I hold on for all I'm worth as the guards continue to try to drag me. My fingers ache, and I think I have splinters from holding onto the step, but I can't let go. I can't struggle back up them either, too many hands holding onto me, pulling me back.

"Theo!" I shout, even though he's long gone by now, back in the sky with Icarus where he belongs. I think I know why she left Volant for him, now. It's an old legend, and one that not many people actually believe, but hundreds of years ago only those who shared a bond with the Avi ever rode them. It was said that Avi could sense this bond and would stop at nothing to locate their true riders.

I think somehow, someway, Theo and Icarus share a true rider's bond.

"Halt!" the Sorceress barks, and everyone does. Not because they're just that disciplined, but because there's magic in her words. Even I can't move, despite how desperate I am to escape. My body feels like lead, a thousand times heavier than it ever has been before. I don't think I could stand even if the room were on fire, the flames licking closer and closer toward me.

"Chain her," the Sorceress says, and the guards are released from the spell. I'm carted across the room, though I think it shouldn't be possible, considering how heavy I am, and then I'm chained to the wall, wrists and ankles cuffed against cold stone. I close my eyes, my hopes finally extinguished.

Time isn't real.

I have no idea how long it's been. It could've been hours or days and it wouldn't have made any difference for me. All I know is that my body aches. My head is pounding from that collision with the stairs and it takes me far too long to realize that my throat hurts simply because I'm thirsty.

"We're going to have fun with you, Princess," someone taunts, their voice sounding far away. The Sorceress. "Your fiancé's only instructions were to make sure you don't return."

She reaches out and grabs my face, then — for the second time today — and I try to tip my head away, but she tightens her hold. The guard beside her is holding a tray, as if he's about to offer her something to eat. Instead of there being food on it, though, there's an assortment of weapons. I whimper.

"Yes, you should be afraid," the Sorceress says, amused. Everything sounds warped. My head is throbbing so hard I can hardly concentrate, and it's a struggle to even follow her hand with my eyes as she reaches for one of the knives. Right as her fingers brush the weapon, the entire tray crashes to the floor.

"Sorry," the guard grunts, immediately dropping to the ground. He seems to struggle with retrieving all the weapons, his hands patting carefully all over the floor for them. The Sorceress scoffs and crosses her arms, waiting.

"Sorceress," another guard says, standing on the stairs with a second tray. "I've brought your lunch."

"I didn't ask for lunch," she says, impatient.

"Really? Because I was told to bring you lunch."

"Imbeciles," the Sorceress mutters. "Guard," she says, addressing the guard beside her. "Torture the princess. And you — what kind of lunch did you bring?" she asks, already crossing the room.

"Yes, Sorceress," says the guard before me, standing again. "Prepare for... lots of fun," he says in a horrible imitation of the Sorceress. My head is still pounding and thinking right now is especially hard, but I can tell that something is... off. For the life of me, I can't figure it out — not with this piercing migraine.

"Soup?" the Sorceress says from across the room. "In the middle of summer?"

"It's a summer soup," the guard claims. The one nearest to me is holding a knife now. My entire body is still, waiting for the pain that's sure to follow.

"I don't hear screaming," the Sorceress says pointedly. She's leaning against the wall, a bowl in one hand and a spoon in the other.

"Scream," the guard before me whispers.

"Huh?" I manage. Confusion sits thick and heavy in the forefront of my mind.

"*Scream*," he insists, and his voice is familiar to me, somehow. I'm still not screaming though, so he waves the knife before my face, impatient, and I get the hint. I let out a high, drawn-out scream, and the Sorceress hums in satisfaction, apparently unable to see the guard failing to slice me open.

"This is delicious," the Sorceress says across the room. "What's in it?"

"Oh, some of this, some of that," the guard answers. "Calming, right?"

"Very."

"Scream, Eleanor," my guard says, and I scream again. The Sorceress slides down against the wall, cradling the bowl of soup as she continues to eat it. I scream in intervals, not wanting the guard to have to risk reminding me again, until the Sorceress suddenly drops the bowl and soup spills all over the floor. My guard turns around, then.

"Is she out?" he asks.

"Like a light," the other replies, before pulling off his mask. And finally, things start clicking into place. Because I recognize that guard.

"*Will?*" I say.

"Who else?" he says, and then the other guard — Ren — pulls off his mask as well.

"What did you do to her?" I ask as Will crosses the room, pulling a key out of his pocket. He answers as he unchains me.

"Gave her a few too many calming tablets," he says. "She'll be out for a few hours, don't worry. We just have to meet up with Theo now."

The second I'm free, my body lurches forward into Ren, my legs not strong enough to hold me up without the help of my bindings. He clutches me to him, caught off-guard, and helps me stand. "Stars, what did they do to you?" he murmurs.

"Lots of stairs," I reply intelligibly. Will hooks his arm under mine and my friends begin leading me toward the stairs. There's too many and climbing them is a pain, considering how badly my head doesn't want me to do anything, but we manage to get to the top. Will releases me, letting me lean against Ren completely as he pushes open the door and peeks his head out of it.

"Can't see anyone," he says. "Ren?"

"Let's wait a minute," Ren instructs, and Will eases the door closed again. A minute later, a pair of footsteps sound outside the door and disappear. Will nudges it open again. "Sounds good," Ren then says, and Will's by my side again.

We venture into a hallway with actual lights and finished walls that I vaguely recognize, and then we walk until the floors turn to wood. A few times we have to duck behind corners or doors to avoid more of the guards, but everything seems to be going well.

Until the alarms start blaring, that is.

They make me cry out, my head way too sensitive for noise like that, and I hardly notice as I'm pulled up onto somebody's back. It's Ren, I realize a second later, and he starts running after Will through the hallways.

We make it out of the building's lower levels and from there it's just a matter of charging through the upstairs dining area. No one in the restaurant seems to realize what's going on but we sprint past them anyway, bursting out onto the street.

Ren's still carrying me, his hands occupied as he holds onto my legs, so Will shoves the whistle into his mouth before stepping forward and slapping his hands over Ren's ears. He blows the whistle just as guards begin pouring onto the streets, and not only from the building we just evacuated.

But Icarus reaches us first. She lands so hard that the ground shakes, and the screech she releases abruptly reminds me of why we use Avi in our military. Not a single guard tries to advance with Icarus standing there like that, her wings extended and her eyes narrowed into slits.

Ren and Will help me onto her back, Theo holding tightly to the reins, and then they follow me up, yelling at Icarus to move. She takes to the skies with speed and I finally let myself acknowledge the fact that I was just rescued. That my friends didn't leave me, even when I tried to make them.

CHAPTER 16

THEO

Despite the hot weather, it's cold all the way up here, especially with the wind blowing through our hair and clothes as Icarus carries us farther and farther from Sudbina. Ren's by my side, facing backwards on Icarus and holding onto the reins with one hand — he's gotten a lot less scared of flying on her, although I'd bet part of that can be attributed to the fact that having something to hold onto is way less scary than dangling from an Avis' beak. Behind me, Will sits next to Eleanor, who's been feeling a lot better ever since we saved her, especially after Will made her some weird herbal healing drink (which he refuses to call a potion.)

I turn around to look at her for the millionth time, still half convinced she has a concussion and is going to tumble off

Icarus at any minute. I guess this is just the result of all my pent-up adrenaline — there's no good way to get it out when you're sitting on the side lines, just waiting for some whistle that you can't even hear.

Icarus had been just as antsy as me, flying around in uneasy circles after we'd dropped Ren and Will off by some guards on the outskirts on the town. We'd stayed long enough to assure that they got the guards knocked out and the uniforms off their bodies, and then we'd left, trusting them to finish the rest of the plan by themselves, equipped with only Will's knife, Eleanor's Avis whistle, and enough Ilman calming tablets to knock a grown woman out for hours.

I crane my neck for the million and first time.

"I'm fine, Theo," Eleanor says. And sure, she *looks* fine, but who knows what she could be hiding under that cool exterior? She's been a princess this whole time! I never would've guessed we were in the presence of royalty.

"I'm just making sure," I tell her. "You'll tell me if you start feeling dizzy or anything, right?"

"Promise," Eleanor says, sounding fondly exasperated. I'm still looking at her. I feel like my skin's crawling all over, curiosity bubbling within my entire being as I use all my concentration to hold back the flood of questions desperate to escape me.

Eleanor sighs. "Just ask whatever you want to ask," she says, and I gasp, spinning around so fast that the hat — which Will had placed on my head for safekeeping when he and Ren had going back into Sudbina — flies off my head. For half a second, it hangs in midair, suspended, before there's a powerful flap of Icarus' wings and we're propelled forward, the hat whipping into the distance and winking out of existence.

"*NOO!*" I shout, launching myself over Eleanor in a vain attempt to reclaim the now definitely lost forever hat, but she and Will catch me and hold me back.

"What?" Ren's asking behind me, panicked. "What's wrong?!"

"The hat!" I yell. "It's — the wind! It just—!"

Will pats my back consolingly. "The wind snatched the hat away," he explains mournfully.

Eleanor sighs. "Honestly, it was probably for the best," she admits. "That was the ugliest hat I've ever seen."

"It had *character*," I hiss. I finally sit back up, but I'm still staring into the distance, hoping the hat will somehow make a reappearance.

"It was ugly?" Ren says, sounding confused. "Eleanor, you said it make me look spiffy."

"Yeah, I was joking," she says. "It made you look like a huge dork."

When I look at Ren, he's gaping. "Why would you make me wear it then?!" he demands.

"We should go back for it," I declare, and intent on listening to my whims, Icarus starts to bank.

"*No*, Theo," Eleanor says. "Come on, you know we'll never find it. Will asking me questions about being a princess cheer you up?"

And I miss our hat, I really do, but Eleanor being *the* Eleanor is still pretty wicked news.

"Why didn't you tell us you were the Lost Princess?" I start without a moment's hesitation, and Icarus corrects the direction of our flight.

"I didn't trust you guys when I first met you," Eleanor says simply. "And then it just seemed weird to bring it up. Plus, I liked feeling normal."

"What happened a year ago?" I ask. "When you left."

"It was my fiancé," says Eleanor. "Our wedding was to occur in a week. He surprised me in my chambers one night and hit me over the head. I woke up in a boat, leagues from Volant and moored on the outskirts of Askund."

"How come it's taken you so long to return?" Ren pipes up.

"I was trying to do it on my own. I couldn't trust anyone in Askund, obviously, and it's almost impossible to get enough money for transportation out here. Mostly I was walking from town to town and scamming for money along the way."

I find myself frowning. I was curious about all sorts of things — stuff about royal life and food and guards — but it all seems stupid now. Eleanor was assaulted. She was forced out of her home by a man who was supposed to love her and had her life turned completely upside down. It's just not fair.

"Are you ready to go back?" Will asks her. The answer seems obvious to me. *Yes.* She's been gone for so long, and under such unjust circumstances, I feel like I'd be dying to get home.

But surprisingly, Eleanor shakes her head. "I was, before I met you guys," she says. "It was all I ever thought about. But since meeting you all, it's been easier to get it off my mind, to enjoy my time away from home. Except now I can't go home," she says suddenly, fiercely. And then she looks up at me and I see fire in her eyes. "My fiancé's trying to take control of the Darkness. If destroying it is the same as stopping him, then that's what I need to concentrate on right now."

Hope flutters in my chest. It just seems like going up against the Darkness — something that no one really has the best idea about how to do, something that's all powerful and terrifying — will be slightly less horrific with my friends by my side.

"Will," I say. "Are you sure you want to come to the Darkness with us? I don't want to force you to do something dangerous."

But Will looks just as determined as Eleanor. "I want to help," he says. And then, quieter, "Plus, maybe if I do this… my dad will see that I'm just as good as a son as I was a daughter."

"You shouldn't have to do something dangerous in order to prove yourself," Ren says immediately, frowning. And I know he's been against diving straight into the Darkness this whole time — I don't blame him for being scared — but it doesn't seem like he's thinking about that. He's just thinking about Will, right now.

"Yeah, well," Will huffs. He shrugs. "Might as well go all out, right? I mean, there's no way he can deny it after this."

"Gonna come out of the Darkness a man," Eleanor says. She puffs out her chest. "I'm ready."

Will panics. "That's not what I meant—"

"Say *goodbye* to Princess Eleanor…"

"Girls can do dangerous things too! I mean, they *do* do dangerous things… I mean — anyone can do them!" Will stammers, face red and eyes wide.

"I'm joking, Will," Eleanor says, and she throws an arm around his shoulders. "If your dad doesn't get that you're an awesome son, that's his loss. We'll always be here to appreciate you, though."

"Yeah," Ren says, heart-felt, and places a hand on Will's ankle. Will smiles.

"Thanks," he sighs. "You know… I never really talked to him about it. The second he found out, I ran away."

That gives me pause. "Wait… so you don't even know how he feels?"

"I can *guess*," Will says, bitter. "He was always telling me how much like Mom I was, and she died when I was a baby. And now he thinks his daughter's dead too! He said as much to you guys."

"Maybe he didn't mean it like that," Eleanor ventures.

Will pulls his knees up to his chest. "Yeah, maybe," he says, though it doesn't sound like he believes her. "Let's just Restore the Light, okay?"

Ren sighs.

"It's gonna be all right, Ren," I promise him. "We'll help you do it. You won't have to be alone."

"We still don't even know if I'm a descendant," he says, holding up a finger. Then he puts up a second one. "*And* we don't know what you're supposed to do to Restore the Light if you are one."

"Well, I think you are," I say, still confident about that. "And the rest will come to us. We won't just walk into the Darkness without a plan. And we still have to find a dark patch, anyway."

"I don't think that's going to be a problem," Eleanor says quietly. She's looking into the distance, and I follow her gaze.

It's still unsettling to see. It looks like it shouldn't be real, like some drawing in a children's book. Rising unnaturally from the ground is this great swath of darkness, a black, impenetrable cloud, curling around itself like a fog moved by invisible wind. Just looking at it sends chills down my spine. Goosebumps crop up all along my arms, and suddenly guilt is eating me.

I'm trying to send Ren into *that?*

Last time when we were in there, we had no idea. But now, the thought of sending Ren into the Darkness on purpose… it makes me feel sick to my stomach. Especially since Ren feels things I don't. Like how he can tell when someone's standing at the front door, or how he knows when it's about to storm. He always makes sure to inform me when a storm is coming, like the knowledge is somehow imperative to me. Even though he doesn't know it, I really appreciate that. Thunderstorms have always freaked me out.

But now I can't stop wondering if going into the Darkness is going to feel different for Ren. For me, it was so unsettling because I couldn't see anything, and because those creatures kept making the creepy clicking sounds and grabbing at us. I wonder if Ren can feel more, though. If there's some other layer of the Darkness that only he's aware of.

I can't believe I'm doing this to him.

"We should stop," I blurt out.

"What? But we're almost there," Will says.

"Right," I say, and then, flying by the seat of my pants, "but we don't need to be there until it's night time, if we want to be able to see. So for now we should rest. Eat and charge up and all that. Plus, Icarus is tired."

Icarus squawks in disagreement.

"I know girl, you can rest soon," I say, patting her neck.

No one argues with me any further. I think it's because they're not too ecstatic about getting close to the Darkness either. We end up landing by an outcropping of trees, all of us climbing off Icarus and setting up camp on the ground.

"Ren?" I say, approximately two minutes after we've sat down. Will's been sorting through his supplies and Eleanor's in the process of adjusting Icarus' harness, making it more comfortable for her while we relax. "Can I talk to you for a minute?"

"Yeah," he says, and he stands, realizing I want to speak to him alone.

I get to my feet after him, telling our friends we'll be right back.

"Be careful," Eleanor says, sounding sarcastic. "We wouldn't want Ren falling on his neck again." I splutter, surprised and startled, but Ren just grabs my arm and marches us away with a red face. We end up ducking into the copse of trees, Ren leaning back against one with his arms crossed as I stand before him.

"That was horrible," he announces.

"Do you think she knows?"

Ren scoffs. "Are you joking?" And then, deciding it doesn't matter. "What did you want to talk to me about?"

"I need to tell you the truth," I say. Because I feel like we have a lot to talk about, what with everything that happened in Sudbina (the kissing *and* the kidnapping), and it all feels jumbled up in my mind. Mostly the kissing, though. Sorry Eleanor.

"The truth?" Ren says weakly. It looks like he's shrunk in on himself, and I wonder what he's thinking.

"Yeah," I say. "Ren... I really like kissing you. And I thought I should feel guilty, like I was messing with your feelings just because it felt good... but I don't think that's *why* I was kissing you."

"And it wasn't for the learning experience?" he says, but it sounds joking. I guess he realized that that was pretty out of character for me, too.

"I don't think so," I admit. "And... I can't really think about it right now — there's a lot going on, and I need to focus on getting home to Hector — but I think after all of this, Ren... we should give it a shot. You know, like. Being together."

"Really?" Ren says, and he lifts his head up, it having previously been tilted toward the ground. His hair falls out of his eyes, then, revealing their blue to me. He looks hopeful. He looks like he's holding his breath.

"Yeah," I say, feeling equally breathless. Is this insane? Ren is one of the most important people in my life. Him and Hector. If this doesn't work out, could I lose him? I don't think I could deal with that. But... "Yeah," I repeat, "I want to," because my stupid feelings are working against me. I wonder if this is how Ren's felt all this time, trying to be my best friend while simultaneously being in love with me. It sure is confusing.

"Okay," Ren says slowly, but he's grinning. He doesn't grin all that often, so I feel giddy knowing I'm making him smile that big. I want to kiss that smile.

Instead, I reach up and brush his hair out of his face. For a second, I cup his cheek, and I just stare at the way the skin under my fingers goes pink. Then I take a step back.

"We just need to Restore the Light," I say. "Then we can concentrate on us."

Ren's smile disappears. He nods, short. "Right," he says, except he sounds far away. I don't worry about it too much. He's waited this long to be with me; I'm sure he can deal with waiting a bit more.

CHAPTER 17

VELOREN

We're outside the Darkness.

I wouldn't know that had it not been announced when we'd landed beside it. We're about thirty paces from its edge, and I know I'll be able to feel it the second we step in — the crawling sensation, the unease. The rest of them won't realize, though. Not when they can't see it.

Right now, it's impossible to tell where the Darkness is through sight alone. That's part of the reason why it thrives so well in Cova. While the Darkness is impenetrable to sunlight, the moon goes through it with ease, and since moonlight never gets into Cova, the Darkness is never weakened.

I'd never been able to figure out why that was. It was easy to assume it was just some sort of flaw, maybe the Darkness' one weakness. But now, I'm not so sure. I think it might be some sort of final punishment. Night's daughter buried her son when she saw he had the Darkness within him, and now the Darkness is vulnerable at nighttime. It just seems oddly fitting, in a sad way.

Except there is no night underground. No day. Just the Darkness and us Covans subjected to it. We haven't always lived this way, though, which is how I figure our nation got entangled with the descendants of the Light in the first place.

I want to say that I can't be a descendant. That Theodore's completely wrong, letting his imagination get away from him as usual, but…

He's lucky. That's the only way I can explain it. All his life, he's been lucky. Sure, he's faced tragedy — his parents' death, having to raise his little brother, being exiled — but it's not rare for things to go his way. That's why he can find and befriend an Avis on a normal day in Silva. Why he can come home with an early paycheck, having somehow convinced his boss he was deserving of it. That's why he can be best friends with someone descended from the Light completely unwittingly, only to discover it's true exactly when he needs it to be.

I never would've thought I might be a descendant if it didn't just so happen to fit perfectly into Theodore's narrative.

I still don't know what I'm going to do. We've been here for hours, night having fallen long ago, and they've been talking and talking this entire time, debating every possibility of how I might Restore the Light while I sit here, panicking.

My mother's words run through my head. *Escape this Darkness, Veloren. There's no destroying it. Not without dooming our people.*

What had she known that I don't? *How* had she known it? If only she were still around now. I wish I could talk to her, ask her what to do.

I don't want to doom my people. I don't want to subject them to more pain and suffering. But Theodore… he needs to get home to Hector. And Stars, everything he said to me… it feels like a dream.

Or a nightmare.

I can have everything I've always wanted, so long as I go against everything my morals are telling me.

"Yeah, I say we give it a try," Theodore says. I sit up straight, realizing I've tuned them out again.

"What are we doing?" I ask, panicking. I still haven't thought of any excuses. Any way to get out of this.

"We're gonna go in," Will says. "We can't see the Darkness right now, so we don't need to worry about those creatures you guys came across last time."

"And what are we doing once we're in there?" I say.

"Meditating," says Theodore. "But that's just our plan for now, you know? It might take us a couple nights to come up with anything better. And if that really doesn't work, we'll need to start thinking about venturing into the Darkness during the day, but that's a problem for future us."

I don't argue. I can't anymore, not without my reluctance becoming suspicious. I'm the only one who doesn't want this, and besides just thinking I'm scared, soon they might realize I have more important reasons for having avoided the Darkness all this time.

My friends are moving, so I stand up and walk with them. Icarus hangs back, clearly unsettled by the Darkness as well. I wonder if she can feel it like I can.

"So you'll just sit down and concentrate," Theodore says to me, sounding encouraging. And what could be the harm in that, right? I can sit and concentrate. I can't possibly harm any Covans that way.

Maybe Mom was wrong. Maybe destroying the Darkness won't hurt our people. Maybe she didn't know as much as I know now — she never traveled around and learned all the stuff I did, right?

I shiver when we cross into the Darkness. I can feel it around me, like a shift in the atmosphere. It feels slightly heavier, like it's just barely pressing down on me. Like there's something watching me, like I'm not quite alone.

"Do you think we're in it yet?" Will says.

"Yes," I say. My friends fall silent. I think they're startled.

"Here should be good, then," Theodore says weakly, and I hear him drop to the ground. I sit down beside him, and I fight to keep my expression blank when he momentarily places his hand on my knee, squeezing slightly before releasing it. "Just try, okay?" he says to me, and he sounds so hopeful that I can't possibly say no.

"Okay," I say, and I swear I can hear the smile in the breath he releases. Will and Eleanor sit down beside us and I close my eyes. I place my hands in my lap and concentrate.

Darkness.

We're in the Darkness, and I can feel it. It's all around me, moving and roiling in an invisible wind, brushing past me, sounding around me in echoes. I think I'm hearing things.

Concentrate.

Think about meditating. About the Darkness. About Theodore and Restoring the light, about Hector and the Covans.

Light.

Descendants of the Light, combatants of the Darkness. Their blood that might run in my veins. No, it *does* run in my veins — believe it. I can't hurt my people by trying. By just thinking. Meditating.

Concentrate.

It's all around me. It wants to consume me. Centuries ago, it stole the eyesight of my ancestors. Those born from Day. Those who belonged in the abovelands, in the sun — blinded. Forced underground. Forced to toil against Darkness.

Darkness.

Not extending from the ground, not a series of saplings spreading in the wind, but *roots*, growing and stretching within the earth, its reach larger and deadlier than ever imaginable.

Concentrate.

Light, light, light. Only those descended from it can put a stop to the Darkness. But how? We can't even see it. Have lived amongst it for centuries. How could we possible fight something that's *everywhere*?

Concentrate.

Think nothing at all. That's how you meditate, right?

I try to stop thinking. Stop hearing. I ignore the sounds of my friends, shifting in the grass beside me, occasionally whispering to one another. I ignore the thoughts that try to venture through my mind, of Light and Darkness and ancestors and abandoned homes. I concentrate on my breathing, on the feeling of air in my nose and lungs. Of the feeling of the earth underneath me, and the feeling of air — no, Darkness — all around me. Pressing down on me.

I concentrate on nothing but what I feel.

And then I see it.

No, *really*. It's a hallucination, I'm sure, something just embedded in my mind, but it's there.

Theodore's explained the concept of seeing to me before. I can make sense of it in that way, as words and ideas, but it's still hard to understand. After all, how can you understand something you've never experienced? How could I possibly explain the concept of hearing or smelling to someone who's never done it before?

So I can get that there's *something* I'm missing out on. Some sense that lets people communicate in ways I can't, that lets them know where things are in relation to themselves.

With that understanding, I assume that right now, I'm seeing. In the distance, something's *there*. And I can't hear it, should have no way of knowing about its existence, and yet I do. The presence of it makes my eyes ache. That's seeing, right?

I stand up, and I walk toward it. My legs feel like jelly, or maybe the ground feels like jelly, and I wonder if any of this is even happening at all.

"Hello?" I call out, and my voice echoes all around me. I realize I can't hear anything else. Not the sound of grass shifting with the presence of insects. Not my friends beside me, breathing and existing. It's just me and this jelly ground and this painful — my mind grasps for a word, a way to describe something I've never experienced before — *light*. That must be what this is. "Is anyone there?"

Of course we're here.

I stumble, falling to my hands and knees. I didn't think those words, and yet they were inside my head, whispered as if they were thoughts of my own.

"Who are you?" I ask. I'm still on the ground, because even when I was walking, I was getting no closer to the light in the distance.

Your ancestors. The descendants.

I feel myself gaping. Can this be real? I know I sat down with this purpose, tried to convince myself that I was a descendant, but it's actually true?

"I didn't realize I was a descendant of the Light," I say weakly. No matter how quietly I speak, my voice echoes as if I've shouted.

No? The voice says. *You don't remember us?*

And just like that, clouds part in my mind, sudden understanding shining through them. I remember leaving Cova, stumbling out of the tunnel and drowning in panic and confusion, having no idea where to go or what to do. I was without parents and all on my own. Having no idea where to go hadn't made matters any better.

Some place with noise. The thought had rung through my mind with sudden clarity, and I'd known it was right. I needed someplace loud enough to drown out my own thoughts, to stop everything that had just happened to me from replaying in my mind. *Silva.*

I'd never realized that those thoughts hadn't been mine at all. My ancestors must've been communicating with me, planting the ideas in my head. How had I not noticed? It's thanks to them that I found Silva. That I found *Theodore.*

Yes, the voice says. *We've helped you in the past.*

I wonder if that's the only time they've helped me. What if they've stepped in at other times? Intervened without me ever realizing?

"Why me?" I ask. "What about the other descendants?"

A pause. And then, *You're the last,* the voice says, sounding solemn. *The last of our kind, of those with Light running through their veins. We've taken great interest in you, Veloren.*

261

This is insane. Like, actually insane. I'm really the last one? The last chance the world has at destroying the Darkness? Panic rises up in my chest, sudden and overwhelming. I can feel it in my throat, restricting my airway, making me dizzy. "Can you help me?" I blurt out.

Can you help yourself?

"I... I don't know," I whisper. "My friends need me to destroy the Darkness."

Your friends need you to. Not you?

"I don't know," I say again. I feel like I don't know anything, now that I'm here. "I don't know if it'll hurt my people. I don't know if my mom's right or if Theodore's right."

This decision must be your own, says the voice. *Is destroying anything you didn't create moral?*

"Help me," I say. "I don't know what to do."

You must make this decision on your own. The voice reiterates. *However, we can offer you this much to consider: what is light without darkness?*

What is light without darkness... is it anything? Was that supposed to be a warning? Or just some kind of backwards encouragement? If they're referring to me as Light... I don't need the Darkness. I've never needed it. I'd gladly get rid of it, if I didn't think it would hurt my people somehow.

But what if that's not what they mean? Light without Darkness... it *can't* be anything. It's just like love without hate, or good without bad. It needs that balance. Are they trying to say I'll cease to exist if I destroy the Darkness?

Listen, the voice tells me. So I do. I'm listening — waiting for them to give me more useful information, hopefully, when I hear it. It sounds far away, but not like another echo. It's just in the distance.

"What is that?"

"I don't know. Where do you think it goes?"

"I can't see anything down there, it's so dark."

"We should go in."

"And leave Ren here? No way."

That's Theodore, I realize. All my friends. What are they talking about?

Concentrate.

"Just looking down there is giving me the creeps."

"It almost… looks like it's moving."

"Will, get away from there."

I gasp, realization flooding in, and the light rushes away from me, farther and farther, smaller and smaller. It's dark again, and the air is heavy with Darkness, and I can hear the grass and my friends. My friends, who are no longer next to me but far away.

I stumble to my feet and my worst fears are proven true. I can feel the difference in the ground, the Covan entrance that they're gathered around, that extends underground and continues for miles and miles in every direction. The entrance that the Darkness originates from, that it's currently hiding in, out of the way of the moonlight.

"Ren!" Theodore says, seeing me. "You're back! You were glowing when you meditated, did you realize that? It was like you couldn't hear anything we were saying! Did you do it? Did you Restore the Light?"

I was glowing? Stars, that's not good. I definitely can't lie about what happened now. "Not yet," I say. "It was weird. And complicated."

"Don't worry, you can try again later," Will says reassuringly. He pats me on the arm.

"Yeah," I say, distracted.

"Ren, check this out!" Theodore says, and he grabs me and pulls me forward. "There's a hole in the ground here. Can you feel it?" he asks.

"Yeah," I say. This is bad.

"Maybe this is where the baby was planted," Theodore says, excited. "The Darkness baby."

"Ew," says Eleanor. "Don't call it that."

"This looks kind of familiar," Will says. *No, no, no,* I think.

"Right?" Eleanor says. "Kind of like that hole we came out of when we were kidnapped."

"You guys came out of a hole?" says Theodore.

"Yeah, Ren led us around underground," Eleanor explains. My heart stops. My blood slows to a crawl in my veins.

"There were just… tunnels? Underground?"

"We wound up in Cova," Will says. "Right, Ren? You said there were entrances all over the place." Fuck. Why did I ever tell them that? They never would've known we were in Cova had I said nothing.

"Yeah," I say weakly. Maybe they won't see the connection. Won't realize that the Darkness is coming from Cova, that I've known this all my life.

"Maybe this is an entrance to Cova, too," Will suggests.

Shut up, I think at him. *Just shut up, Will, be quiet.*

"That can't be good," Eleanor says. "It's right in this dark patch. Do you think the Darkness could get into Cova that way?"

"Huh," Theodore says. He's thinking about it. And he doesn't give himself enough credit. He's always saying I'm the smart one, but it's him. He makes connections that other people wouldn't. Sees things from perspectives that others don't. "Wait," he says suddenly. "If it got into Cova, it could spread down there, and then come out somewhere else. Right?"

"Maybe," says Will.

"Ren?" says Theodore.

"Maybe," I choke out, crossing my arms. *Please don't press me on it.* Can Theodore see through me? He has this horrible habit of knowing what I'm thinking, what I'm feeling. Can he see my guilt? My apprehension?

"Yeah, maybe it isn't down there," Theodore says quietly, thinking it over. *Yes*, I encourage him silently. "But I could go check," he blurts.

"*What?*" says Eleanor.

"I could just walk in," Theodore says. "I'll know if it's down there if I suddenly can't see anymore."

"But if it really is the Darkness, won't there be creatures?" Will points out, sounding frantic. I'm panicking. My heart is loud in my ears, but not loud enough to muffle what Theodore says next.

"We need to check," he says, brushing Will off. "Besides, it's probably not even down there. I'm sure Ren would've realized by now if it were, since he can feel it."

My whole body feels like lead. Stiff and unmoving. What can I do? What can I say? Stars, am I even breathing?

"Theo, I don't know if this is a good idea…" Eleanor says, reluctant.

"Sure it is!" Theodore argues. "I'll just be in and out, I promise."

And then he starts walking, heading straight toward the hole. The creatures will be able to tell he's an intruder, I just know it. He'll walk differently than we do. Slow and unsure. His breathing will be different — faster, panicked. They'll hear him from a mile away, and they'll descend on him. They'll rip into him and tear him to shreds. They'll kill him just like they killed my parents.

My whole body jumps into action. I'm running before I even have a chance to process it, my fingers curling around Theodore's wrist. "Don't!" I say, cold all over.

When Theodore speaks, his voice is hard. Distant. I know at once that I've made a mistake. That he was bluffing, playing me like only he could. Of course he noticed something was off with me. Of course he picked up on my unease.

"Why not, Ren?" he says coldly. "Know something I don't?"

I swallow. Fuck. All this time, I've kept it from him. Why did I have to slip up now? What's he going to think?

Eleanor and Will are silent. I think they realize that something's going on. Something bad. Something big.

"I'm sorry," I blurt out. I'm still holding onto his wrist, I realize, and I let go of it in favor of wringing my hands together. "Theodore, there is Darkness in Cova."

I expect silence to fall, or for my friends to gasp, but Theodore just continues, taking my admittance in stride.

"And you didn't think that information was worth sharing?" he scoffs. "That's *pretty big*, Ren."

"I know," I say. "I'm sorry."

"Why wouldn't you tell me?" he demands. "What reason do you have for keeping it from us?"

"Theo, I don't think we would've figured anything out any faster..." Eleanor says timidly, peacekeeping.

Theodore ignores her. It doesn't matter that the information wouldn't have told him how to Restore the Light. It's the fact that I had information he didn't and kept it from him. We both know that.

"Theodore..." I say.

"My *brother* is waiting for me in Silva, *alone*," he rants, his voice shaking with anger. My throat feels completely dry. "Why didn't you say anything?!"

"I-I forgot—"

"Bullshit," Theodore interrupts me. "Try again." I've seen him mad before, but his anger's never been directed at me. I feel like I'm melting under his fury.

"I couldn't tell you, okay?!" I finally say, and the words drag the air from my lungs, leaving me standing there, breathless.

"*Why!*" Theodore roars, and he steps toward me. I stumble backwards, but he reaches me. His hands fist in my shirt and hold me there. "Tell me, Ren."

"Because…" I whisper, and I utter the secret that I've kept this entire time, the one I so foolishly thought I wouldn't have to forfeit. "I don't want to Restore the Light."

And now silence does fall. It's even heavier than the Darkness. It's suffocating, and I feel like I'm choking on it. Can anyone else breathe, right now?

I rush to explain, because no one's demanding answers, but surely they must want them? I can make them understand. "It'll hurt my people, Theodore," I say, my words rushed and combining together. "Destroying the Darkness… it'll hurt Covans. My mom told me that years ago."

Theodore's still silent. Still holding onto my shirt. I turn toward Eleanor and Will, hopefully looking at least one of them in the eye. I plead, "Can't you understand? I wanted to find some other way. To contain it, maybe…"

"You don't love me," Theodore says. It's quiet. Barely audible. I hear it anyway, and I flinch in shock.

"What?" I say. It comes out as a whisper.

"You don't love me," Theodore repeats, louder this time. And then he yells. "And I'll *never* love you," my breath catches in my throat, sticks there. "You weren't avoiding the Darkness because you were scared, or because you thought you weren't a descendant. You just didn't want to help me! You never wanted to help me!"

"Of course I want to help you—"

"Shut up!" he screams. "You don't care about me. You don't care about Hector! You only care about *yourself!*"

"That's not true!" I argue.

"I don't need you," he says suddenly, and he sounds calm again, farther away despite the fact that he's just right there. His voice is low with rage. "I learned as much as I did without your help. I can Restore the Light on my own, too."

"Theodore, you can't," I say. "You were right, I am a descendant. But there's more to it than that. There's a balance — what's light without darkness?"

"Stop spewing nonsense at me," Theodore snaps. "You're still just trying to stop me! I need to get back to Hector, not that you care."

"I do care!" I sob. It's only then that I realize I'm crying. How could I have done this? How have I managed to so royally screw things up? "We can't just destroy the Darkness, there'll be consequences!" Because I'm sure of it now. That's what that voice was trying to convey to me.

Theodore scoffs. It's not just that he doesn't believe me, it's that he doesn't even *want* to. I've annihilated the trust he had for me.

"Eleanor, Will," Theodore says. "You don't need to follow me if you don't want to. I know it'll be dangerous. Icarus will take you guys home, if you ask her." With that, he starts in the direction of Cova's entrance. I go after him. "Don't follow me, Ren," he bites out. And I don't know what to do. I have to follow him, right? I can't just let him go in there. But if he keeps yelling at me, he'll just attract the creatures even sooner. Which way is safer for him?

Without another word, he's gone. He'd charged right into the tunnel as I'd stood here, debating with myself. I feel sick to my stomach, and then I realize I'm sobbing, loud and uneven, my lungs aching because I can't get enough air.

Eleanor hugs me. Her hair's all in my face. "I wish you'd told us sooner, Ren," she whispers. "I'll try to keep him safe in there, okay?"

"Th-the creatures," I stammer. "They'll know you're not Covan! They'll kill you!"

"We'll be careful," Will says. His hand is on my back. How long has it been there?

"My m-mom," I say. "*She* was careful..."

"Your mom…" Eleanor breathes, but I don't really hear her. I'm shaking in her arms. Theodore's all alone in that tunnel and I'm nowhere near him. I can't keep him safe. What am I going to do?

"Help him," I beg, and I start speaking faster, desperate. "You have to walk confidently in the tunnels. Only touch the walls when you have to, or they'll know. If they find out you're not Covan, run. Find the nearest exit you can. Turn left at every corner and you'll come across one eventually."

"Okay," Eleanor says. She sounds afraid, and I think it's because she's picking up on my own fear. I feel her lips press against my cheek, and her hand briefly brushes through my hair, and then she steps away from me. Will does too.

They both walk into the tunnel, and I collapse to my knees, shaking. Everything, everything is ruined. What in the world have I done?

CHAPTER 18

THEO

I shouldn't be so surprised by how dark it is down here. I should also probably be more scared than I am. Except I can't feel anything except anger. Betrayal.

I'm marching down Cova's tunnels, fury fueling my body. I swear things have passed by me — creatures of some sort, surely — but they haven't bothered me. I don't know why and I'm not questioning it, too busy thinking about Ren to concentrate on anything else.

Ren, who betrayed me. Ren, who I thought was firmly on my side, who I thought I could always depend on, who was secretly working against me this entire time.

"Theo!" someone calls, and I stop in my tracks. It was Eleanor's voice, and I feel a sense of relief flood through me. Somewhere in the back of my mind, I was hoping I would be followed. I'm not exactly sure what I'm going to do down here, but I'm desperate, and I'm thankful that I'm not alone.

"Eleanor?" I call back.

"Wait up!" she says, and then two pairs of footsteps run toward me. For a second I panic, thinking it might be Ren with her, but Will calls out a greeting when they're close enough. Good. Ren should know better than to follow me when I feel like this.

"What are we going to do?" Will asks as I start walking again. I have no idea where I'm going, no idea where anything is, and no idea how Ren ever lived like this. How he *still* lives like this.

Stop thinking about Ren.

"We're going to Restore the Light," I say, all false confidence. It can't be that hard. Five minutes of sitting with his legs crossed and his eyes closed and Ren started glowing. That just makes anger pulse through me again, hot and fresh. To think that it was really as easy as I wanted it to be, that I was right about Ren all along, and that he betrayed me. I don't think I've ever been so hurt.

Because underneath my front — and that's all my anger is, a front — I'm *hurt*. My best friend, the boy who says he's in love with me, withheld vital information this entire time. He listened to me talk about missing Silva and my fears for my little brother and said *nothing*. He knew about the Darkness, about its presence in Cova, about its connection to his people, probably, and he just let me go on this wild goose chase from nation to nation in a desperate scramble for any scrap of information that could get me closer to Restoring the Light.

The crap he said didn't even register in my mind, not really. Something about disrupting the balance. Something about Covans. Something about, *you were right, I am a Descendant*.

Stop thinking about Ren.

"We need to be careful," Eleanor says, her voice level. "Ren said the creatures will attack us if they realize we aren't Covan, so we need to walk confidently."

"Got it," I say coolly. I ignore the niggling sense of panic and doubt trying to spring forth in my mind. I know Ren's right about Cova, however much I might not want him to be. If he says the creatures are down here and want to kill us, then they're down here and want to kill us.

It's hard to figure out what we're going to do when we can't talk about it. I can tell we're all thinking the same thing — that the creatures might hear us and understand us — so we stay silent. The farther we walk, the more unsure I become. This was probably a huge mistake, charging down here in the wake of my anger, but it was all I'd been able to think of doing in the moment. I thought I'd get down here, beat up some imaginary source of the Darkness, and return to Silva a hero.

Plus, now that I'm on high alert about the creatures, I swear I can hear them. Sense them. They haven't tried to kill us yet, so I assume we're playing the part of diligent Covans walking-home-from-wherever-Covans-go pretty well.

We can't keep walking forever, though. And I'm just about to risk speaking, suggesting that we find somewhere to stop, when I hear voices. None of us mention it, knowing doing so would make us seem out of place, but I keep walking toward them despite getting the feeling that Eleanor and Will want to go a different way.

I don't know if my senses are adjusting to being in complete darkness — I think hours have passed, and my aching feet can definitely attest to how far we've walked — but when we get closer to the voices, I *feel* the room open up. We're no longer in a small hallway but a spacious room, and I pull Eleanor and Will into it with me. I think it's some kind of park or public space, which is exactly what I was hoping for.

"Come on," I say, confident we'll be much safer here. As long as we don't start stumbling into people, that is. Everyone here can clearly navigate just fine — I can hear kids shouting and running around as they play — so we need to stay out of their way if we don't want to blow our cover. I end up leading Eleanor and Will farther into the area while sticking to the wall, and eventually I just sit down and lean against it. I hope it's not totally out of character for a Covan to do that, but I have no real way of knowing.

"What are we going to do here?" Eleanor murmurs. I'm glad she's talking quietly because I'm suddenly unsettlingly aware of how much better everyone else's hearing is around here. If any of them concentrate on our conversation, they'll probably be able to hear it. Knowing that, I decide to talk in code.

"I just want to sit and meditate for a little," I say, hoping they'll understand.

"Really? But you're not—" Will begins, before I interrupt him.

"A dedicated meditator? No. But I figure it can't hurt to give it a try," I say with a laugh.

"Actually, I was going to say—"

"That I should leave the meditating to our friend? Well, he's not here right now. And I don't exactly trust him to meditate, anyway," I add darkly.

"Oh!" Will says in sudden understanding.

"You know, I don't think *meditation* is something anyone can do," Eleanor says.

"Just let me try," I snap, and my friends fall silent, thankfully. I breathe out slowly, crossing my legs and folding my hands in my lap. I try to remember what Ren looked like, if he did anything special, but he just looked like Ren.

At first, he'd just sat there, obviously uncomfortable and aware of our attention on him, but as time had passed, he'd relaxed. That scrunch in his brow had smoothed out, his expression clearing, and every line of tension in his body had disappeared. Not too long after that, he'd started glowing.

I try to imitate him now. I try to concentrate, to clear my mind and find peace or whatever the hell it is you're supposed to do when you meditate.

Everything just seems louder.

Kids are laughing as they play, calling each other's names, breathless and excited, their feet smacking on the ground as they run. Adults talk, their voices level and calm, their laughs ringing out like my parents' used to through the house, their words falling hushed whenever some sort of gossip arises.

Concentrate.

Everything's so loud. Except for my friends — they're quiet. Or they're trying to be. Their voices are still distracting, though.

"Do you think he'll be able to do it?" Will says, hushed.

"No. I think Ren wasn't lying about being a *you-know-what.*"

"Me neither. I think we need him."

"We don't need him," I snap, making both Eleanor and Will gasp. "And can you guys shut up? I'm trying to concentrate."

So I keep sitting there. And I keep concentrating. I focus on my breathing, and then I focus on the ambience, and then I focus on begging the Stars to give me *something, anything, please*, but nothing happens.

"Theo," Eleanor says quietly. "It's been an hour. I think it's time we try something else."

I huff, frustrated, before pulling my knees up to my chest and burying my face in them. My whole body shakes and it takes everything in me not to start crying. I feel so defeated. Hopeless. What in the world am I going to do?

Only Ren can do whatever meditating thing he did. And only he can Restore the Light. But he's not willing to do it, which means it's never going to happen, and I'm never going to get to live in Silva again. At this point, it seems like my only choice is going to be sneaking Hector out somehow. I'll have to pull him out of school, disrupt his education, and find a place for us to live somewhere else. Our savings from Silva will be made useless with us traveling illegally, which means we'll have to start anew. We could either settle down somewhere in Askund, where documentation and licenses don't matter, or we could sneak into someplace like Udula or Ilma and try to make a new life there. We could get illegal jobs; ones you don't need to be an actual citizen to get.

But no, Ilma's totally out of the question. We'd constantly be on our toes, worried about having our secret living situation discovered. That means it'll be Udula for us, unless Eleanor can pull some strings and get us a citizenship in Volant, although even that doesn't sound very likely.

Stars, everything's going to be so different. Hector's going to hate me. Silva is our *home*, I doubt he'd ever want to leave, and I'd be forcing him to. Not to mention the fact that I'll have to break the news about Ren to him. I'll have to explain why we're not living with him anymore, why we no longer talk to him.

And then there's my own feelings to deal with.

Maybe I can get over them in time, can squash down what Ren's helped grow, the seeds he's planted. The entire forests I've stumbled across, bewildered over the fact that I'd never seen them before.

Maybe I can destroy those, can start fires and raze the copse of feelings. But even if I manage that, there's no getting rid of the land they grew on. The soil that nurtured them. There's no getting rid of the years of friendship and love I have for Ren, no matter how badly I might want to.

And Stars, do I want to. Maybe I'm being irrational right now, anger and adrenaline still coursing through my veins, but I don't see how I'm supposed to forgive him after this. I never would've thought he could work against me, could hurt me so badly that I'd abandon him in the middle of a field, surrounded by absolutely nothing familiar, and yet here we are.

"Theo," Eleanor says softly. "Are you okay?"

I shake my head against my knees. No, I'm not okay. I abandoned my best friend. And he betrayed me. Everything's different and horrible and the last thing I should want right now is to fall into Ren's arms and hug him into oblivion, and yet…

"Yes," I say, and I pride myself on the fact that my voice doesn't shake. "Just need to keep thinking, is all."

"We'll figure something out," Will assures me. His hand lands in my hair. I think he was aiming for my knee, but given the fact that I'm using my knees as a face-rest…

"Yeah," I sigh. "We'll figure something out."

We're lost. Of course, we've kind of been lost ever since we entered these damned tunnels, but now we're *really* lost. I think it's night time, because we've stopped coming across other people so often, so I figure it's just us and those heading to their homes, now. Except we have nowhere to go, which means we might be discovered soon. How odd is it for Covans to still be out in the middle of the night?

"Good evening," says a Covan as he passes us. That's been happening a lot, because Covans are really friendly. They greet everybody they walk past — maybe because anyone you pass could be someone you know — and some even start up little conversations, the kind that leave you feeling warm inside, realizing just how much you love people and all the little things they do.

"Good evening," the three of us chorus politely. I wonder if he can hear the smile in my voice. Somehow, general pleasantries are bringing up my mood.

And then three, four, five paces behind us...

"Good evening," the man says again.

"Good evening," another man grunts in return.

I don't stumble, don't come to a complete stop, but I feel my expression morph into a glare. That didn't sound like Ren, not really, but if Ren were following us, it would make sense that he'd try to disguise his voice. Apparently, he's not very good at it.

"Well," I say to my friends, suddenly sure that Ren is behind us. "I guess it's time to tell you guys."

"What?" Eleanor says, sounding confused. I don't blame her. We haven't really been talking much, but I hadn't suspected Ren of trailing after us before now. Did he just *leave* Icarus? That bastard. She's probably worried and scared, sitting up there all on her own.

I want to hurt him. I think I might have already — I can hardly remember the things I yelled at him — but I don't feel done yet. "That I'm officially on the market," I say, straining my ears for any noises from the person behind us. A gasp, maybe. "You know, now that Ren's betrayed me, I want to start getting out there. Find out what it's really like to be loved by someone."

"Really?" Will says, bewildered. "I got the feeling you liked him back, Theo."

I scoff. "No way," I say, rolling my eyes for no-one's benefit but mine.

"You're just hurt right now," Eleanor says. "Even if you don't have romantic feelings for Ren, you *do* love him. You two will make up after this."

"Don't count on it," I mutter.

A second of silence passes between us.

"I won't let you visit my castle if you and Ren aren't friends anymore," Eleanor says.

I gasp, offended, and behind us, there's a snicker. I spin on my heel.

"Give it up, Ren!" I shout. "I know you're following us!"

"Well *excuse me* for trying to keep you from getting yourself killed," Ren snaps.

"You should've just let it happen," I seethe. "Then you wouldn't have to worry about whether you're betraying anybody."

Ren groans, clearly frustrated. Good. That's better than having to see him cry again — or hear it, in this case. A vindictive part of me had relished in making him cry, but a much bigger part had wanted to make it stop, to just drop the whole thing.

"Stop arguing," Will says.

"I'll stop arguing when Ren stops being a horrible friend," I say snidely.

"Restoring the Light meant *hurting* Covans!" Ren roars, and I remember him saying that earlier, but I hadn't wanted to believe it. I still don't.

"Guys!" Will says.

We ignore him.

"You could've told me that!" I say. "We could've looked for a different solution *together*."

"Are you kidding?" Ren scoffs. "You're so stubborn — you really think you would've accepted that? That you wouldn't have just been mad at me for even suggesting we not Restore the Light?"

"You *guys*."

"Of course I wouldn't!" I say. Except I'm not entirely sure. I mean, I totally would've been freaked out. I would've panicked and wondered what to do about Hector, for sure, but I don't think I would've turned on Ren. Not if he'd just come out and told me the truth.

"*GUYS*," Eleanor and Will roar, their voices echoing down the tunnel.

"*What?*" I say, just as I hear Ren suck in a breath.

"I just… feel like we're not alone," Will says.

Silence falls. We all pause, standing there completely still, hardly daring to breathe. My throat feels tight, and my eyes search uselessly through the dark for any sign of the creatures.

"Ren?" I question quietly, our argument momentarily forgotten.

"He's right," Ren says. The hairs stand up all over my body. My skin feels itchy, all the sudden, like I can feel their eyes on me, except I know that's illogical. I don't think they can see, either. "We're not alone."

"What are we going to do?" Eleanor whispers.

I hear something. The shuffle of a footstep. And then, to our other side, the eerie clicking sound they make. They're growing restless.

"*Run*," Ren says, and in the next moment, my hand is in his, his warm fingers laced with mine, my calloused palm pressed to his. I reach for whoever else's hand — Eleanor, maybe — and then Ren's pulling us along. I think we're all holding onto someone, hopefully.

"Where are we going?" I demand, struggling not to trip over my own feet as we keep up with Ren's unrelenting pace. Behind us, the sound of clicking explodes, and it follows after us like a tsunami. I get this horrible mental image of the creatures crawling along the walls and ceiling after us.

"Anywhere!" Ren gasps.

We take turns at random, or maybe Ren actually knows where he's going. To me, we're sprinting through a landscape of nothingness, being yanked around corners that aren't really there as monsters plucked straight from a nightmare follow after us.

Will cries out suddenly and my stomach turns over. Wordlessly, we speed up, but it's no use. The creatures are faster than us, and soon we're not so much evading them as just running into them, body slamming the creatures and yanking each other around them as we continue to run. Several have touched me, and a few even managing to get their claws on me, but so far none of them have gotten me like they did last time. I figure as long as we can stay out of their grasp, keep them from sinking their claws in to the bone, we'll be fine.

It's impossible to keep running. They're everywhere, the presence of them so thick, their clicking so loud, that I know there's nowhere else to go. This won't work.

"Ren!" I say. "You have to destroy the Darkness!"

"I can't!" Ren shouts, sounding angered even in his exhaustion.

"If you don't, we'll all die!" I say, and Ren stumbles. I got through to him. He knows I'm right.

"How am I supposed to meditate like this?" he demands.

"We'll hold them back," I say, despite my uncertainty. "Just do it as fast as you can, okay?"

"Fine," Ren pants, except he keeps running just a little bit more, and then he yanks us around one last corner. It sounds different, like we're not in a hallway anymore, and somehow none of the creatures are in here yet. I think we're in a room. My thoughts are confirmed when a door slams shut behind us, and then the sound of a lock clicks into place.

"Where are we?" I say.

"My house," Ren says, panting. He brushes past me. I don't have the presence of mind to snap at him when he squeezes my elbow as he does.

"Your *house?*" I say, incredulous, but Ren doesn't respond. I think he might be sitting already, trying to meditate. The creatures are outside the door, throwing their bodies at it from the sound of things, but nothing could hope to obscure the sound of their monstrous clicking.

"We're all gonna die," Will announces.

"No we're not," Eleanor assures him. "Just let Ren concentrate."

So we let Ren concentrate. For about ten seconds, that is, and then the door gives.

Automatically, I retreat toward Ren. He's sitting against the back wall, and me, Eleanor, and Will gather in a half circle around him. I have nothing but my hands to fight off the creatures, but I do my best. They grab for me and I shove them away. They try to get past me — maybe smarter than we realized, having figured out what Ren is up to — but I kick them back.

It's exhausting, not to mention terrifying. They're stronger than me, and while it seems like I'm not actually their intended target, several of them end up scratching me in their attempts to get to Ren. It's not made easier by the fact that I can't see any of them, can't defend myself or attack until they've already gotten to me.

Hurry, Ren, I think at him.

And then he starts glowing. I didn't think it was possible — no light is supposed to be able to penetrate the Darkness — but Ren's sitting there, glowing like the moon as if the laws of nature don't apply to him. My eyes adjust slowly, and finally I can take in the room, can see my friends and Ren. His whole body is lit up, but it's his eyes that are really glowing. I thought they'd be closed, but they're wide open despite the fact that I know he's not really seeing any of us. He seems far away.

The creatures don't want to get any closer to Ren's light, which I'm thankful for, because they're even more terrifying now that I can see them. They're all hunched over, their bodies jutting out in weird places and their gray skin stretched over the protrusions. Their arms are longer than their legs, dangling toward the ground, but it's their knife-sized claws that actually drag against it.

Lastly, their faces. Something I keep trying not to look at but my eyes are darting toward anyway. Their eyes are milky white, as unseeing as anything else down here, and they have beaks like a bird, protruding far out of their faces, yet still lined with teeth. Beaks snap and click as the creatures circle around us, moving endlessly but not daring to get any closer with this light pouring off of Ren.

The three of us shrink closer to him, panting and bleeding, and I try not to let the horror of the situation make my legs collapse out from under me. There's *so many* of them. Not just in the room, and not just on the ground, but still flooding in from the door, shifting and shoving their way through each other. They climb on the walls and the ceiling, just like the grotesque image I'd had in my mind only minutes ago. Only our tiny ring of light remains free of their presence, and even then I'm not sure how long it will last. They keep trying to edge closer, clicking furiously whenever they step into the light.

"Hurry, Ren," I urge him, aloud this time. He's sitting completely still, his eyes swallowed in light, and I step closer to him, letting my leg brush against his arm. I'm not quite sure which one of us it's supposed to comfort.

VELOREN

It was difficult getting here. Almost impossible to concentrate with everything happening — not only because of the sheer noise of it all, but also because of all my feelings. The panic, the desperation, the pain.

I shoved it all away though, struggling to concentrate, to think of nothing. And then, finally — the light. This time I didn't hesitate. I leapt to my feet and raced toward it, panting and calling out as I ran.

"I'm ready!" I shout now, stumbling over my feet on the jelly ground. The last time I was here, I felt oddly disconnected from everything around me, including my feelings. Now, the urgency of the situation remains. "I've made my decision! I'm ready!"

You are? the voice says.

"Yes!" I pant. "I need to destroy the Darkness! How do I do it?"

The voice remains silent. I just stand there, shaking and scared and impatient, when it finally responds. *Veloren*, it says. *Your decision is disappointing.*

I gape. "You said it was mine to make!"

And yet you did not make it, the voice says. *This decision wasn't yours.*

"Maybe not," I admit. "But we'll die here if I don't do it. I need to destroy the Darkness."

So you no longer fear for the lives of your people? You admit that your own life is more important than theirs?

"What? No!" I say. "That's not true—"

What would you do if we told you that destroying the Darkness would be the same as killing them? That the disruption of balance between Dark and Light would be their death sentence; that those who have their whole lives down here, who live and love and exist as vibrantly as you ever have, will perish. Does your decision remain the same?

My answer dies in my throat. My body feels weak. So Mom was right, huh? Destroying the Darkness is the same as destroying our people. I can either kill them, *all of them*, to save my friends, or sacrifice our lives for the rest of my people.

It's a no brainer. I think I'll just sit here forever. Wait for it to happen. That way I won't have to watch my friends die. Maybe I won't even feel it.

"Is there nothing I can do?" I whisper, defeated. The light grows a little more intense, and my eyes ache. I want it to leave again. I just want it to just be me and the nothingness I know.

There is one thing, Veloren Selcouth, it tells me. *Because there is a difference between destroying the Darkness and Restoring the Light. But you must understand that there will be consequences.*

My heart leaps. "What?" I say. "What can I do?" I'm growing more desperate now, because I think I can hear my friends. I think they're shouting, and I don't want them to die — I don't want anyone to die. "Please! I don't want to destroy the Darkness! I never did! What can I do?!"

And I wait, desperate, panicking, until the voice speaks. *Take it,* it says. *Take the Darkness within yourself, and there shall be no need to destroy it.*

"Take… the Darkness?" I say.

Yes, it says. *The Darkness is no curse. It existed within a person originally. Not until it was abandoned did it grow corrupted.*

"So… it would exist in me," I say. "I'd be the Darkness."

You'd have the Darkness.

"What'll it do to me?" I whisper. My friends are shouting. I know it now. I can hear them crying out.

We are unsure, the voice says. *The Darkness has changed much since its beginning. However, Light courses within you as well. There's no telling what the combination will do. Only know that your life will surely change.*

I swallow. My fingers are shaking, so I clasp them together. But then my knees take up the movement.

What'll it be, Veloren? the voice asks me. *Will you take the Darkness?*

THEO

Everything hurts. Not just the injuries, but the exhaustion. I think my body will give out any minute. I can't imagine what'll happen to Ren when he comes to — if he'll find us here, all laying around him, dead.

"Ren!" I shout, because we're desperate now. The creatures have grown steadily less scared of the light, and one by one they're jumping into it. We can't kill them, either. It seems no matter how many times we bat them away, they return, uninjured. Even the ones stabbed by Will and Eleanor's knives seem fine, despite the black, sluggish liquid that spills out of them.

"Ren!" Eleanor shouts next, and then Will. We just keep calling his name, hoping he'll hurry up, or maybe come out of it. I don't want him to find us dead. I know I was mad at him, but it seems useless now. You can't be mad at someone you love — not when you're on death row.

One of the monsters lunges at me, swiping at my feet. My legs give out, and I lay there on the ground, panting. It's hopeless. It's all over.

And then Ren lights up like the sun.

It's *blinding* — so painful in its existence that I can't even look at him. But after my eyes close, I force them back open, blinking through tears.

The room is completely lit up. It's clear — through the creatures that are steadily retreating, screeching now instead of clicking — that this place was a home. One well lived in, well loved.

Except in the center of the room, the floor is brown. It looks disconcertingly like old blood.

I can see the Darkness. I know that doesn't make sense, but it's true. I can see it moving, swirling, just like I'd been able to from the outside. But then, suddenly, it stops. Completely halts. It's this thick fog, and it's just stationary, hanging motionless in the air.

And then, all at once, and in complete silence, it *moves*. Not in the slow, patternless way like before, but with intent. It rushes toward Ren, *into* him, and I let out a shout that I can't hear. Not over the deafening sound of the silence.

The Darkness floods Ren, envelopes him. I don't know what's happening, and I can't move. I just watch, horrified, as it assaults my best friend. His hair is blowing around like he's in the center of a tornado, and it looks like he's in pain. The more of the Darkness that he takes in, the dimmer he glows. I watch as the light fades out of him, more and more, until just his eyes are glowing, his body completely still as he sits there and takes it.

And then, finally, it stops. I can't see the Darkness around him, around any of us, and then I can't see anything at all, because the light in Ren's eyes goes out. It's pitch black again, but it feels different. Somehow, the air feels lighter. I can move again.

"Ren!" I shout, and I'm not the only one. I stumble toward him in the dark, the first one to make it to his side, and I feel around for him. He's no longer sitting up, but laying on the floor, and as I slide my hand up his chest to find his face, I realize it's lolling against the ground.

"Is he okay? Is he hurt?" Eleanor demands. I can't answer her.

"Ren?" I say. I'm shaking him, touching his face, gripping his wrist. Is there a heartbeat? Can I feel it? Or is that my own? "Wake up," I beg him. I'm holding him so hard, my fingers digging into his delicate skin, and I want to apologize but I *can't*. I can't even loosen my hold. "Wake up, Ren!" I tell him.

Eleanor's crying, and Will's whispering something to her, but I tune them out. They're wrong. He's not dead, right? I think that's his heartbeat. I think I can feel it.

"*Ren,*" I say, and I plant my hands on his chest. I grip his shirt and I shake him because this idiot fell asleep at the most inappropriate time. "Wake *up*, Veloren!"

Ren coughs, and I sob. Then I stop shaking him, because maybe he can't breathe — is that why he's coughing?

We're all talking, our voices clamoring over each other. We just want his attention, want to know if he's okay.

"Theodore?" he croaks. His voice is quiet, but his hand touches me. It brushes my cheek, and I grab it with both of my own, flattening it against my face, and then I just hold onto him. I think he can probably feel me crying, touching my face like he is, but I can't bring myself to care.

"Right here," I tell him. "I'm right here Ren, you're okay. You're okay, right?"

"Yeah," he says, but he sounds distracted. He tries to sit up, letting out a groan, so I shuffle through the darkness until I'm behind him, his head in my lap. I brush my fingers through his hair, cup his face, touch him as much as I can because Stars, he's really all right. "I'm sorry," he says.

"What?" I say.

"I'm sorry," he says, sucking in a breath. "I'm sorry for betraying you. I'm s-sorry I didn't tell you sooner. Theodore, I'm *so sorry.*"

"Shut up," I say, and I lean over him. I press my forehead against his, but then I sit up, just so I can press a kiss against it instead. "I was stupid. You had your reasons. And yet you did it anyway," I breathe. "You destroyed the Darkness."

Will laughs. It sounds incredulous and relieved, and I find myself echoing it.

But, "I didn't," Ren says. Silence falls.

"What? But... it's gone," Eleanor says. "I *saw* it."

"I Restored the Light," Ren clarifies. "But I didn't destroy the Darkness. I... took it."

"You *took* the Darkness?" I say.

"Yeah," Ren says. "I have it in me."

We're all silent, shocked.

"What does that mean?" Eleanor finally asks.

I feel Ren shrug against me. And then he admits, "I don't know."

CHAPTER 19

THEO

We return to the surface. There are Covans everywhere in the tunnels, no doubt able to tell that something is different, even if they can't see it, but we don't stop to chat with them. We only waited long enough for Ren to regain enough energy to get to his feet before practically dragging him through Cova.

We surface somewhere different from where we entered, but it doesn't matter. I spare a moment to blow Eleanor's Avis whistle, hoping we're within a couple miles of Icarus, and then I drop to the ground beside Ren. His eyes are closed, his head resting on Will's bag. He's completely worn out, exhausted in every sense of the word.

Eleanor and Will are just as concerned about him as I am, but they're giving me some alone time with him. They're setting up camp (with everything except the supplies in Will's bag) as I hover over Ren.

"Are you awake?" I ask him, my voice quiet in case he isn't.

"Yeah," Ren murmurs.

I know I shouldn't disturb him. He looks tired, and honestly, why wouldn't he be? He *took in* the Darkness, all of it, and I feel exhausted just thinking about that. But I'm horrible when I get curious, and this question has been dancing around in the back of my mind ever since we left Ren's old home. Or, what Ren *thinks* was his home.

"Can I ask you something?" I say, after plopping onto the ground next to him. "You know, as long as you're feeling all right…"

"I feel fine, Theodore," Ren says, and he reaches out and tangles his fingers with my shoelaces, of all things. He just holds onto me. "What did you want to ask?"

"How sure are you that that was your home?" I say, staring down at him intently. Ren frowns, and with his eyes closed like that, it almost looks like he's having a bad dream.

"A hundred percent," he says, and it sends shivers down my spine. "Why?"

"It's just… when we were there, you started glowing like crazy, and I could see the whole place," I explain. "But Ren… it looked like there was blood on the floor. Old blood, but still."

I wouldn't have noticed Ren's reaction if he weren't holding onto my shoelace. But as it is, his fingers clench around them, and it makes my shoe grow tighter around my foot. Finally, he speaks. "Well, that makes sense," he says, sounding overly casual. "My mom died there."

In the distance, something crashes. I think it was a support beam in my brain, knocking over a box labeled something like *Facts Theo Knows For Sure*. Out spills *Ren's Parents Are Horrible Abandoners* and suddenly I'm questioning if the sky is really blue. His mom is *dead*? She died right in his home? What, was he there? Why did he never tell me?

Suddenly, I realize I'm asking all of this out loud. Ren sat up without me noticing, and his head's bent toward his lap, his hair hanging all in front of his face.

"I don't know, Theodore," he says, his voice so quiet I have to strain to hear him. "One of those creatures slashed her in the stomach when I was little, and Dad went on a rampage, saying he was going to kill them all. Mom told me that I had to leave, and never come back."

"And that destroying the Darkness would hurt your people," I conclude, and Ren hums in agreement.

"Yeah. I think our ancestors must've talked to her too, if she knew that. Stars, she was bleeding all over the place..." he says, and he sounds far away now. I feel horrible. I shoved him into this memory, and I know exactly how that feels, like you're living it all over again. For a second, somewhere in the back of my head, thunder crashes, and a branch snaps.

Ren shakes his head, and his breath shudders out of him. "I don't know why I never told you," he says. "At first, I didn't want you to know I was homeless, and then I didn't want you to know I wasn't from Silva, and it just escalated from there. By the time I realized it wouldn't be so bad if you knew, it felt like it was too late."

"It was never too late," I say, and I reach out to touch him, rubbing my hand along his back. "Stars, and there I was," I say, exasperated, "weeping and wallowing all over the place about *my* parents. And you'd been alone like that for years."

Ren shakes his head. "I wasn't alone, Theodore," he says gently. "I had you." And he finally looks up at me.

I don't manage to stifle my gasp in time.

"What? What is it?" Ren says. When I don't answer right away, he tugs on my shoelace. I don't comprehend it. I'm just gaping at him as I stare. "Theodore?" Ren finally says, desperate.

"It's nothing," I say, snapping out of it. "Just — your eyes. They're different."

Ren frowns. "What do they look like?"

"They're black," I say. "The irises, I mean." And then I lean closer. "They might just be a really dark gray…" I grab his face and tilt it upward, trying to get the light in his eyes, except I can't. It's like they're swallowing up all the light they touch — there isn't even a reflection in them, even though the sun's steadily rising.

He's still frowning. "What did they look like before?" I let go of his face in surprise, sitting back.

I'm thrown for a loop. I swear I would've told him his eye color at some point in time, but for the life of me, I can't remember ever doing so. For a second, I can't get any words out of my mouth. "Blue," I finally manage. "This pale… blue."

Ren bends his head down. Like this, with his eyes downcast, you almost can't tell they're an unnatural color. "Did you like them better that way?" he asks.

"What? No," I say abruptly. "Ren, I don't care what you look like, I'll lo— um, *like* you no matter what. And your eyes look pretty badass now, actually."

"Okay," Ren says, but his head's still bent down, and I can tell I haven't said the right thing yet. I scoot closer, grabbing his hands.

"I couldn't care less what you look like," I repeat. "But… if it makes any difference, you're really attractive, Ren. Heads turn when you walk by."

Ren gapes, his head flying up. "You're lying," he accuses.

"I'm not," I say with a laugh. "I have a really hot boyfriend."

Ren laughs in disbelief, and then his smile freezes, and melts. "Wait," he says. "Did you say boyfriend?"

"Maybe," I say, just to be a dick, and then I kiss him on the cheek before getting to my feet. "Go to sleep, Ren. I can tell you're exhausted."

VELOREN

I can't sleep.

I know I told Theodore I was feeling fine — and I am!
You know, if I don't really think about it — but I *am* thinking
about it. All my attention is on it, on what's different about me,
ever since…

I shiver.

I'll take it, I'd said. For a moment, there'd been nothing. I
thought I was too late, that maybe the Darkness had already won
against my friends. But then, suddenly, the light had
disappeared. Not like before where it'd grown smaller and
smaller before vanishing, but just winking out of existence
entirely. The total darkness that had followed was not like what I
was used to. It was crushing, all-consuming, and I drowned in it,
every ounce of my existence rejecting what was happening to me,
what I was becoming.

I want to think I'm still the same. That it's still just me in
here, that I took in the Darkness and didn't change, *won't*
change.

But I can't shake this feeling. The feeling that
everything's different now.

It's in me. The Darkness — it's *in* me.

Consume.

Ignore it. These intrusive thoughts — they keep popping up. It's like when I was with the Light, the thoughts that aren't mine echoing around in my head as if they are.

They aren't, right?

Consume.

I don't even know what it wants me to consume. Food? Is it hungry?

Except the Darkness... it was always expanding, wasn't it? Spreading throughout all of Cova, and then out of it, escaping from every exit it could find. Is that what it wants from me? Or Stars, is it going to escape and spread? Is it going to act like an infection? How can I possibly contain it?

Consume, consume, consume.

"Theodore!" I gasp, sitting upright. Was it louder that time? My fingers grip my knees as I sit up, panting, shaking.

"Ren? What's wrong?" Theodore says, but his voice sounds far away. "Guys!"

What's going on? The Darkness, it's in me. A part of me. It's in my eyes, my blood, my lungs. I whimper. I think it's trying to escape.

Consume, it tells me.

"What does that mean?" I say.

"What's wrong with him?" someone else says.

"Woah — his eyes!"

"It's spreading from his irises, what does that mean?"

"What does that mean?" I echo. *Consume*, I think. No, *it* thinks.

It feels like the world is rushing all around me, thoughts and sounds, places and smells, consuming me and overwhelming me.

"*It's cursed,*" someone says. Far, far away, their voice only an echo. It sounds like my mom, but I know it's not.

"*It's not,*" another voice replies. "*It needs only your love.*"

But she scoffs. She must not believe them. And then I'm cold — freezing, in fact — and so very alone. This infuriates me. Why was I not worthy? Why was I not loved?

If I can't be loved, I'll be hated. I'll accept it. I'll consume whatever feelings I need to. And if anyone dares to oppose me, they'll find themselves as alone as I was. Alone and cold, abandoned and disposed of.

Everything could be mine. The people that lived amongst me — mine. And the creatures born of my anger — mine. Each of them fit to feel, to love and hate, it didn't matter. Regardless, I consumed.

Consume.

"Ren? Come on, are you okay?"

I gasp. Shake my head. The feelings — the thoughts and experiences — they rush past me again, away, and I give them a good shove while they're at it. I can hardly get enough air in my lungs, and I realize I'm holding onto someone's shirt. "That's it," they're saying. "Just breathe. Concentrate."

"His eyes… normal again…"

"Theodore?" I say.

"That's right," Theodore says, and his knuckles brush against my cheek. "Are you okay?"

Good question. *Am* I okay? I feel fine now. And it's not like I'm in pain. But what if the Darkness comes back? Forces more of its... memories, if that's what they were, on me? What then?

"I think so," I say. "But... the Darkness. It wants to consume."

"What does that mean?" It's Eleanor who asks it. And suddenly, I'm glad she's here. I missed her. I mean, I know she's been here the whole time, but I really have come to love her in the time since I've gotten to know her. I don't even realize I've reached out for her until she grasps my hand with hers.

"I'm not sure," I say, except I think maybe the Darkness was trying to explain it to me. Consume... It hadn't wanted territory, per se, but the people within it. It wanted their feelings, their experiences, all because its mother never loved it. "I think... it wants to be loved."

Silence. I guess I should've expected that. Who could love the Darkness? This thing of evil, this thing that's been spreading and consuming, hurting and scaring people for centuries now. How could anyone possibly—

"Well, that'll be no problem," Theodore says cheerfully.

"What?" I say, torn out of my thoughts, because I was just resigning myself to trying to love the Darkness all on my own. Like, a greeting it every morning and telling it I love it, kind of thing.

"The Darkness is a part of you now, right?" he says. "And I love every part." I huff out a laugh, turning my face down toward my lap because I know there's no way I'm not blushing at that.

"Me too," Eleanor says, squeezing my hand.

"Yeah, me three," says Will, and he crouches down beside me. I lean against him, and I think about apologizing for how mean I was to him at first, but I can't get the words out. One day, I think.

I can feel their love already, and not just in my head. It's like their words and the meaning behind them have flooded into my body, warming it from the inside out. It wasn't until then that I realized I was cold.

The last few days have been a learning experience. Not just about the Darkness within me, which is ever-present and as much of a living thing as I am, but about the world in general.

See, I took all of the Darkness into me. *All of it.* And people have noticed its absence. They've also made the connection between the absence of the Darkness and the miscellaneous group of teenagers that have apparently been going around to different kingdoms and asking questions about Restoring the Light.

There are all sorts of search warrants out for us. Ones from Silva, demanding the return of their hero (funny how Theodore can turn from a criminal into a hero that easily).

There are ones from Volant, searching for the rumored-found Lost Princess, and even more from Volant of the shadier sort, offering all sorts of rewards if the Lost Princess remains lost. And there are even ones from Ilma, asking only for the return of a worried man's son.

So, of course, we've been on the run. I know that might not make sense, but we have no idea which warrant people are looking for us for. The first couple of people to find us posed as travelers from Udula, informing us that they could escort us back to Silva, and wouldn't take no for an answer despite the fact that we insisted on taking our friends home first.

"I don't trust those guys," Theodore had said approximately twenty minutes before we realized we couldn't trust them.

"Is it because of that guy's cowboy hat? Because I swear, Theo, it's not ours," Eleanor had said.

"It looks the *same*," Theodore had muttered darkly.

In the end, the travelers turned out to be some of the few wanting to keep Eleanor from returning home, so we ditched them at the first chance we got (though not before Theodore triumphantly stole their hat). After that, we resolved to accept help from no one on the rest of our journey. Even though we *do* kind of desperately need help. Traveling is much harder without Icarus, who we still haven't found.

As for what we've learned about the Darkness... well, we're still learning it. For example, at night, when the Darkness was always said to be weakest, my eyes turn blue again, and the

Darkness rarely talks to me. But when I'm angry or scared or upset, the black in my eyes escapes my irises and floods into the whites of my eyes. Theodore says it'd be unsettling if it weren't me, but I have a feeling he's just trying to be nice.

Still, the Darkness is certainly much happier ever since my friends professed their love for me, and now it says more than just *consume*.

For example, yesterday we were walking along the dirt path when it'd said, *watch out*. I'd had a second to think *what?* before immediately stepping into a pothole and twisting my ankle.

Everyone had gone about frantically apologizing to me, Theodore offering to give me a piggyback ride for the rest of the day (even though he's definitely not strong enough to carry me for that long), but I'd just sat there, lost in my thoughts. The Darkness was aware of things I wasn't. *And* it was on my side. It hadn't wanted me to trip, at the very least.

I'd conveyed these thoughts to my friends later from my position on Eleanor's back.

"It *talks* to you?" Theodore had said, finally putting an end to his silent treatment. He was offended that I'd let Eleanor carry me instead of him.

"Yeah, sometimes," I'd answered. Despite the fact that this knowledge had made the rest of them uneasy, it doesn't really bother me anymore.

Now, Theodore says, "Plug your ears, Ren." I sigh, coming to a standstill and shoving my fingers in my ears.

Cursed, says the Darkness, and I can't help but agree. When Theodore blows the Avis whistle, I can still hear it, but it's not quite as piercing. We've been blowing it periodically every day, hoping we'll finally be close enough to Icarus that she'll hear it and find us. So far, we haven't had any luck.

I can tell Theodore's upset despite the fact that he's pretending not to be. Icarus may have been our primary source of transportation, but she was never just a ride, not to Theodore. She wasn't even a pet — she was a friend. They had a real bond, the two of them, and Theodore's worried about her. I can tell.

It doesn't even occur to me to try to use the Darkness to my advantage until much later in the day, when it's complaining for the fourth time about that whistle. Because it knew about that pothole, right? And sure, that was right in front of me, but if it could sense that, maybe it can sense even father...

"Let me try something," I blurt, interrupting Eleanor's suggestion to stop and eat lunch. Without any further explanation, I sit down right there in the middle of the path and close my eyes.

I expect it to be like before, when I meditate. Some closing my eyes and thinking, clearing my mind and concentrating. I'm expecting the invisible world of jelly again, to maybe ask some phantom figure of light if it knows where our bird is.

This is nothing like that.

The second I close my eyes and even *think* about concentrating, it feels like I'm falling, like I've stepped off a cliff and am descending into a pit. There's no time for me to scream, because almost as soon as it started, it stops, my body jerked to a sudden halt. I can feel the Darkness — thick and heavy like it was before — except it's no longer so intimidating, and there aren't any creatures here. They were all put to rest when I took in the Darkness.

"Hello?" I call out.

How nice of you to visit, says the Darkness.

"Right," I say. "Um. Can you help me find Icarus?"

There's a lot of things I can do, it informs me. I wait, channeling patience, and then it says, *Yes.*

Again, I didn't know what I was expecting, but a sudden and total awareness of everything around me wasn't it. I'm not seeing, not really, but I'm aware of everything like never before. It's not a knowledge of where things are based off sound and memorization. It's like another sense entirely, where everything and its place, its existence, is just *known* to me.

I'm outside of my body. I mean, I'm probably not really, but I feel like I am. I can sense myself — sitting there on the ground, my eyes wide open and completely black — with my friends gathered around me.

"How long is he gonna sit like this?" Eleanor murmurs. Her voice sounds like it's on another plane of existence.

"Until he figures out whatever he's trying to do, I guess," Theodore says. He's crouched next to me.

"The Darkness isn't consuming him, right?" Will questions tentatively.

308

"I don't think so," says Theodore. "I don't think it's evil, either. The legends were probably wrong, calling it a curse. It's just misunderstood."

And Stars, does the Darkness like those words. It likes *Theodore*. Seriously, everything within me seems to thrum with delight, and I have to shake myself out of it, for once not sure if my overwhelming affection for Theodore is my own.

"Come on," I say aloud. "We need to find Icarus."

The Darkness is reluctant to leave my friends so soon, but we go anyway. I feel larger than life, like seriously ten times my size. My awareness spreads out in every direction, tendrils of it snaking away from me. I can feel towns in Askund, people walking along different paths, the tunnels underground and the Covans within them. And then, far, far in the distance — Icarus.

She's lying beside the entrance we originally disappeared into, curled around it like a cat, no longer scared to get so close now that the Darkness is gone. She croons lowly, clearly depressed, and my heart aches for her.

"Icarus!" I say, not really sure if she'll hear me, but she does. Her head perks up, and she looks all around. I can tell she's confused. "This way, girl!" I encourage her. I narrow my awareness — the towns and people and Covans disappear — until it's just me and her, and far, far behind us, my friends.

Icarus squawks as she stands up, and her massive wings — Stars, I never realized she was this big — unfurl. I'm suddenly glad I don't normally have any idea of what shape she takes, because I don't think I ever would've agreed to get on her had I known. Her wings beat a few times before she leaps into the air, and she starts flying toward me. She follows the trail of me and the Darkness, and I follow it too, leading her closer and closer to the rest of us.

I'm back in my body in no time, Icarus only a few miles away, and I gasp. My awareness of everything around me dissipates as I push myself to my feet, stumbling a bit. How long was I sitting there?

"Ren!" Theodore says, sounding relieved. "What'd you do?"

"Blow the whistle," I say. "She's almost here."

"I — what?" Theodore says, but I already have my fingers in my ears, waiting. Moments later, Theodore blows the whistle, and in the distance, Icarus screeches.

When she gets here, her and Theodore are a force to be reckoned with. He yells in delight, and I just back away and pray not to get hurt as they start playing together, chasing each other around. Theodore's laughing and Icarus is making the most delighted chirping sounds. At one point, she even snatches him in her talons and flies him into the air as he laughs. Stars, that boy is insane.

The only bad thing about Icarus' return is that it means our adventure really is coming to an end. I can't quite figure out how I'm going to manage to say goodbye.

CHAPTER 20

ELEANOR

I never thought I'd forget how to wear a dress, and yet here I
am. It's stiff and itchy and nothing at all like the clothes I've
grown used to wearing. It's probably sad that I miss my old
clothes, sewn together countless times and definitely never going
to have the dirt washed out of them.

My ribs ache — not from the corset, but from the
number of hugs I've been subjected to. Not that I'm arguing, of
course. I've sworn all my friends to secrecy, never to mention the
fact that they saw me crying like that. I sat in my dad's lap for
almost an entire hour, just hugging him and crying into his chest

as he brushed his fingers through my hair, my mom having abandoned her own thrown so she could press kisses to my forehead.

Warren's long gone, thrown into the dungeon for all sorts of crimes to be tried on later, and my friends have been cleaned up just as well as I have. Like, scarily well.

Sure, I barely recognize myself with my hair washed and brushed and braided, but I recognize my friends even less.

The three of them are wearing Volation dress-wear, each tailored to their bodies. Theo's curly hair is no longer matted and tangled. His clothes are mostly white, a situation just begging for something bright red to be spilled on them, which he seems similarly worried about. Ren, with his hair long enough to normally hang in his eyes, has it pulled back into a bun (which he looks horribly uncomfortable about). His clothes are dark, matching his eyes, and he can't seem to stop putting his hands in his pockets, even though you're really not supposed to do that with these kinds of clothes.

Will's the only one who seems genuinely excited about his appearance. His hair, which before was cut choppily, is now short and neat and perfectly styled. His shirt hugs him in all the right places and he keeps straightening his tie simply for the act of straightening it.

They stay for the Princess' Return banquet, eating their fill and dancing the night away with me, but come morning, it's time for them to go. They're gifted metals and awards for their good deeds (and their success in returning me home), but most importantly, my father allows them to keep Icarus. I think we're all amused by that declaration, because there's no way Icarus would stay here even if we tried to make her.

She's equipped with official Volation flying gear, much safer than the harness I made, and then it's time to say goodbye.

"Promise you'll visit?" I say, enveloped in Theo's arms.

"Promise," he says, and steps away. He falls automatically into place beside Ren, and I refrain from smirking at Theo when their fingers tangle together.

"You'll have to bring Hector," I instruct. "I want to meet him."

"And he'll want to come," Theo laughs.

I plunge into all their arms one last time, holding back tears, and finally let them go. For the first time, I watch Icarus fly off without me.

WILL

I think I'm going to throw up.

I mean, I haven't eaten anything all morning, but I still think it might happen. I can't seem to sit still, and as we get closer and closer to Ilma, I consider telling Theo to just take me back to Silva instead. They wouldn't mind having another roommate, right?

Calm down, I try to tell myself, because my friends have told me the same thing a million times. Based on the search warrants we've heard of, Dad really does want me home. And Eleanor has loudly claimed (multiple times) that I was an idiot, running off that day before he could even say anything to me. She's convinced he doesn't hate me, and I've tried to let her conviction rub off on me.

"I think I see Ilma!" Theo announces.

"Oh Stars," I mutter, and Ren reaches out and grips my elbow.

"You're going to be all right," he promises. I consider throwing my last water tablet off of Icarus to be lost forever. Can't go home if I can't breathe in water, right?

But I don't decide fast enough, and the next thing I know, we're landing at the edge of Ilma, looking down at the buildings beneath the clear water.

"I'm gonna miss you, Will," Theo announces, abruptly throwing his arm around my shoulders.

"Really? 'Cause I could go home with you. You know, if you're gonna miss me that much."

Surprisingly, it's Ren who laughs. "You can definitely visit anytime," he promises, and he slips into the hug as well. He can't see me grinning, but I think he must know I am. It's almost amusing, thinking of how much he used to hate me.

"Okay," I say finally, letting out a shaky breath. "I'm gonna do it," I announce. And we have our last hugs, long and tight, before I swallow my tablet and take a step into the water.

"Visit me sometime soon," I say. "If they're taking too long, come get me yourself, Icarus."

She chirps in delight and I dive into the water before I can lose my nerve. It's a shorter swim than I remember, unfortunately, and soon enough I'm walking through Ilma. Everyone's looking at me, it feels like, and I hurry as fast as I can, trying to get to my dad before the rumors do.

Maybe it's ridiculous, but when I get to my house, I knock.

It's only moments before the door swings open. I watch as Dad takes me in, his eyes wide and his mouth open, before he steps out of the house. "Oh, thank the Stars," he says, pulling me into his arms. I'm shaking, crying as I hug him close.

"Dad," I say, hugging him as hard as I can, and he lifts me up, definitely too old to be picking me up but doing it anyway. He shakes me from side to side, my legs dangling, until I laugh, begging him to put me down again.

"Forgive me," he says, "but I don't know what I should call you."

I grin. "Call me Will."

And I don't know what kind of reaction I was expecting, but this wasn't it. His mouth opens, and his eyes light up. "Oh!" he says. "You named yourself after your friend! You four are all anyone's been talking about."

But, "What?" I say, confused. "What friend did I name myself after?"

"Will?" Dad says, sounding confused. "With the curly hair?"

I find myself glaring. They used fake names, really? And Theo used *mine*?

"Come on," I say, slumping past my dad and into the house. "Let me tell you everything that's happened."

THEO

I know it was just me and Ren in the beginning, but it feels terribly lonely now, with just the two of us on Icarus. The only thing distracting me from how much I miss my friends is how excited I am to see Hector. I think Icarus can pick up on my feelings because I swear she's flying faster than usual, zooming toward Silva as quickly as she can.

When I see it, happiness blooms in my chest. I can't believe how much I've missed the sight of these trees, gigantic and towering just like they should be. Excitement thrums through me and I reach over and grab Ren's hand.

"We're close," I say, even though we're still probably an hour's flight away. Silva's trees really are monstrously big.

Ren scoots in front of me before leaning back against my chest. I hug him tight, resting my chin on his shoulder for the remaining duration of the flight.

Silvans are waiting for us. They're standing out on all the branches, jumping and cheering and shouting as Icarus flies us through the trees, spinning and landing appropriately in order to weave through all the branches. We don't stop to greet any of them though, because my heart's set on one single destination, and Icarus knows what it is.

We stop outside the town center first, Icarus landing so thunderously that the branch shakes, and I run inside a couple shops, ignoring Ren's obvious confusion. I don't even want to know how he realizes I didn't bring us straight home. I'm done and climbing back onto Icarus in less than a minute, and by the time we reach our house, I think my heart might explode because of how fast it's beating. My feet meet the branch beneath me with a thud.

"*Hector!*" I yell.

I don't know how he missed the commotion all throughout Silva, or the news which surely must have spread by now, because I swear we're in all the newspapers, but Hector wasn't expecting us. He races out of the house, wearing one sock and dressed in pajamas, and skids to a stop on the branch across from me, gaping in sheer astonishment.

"Theo…" he says, heaving. There are tears in his eyes. And I know it hasn't been that long, but I swear he looks taller.

I don't wait to find a good branch to cross over on — I just take a running leap from mine to Hector's, stumbling when I land before I race toward him. He meets me halfway, jumping into my arms as I grab him and spin him around, sobbing.

"Fuck, I missed you so much, Hec," I say, squeezing him as tight as I can.

Hector laughs through his tears. "You just said the F word."

"Shut up, you brat," I say, and then Ren's beside us, and he piles onto the hug as well.

"Don't tell me *Ren's* showing affection?" Hector jokes, and Ren scoffs, fake-offended.

"This is why we shouldn't have Restored the Light," he says, and I punch him, amused but also unable to believe he's joking about that, the bastard.

"Here," I say, thoroughly pretending there aren't tears in my eyes, and I pull away so I can hold out the bag from my short shopping trip. Hector takes it, confused, and peers inside. "Told you I'd bring you home something good for lunch, didn't I?" I say.

Hector doesn't even say anything. He just barrels back into my arms, and this time he's out of jokes, just sniffling as he hugs me.

"I really missed you, Theo," he whispers.

"I missed you too, bud," I say. "Promise I won't leave you again."

"And you won't get in trouble?" he prompts.

"I think I'm famous now," I say. "They'd be insane to try to exile me." Icarus squawks in agreement and Hector jolts in my arms, finally noticing her, before he takes a step back and gapes up at her.

"No way," he whispers.

"Yes way," I tell him. "How 'bout a ride?"

EPILOGUE

The Volant Times

Return of the Lost Princess by **Elena Ruth**

Since Princess Eleanor's disappearance, countless theories have arisen, almost everyone capable of producing their own speculation as to how and why she disappeared that night. However, few — if any — thought that her betrothed, Warren Helbig, was the culprit.

Princess Eleanor took the time to sit down with me and briefly explain the events of her year spent in Askund for those of you who missed the full story at the Princess' Return banquet.

"Most of it was hiding out and trying to earn money as I hiked back to Volant," she said. "Toward the end, however, I came across two travelers from Silva — Theo and Ren. It's because of them that Light was Restored."

When asked what all this might mean for the future of our nation, Princess Eleanor had an answer readily prepared. "The fact of the matter is that the Darkness never would've grown like it did without prejudice. So many of us spent years worrying over the Darkness spreading to the reaches of our own nations when in reality, the people of Cova had been living with it for years. Now, it's time for this prejudice to end. The people of Cova, should they wish it, should be allowed to return to their lands of old, and Askund shouldn't remain a land of lawlessness."

The princess makes a good point, and I expect further discussion of this topic will begin to arise in the kingdom and throughout conferences between our nations' leaders.

Finally, there's been speculation about there being a reunion of the Heroes

of Light — our own princess along with her
friends, Theodore Laurent, Veloren Selcouth
(not only a Covan, but a Descendant of the
Light and our Container of Darkness!), and
William Endring — at Princess Eleanor's
Birthday Ball. Be sure to attend if you
want a chance to meet the Heroes of Light!

VELOREN

"Hm," I say. It's still weird that everyone just *knows* I'm Covan,
now. It's weirder still that everyone doesn't hate me for it. "It's
weird being in the paper," I voice aloud.

"It's weird getting The Volant Times in Silva,"
Theodore returns. It is weird, but it's not bad. The nations have
been a lot more connected since we Restored the Light. And
then, "You hungry, babe?" Theodore asks, brushing his hand
through my hair. I am hungry, but the idea of getting up and no
longer using Theodore's lap as a pillow isn't a good one.

"Not if you're cooking," I joke, except I not-so-secretly
am serious. I didn't know it was possible to burn noodles, but
Theodore managed to do so last night. Even Hector couldn't
force them down, and he always attempts to eat the crap
Theodore makes.

I don't notice Hector enter the room. I should, because he traipses around like an elephant at all hours of the day, but I'm too distracted. Theodore does that to me, unfortunately.

"Gross," Hector announces upon noticing us. He likes to pretend that he's totally disgusted by any displays of affection between the two of us, but it's obvious that he's actually happy about this new development.

Twerp, the Darkness says. I scoff to myself, because underneath the insult, I can feel the affection.

"Hector, how about I make some dinner?" Theodore says suddenly.

"I want Arlo's," Hector immediately answers.

Theodore huffs. "You know what? Fine," he says, and he stands up, making my head thump onto the couch. I push myself up with my elbows, disgruntled. "Let's get Arlo's. And from there, we can pick up Will and head to Volant. You good with leaving a day early, Hec?"

Hector's already gone, having sprinted out of the room whooping. He's been going on and on about meeting our new friends (*well* excuse me *if I've never heard of you guys having friends before,* he'd said sassily) and I know he's especially excited about meeting a princess.

"You really want to leave early?" I say in Theodore's direction.

"Yeah, if that's good with you," he says. "Will keeps threatening me in his letters. He says he can't convince his dad that I didn't come up with his name."

I snort, swinging my legs over the couch and finally standing up. "Guess we should get packing, then," I say.

"Guess so," Theodore says, but somehow neither of us get started. I end up on the couch again, Theodore in my lap and his hands in my hair, until Hector screeches at us to get moving already.

It's hard to listen to him, though, especially when something about Theodore makes me feel like I'm being enveloped in light. My love for him swells and swells, overwhelming and blinding as always. It's not until Icarus sticks her head through the window and squawks that we actually get a move on, and even then we remain linked at the hands.

I kind of feel like the luckiest guy in the world.